LOST WITH A SCOT
THE LEAGUE OF ROGUES
BOOK XVII

LAUREN SMITH

ISBN: 978-1-956227-22-2 (e-book edition)

ISBN: 978-1-956227-23-9 (print edition)

❀ Created with Vellum

CHAPTER 1

September 1821
Ruritania

Anna Zelensky was lost. Dark branches reached overhead to block the crescent moon. Roots protruded from the black soil to trip her as she tried to run. She couldn't say what she was running from, but she knew if she didn't escape it she would die.

"*Help*." Her voice was reduced to a raspy whisper. "Someone, please, help me."

It seemed she was always running from something in her dreams. Something was coming. Whatever it was, it wasn't good.

The shadows of the trees lengthened, and she heard breathing in the dark wood.

She started to run again, fleeing whatever now lurked in the dark.

She skidded to an unceremonious halt as her eyes lit on

1

the old oak tree. She knew it, had passed by it many times throughout her childhood. It was a marker for . . .

"The enchanted well," she breathed in relief knowing where she was now. She changed direction toward where she knew the oak marked the well-worn path. Her gaze darted about, searching for the circular cairn of stones, knowing she should have seen it by now, but it remained out of her reach. Her lungs burned and her feet were bruised from the uneven path, but she pushed herself to reach the well. Most people avoided it—it was said to have been created by vengeful fairies, full of dark magic. But she had never feared it. She'd been told that there was magic in her blood. The well would help her—it always had before, at least in the land of dreams.

In the midst of a clearing, the gray stone well was revealed to her desperate eyes. She ran toward the edge, her hands gripping the cool rocks. She peered over the edge into the water below, which was still and glossy as a mirror. Her face was reflected back at her.

The surrounding woods trembled with the howls of the beasts that were now close enough to smell her fear. She knew she had but moments before she was attacked.

"Help, *please* . . . ," she whispered to the water. The surface rippled, and her reflection vanished. A tall, dark-haired man with solemn gray-blue eyes peered back at her. He was beautiful, his face full of hard angles, strength emanating from his features as he gazed back at her through the water. Her lower belly quivered in a foreign longing that she'd never known before she first saw this man in the water.

Slowly, he reached for her through the water. His hand

broke the magic seal between his world and hers. Milky water droplets from the crescent moon shining above dripped down his hand, making her realize he was truly reaching for her, that she could *touch* him.

"Take my hand, lass," the man urged in a low, rich voice with a Scottish accent. She'd never been to Scotland, but she knew of it from tales her mother told her. It was a wild, faraway land that matched the man in the water.

The howl of beasts in the woods made her suck in a breath in terror. She glanced at the woods, then back at the man in the water.

"I don't know how to leave. I don't know how."

"Ye've got to trust me," the man said. "I canna protect ye if ye arna willing to take my hand."

Anna thrust her hand out, grasping his and pulling hard.

She flew awake with a little cry, and it took her a moment to remember where she was. Her silk nightgown was damp with sweat, sitting up in a plush four-poster bed. Her heart was still beating hard in her chest, but her brain was catching up and realizing, *It was just a dream. It was just a dream.* She wasn't in the woods; she had been dreaming. Anna was in her large four-poster bed at the Summer Palace, her family's royal residence. She was safe. No beasts were hunting her, no branches had caught and torn her clothes. She hadn't really been in the forest; it was just a dream like all of the others. She'd dreamt so many nights of the man's face in the well. But tonight's dream felt more . . . *real.* As if it had truly happened.

She stared at the embers burning in the hearth across

the room as her mind seemed to finally accept that she was safe.

"My lady!" Her lady's maid, Pilar, a dark-haired Spanish woman, appeared in the doorway that linked their rooms. Pilar stared at her with worry. The candle she held illuminated her in the dark.

Anna rubbed at her face with her palms, gently massaging her cheeks. "I'm all right, Pilar, truly. It was just a terrible dream. I've had so many of late."

Her maid came to her bed and set the candle down on the nightstand, then eased beside her and put an arm around her shoulders, giving her a gentle squeeze. Pilar had been her maid for ten years. She'd come to work at the palace when Anna was only twelve, and Pilar had been a girl of sixteen then. Pilar was more like a sister to her than a maid in many ways, and she trusted the woman with all her secrets. Along with her parents and her twin brother, Alexei, Pilar was one of the people Anna trusted most.

"It was that dream, the one where I'm in the woods and the man in the enchanted well tries to save me."

Pilar was silent a moment. "Your grandmother had enchantment in her blood. Perhaps you do as well. She was gifted with the sight, and most of her visions came to pass. Do you believe what you saw was something that will happen?"

Anna considered it. Was she like her grandmother? She'd always been told she was. But visions of the future? A man couldn't reach through the water like that and save her.

"I don't think monstrous beasts in the woods and the

wishing well are real, at least not as they are in my dream," she admitted. "Perhaps my imagination is overactive."

"Water is a powerful thing to dream about, milady. Do you trust the man you see in the water?" Pilar asked.

"I . . . I do." Was it possible to trust someone she had never met and likely wasn't even real? She'd seen him so often and for so long that she could answer no other way. Trusting him was like trusting herself.

"Go back to sleep, milady. Dawn is but a few hours away, and you need your rest."

Her maid kissed her forehead, and Anna lay back in her bed and pulled her blankets back up around her. She had many court duties to perform in a few hours—the life of a princess was never truly her own.

She'd only just started to fall asleep again when a bitter smell teased her nose. She shifted uncomfortably but couldn't escape the scent. She opened her eyes and peered into the darkness, trying to see what was causing the smell. The distant light of a red dawn illuminated the edge of her window. The light flickered and wavered, dancing with the shadows nearest it. That wasn't right . . . there were no trees outside her window that would make the light move if stirred by a breeze.

She took a deeper breath, and the bitter scent turned acrid, a smell she recognized with horror.

Smoke . . .

The light on the windowsill wasn't dawn's early light, but a fire's angry glow. She threw off her blankets and shoved her feet into the pair of walking boots she kept by the foot of her bed.

"Pilar!" she shouted as she ran to find a gown that she

could get into quickly. Her maid burst into the room, still in her nightgown, and sniffed the air.

"There's a fire!" Pilar gasped. "Oh God . . ."

"I know. Dress quickly! We must go!" Anna pulled on a dark-green gown with laces up the front, but her hands were shaking so badly she just hastily knotted the ribbons.

She had to find her parents and brother, and then she needed to help the servants and palace staff escape. Once Pilar was dressed, they quickly exited Anna's chamber into the corridor. Smoke drifted along the arched ceilings of the palace above them.

"Cover your nose and mouth. Try not to breathe in the smoke," Anna warned her maid. They lifted their shawls up around their faces as they bent low while running to avoid the smoke gathering above them.

Screams and shouts filled the hazy corridor. The crack of pistols and the firing of rifles in the distance was eerie and terrifying as they echoed down the halls through the smoke. Suddenly, a figure loomed out of the shadows and crashed into them, knocking Pilar to the floor. When Anna heard her maid's cry, she hurried over and pulled Pilar up to her feet.

One of the palace footmen barreled into them. He tried to rush past them, but Anna caught the man's arm. He was trembling, and she saw blood on his chest.

"What happened?" she asked. "Are you all right?"

The man's eyes grew wide with terror as he looked into her face. "It's not my blood. It's the cook's. They murdered the cook and the scullery maids . . ." He shook his head as if to rid himself of a nightmare. "Men are here for you, princess. They are coming for you. You must escape! *Run!*"

Then he turned at the sound of heavy boots thudding around the distant corner of the corridor. "I'll hold them off."

He pulled out the short sword that all footmen carried when they were in the palace. It was ceremonial and barely sharp enough to cut bread. If he tried to fight anyone with it, he would be killed.

"No, come with us." Anna was not going to let the man face whoever was coming for her. If she could find a blade or a pistol, she could fight as well as any man, and she would, too, to save her people.

"Someone must hold them off. Not even you can fight them. There are too many!" the footman said. "Go and live, princess."

Pilar gripped her arm and jerked her down the hall and around another corner. A moment later, they heard the clash of steel and the shouts of men at war.

Thoughts of her parents and the dangerous men who had come to burn down her world were pushed to the side as she heard Pilar's whimper of fear as they quickly moved from shadow to shadow down the hallway. She would find out what was truly going on once she could ensure Pilar's safety. If her parents and Alexei were not outside to greet her, she would find a way back into the castle to search for them.

"We must find Alexei," she whispered to Pilar as the smoke and flames forced them to turn from the hallway that would lead to her brother's rooms. Her stomach dropped as the darkness ahead of them crackled with the destructive force of the fire. Her body was moving by itself, her mind screaming about his safety, and the heat of the flames singed the air around her. Pilar pulled her back.

"The gardens," Pilar said. "We can reach his rooms from the southern gardens."

Encouraged by their new plan, Anna hurried with her maid toward the door that led to the south part of the royal gardens.

When they stepped into the cool, clearer air of the gardens, the smoke thinned. They were alone, at least for now, but a wall of fire separated them from Alexei's rooms.

Anna stared at the flames. "We have to find a way to get to him." She would never leave her twin behind. They were inseparable, two halves of a whole . . .

"We can't, my lady. Alexei has his best friend William, one of the loyal palace guards, who was assigned as his bodyguard. William will watch over him. My duty is to take care of you. We must go. Milady, please!" Pilar begged, her face streaked with tears.

Only her maid's fear made Anna agree to find a way to escape the danger on the palace grounds.

She prayed that William would be able to see him safely out of the palace.

More fighting broke out somewhere in the palace, and the horns of Ruritania sounded as the loyal palace guards fought against whoever had started the battle to defend the Crown. Flames leapt along the tops of the roof of the Summer Palace, devouring all the wood and blackening the stone. Anna stared up at the growing inferno from the garden, her body frozen, her mind blank with grief and fear. Her whole world was *burning*.

"My lady!" Pilar hissed, tugging hard on Anna's hand.

Once more, they were running through the hedgerows of the luxurious palace grounds. A figure suddenly leapt out at them, and Pilar screamed. Anna took up a defensive stance, ready to protect herself and her maid however she could. She'd been trained in the use of many kinds of weapons, including her own hands.

"Anna?" a familiar voice croaked hoarsely in the dark.

"Alexei?" She ran to the cloaked figure and threw herself into his arms.

"Thank God you're both unharmed." Her brother coughed from breathing in the smoke. But he held her close, hugging her so tightly she almost couldn't breathe.

She was almost laughing insanely with panic and relief, but her twin wasn't. His face was hard and his eyes full of pain.

"Alexei . . . ," she began uncertainly.

"You have to go to the harbor. Board the *Ruritanian Star*. It's waiting for you."

"Me? What about you? Where are Mother and Father—?"

"They're *gone*, Anna," he rasped.

"Gone . . . What do you mean, *gone*?" She felt a wild hysteria building as she tried to process what he was saying.

"Uncle Yuri killed them. He almost killed me. If not for William, I would be dead." Her brother's face was dusted with smoke and streaked with tears. "He has turned half the army against us. We never even knew the *devils* were inside the walls until it was too late." He ushered her and Pilar into the shadow of the garden wall at the edge of the palace. "Now go. Run to the docks. Take this." He pressed a heavy coin purse into her hands.

"Aren't you coming with us?"

Her twin smiled sadly. "I must stay and rescue any who are still loyal to us. Now that Father is gone, I am king, and I must stay with our people. Yuri will not spare them in this fight. The *Star* will take you to London. Speak to King George. Bring back soldiers to help us. I need you to do this for me . . ."

She was shaking her head, not wanting to leave him. "No. Alexei, I can't—"

"You can, sister. You have always been braver than me —that is why you must go. You have the heart of a queen, and King George will want to help you once he hears you speak of these atrocities. When it's safe, I will send for you. Until then, William and I will be fighting to take our home back."

Anna threw her arms around her brother's neck. "Keep your promise, Alexei. I cannot live in a world without you." She kissed his cheek and let him go, even as her heart was breaking.

She and Pilar ran for the woods on the edge of the castle grounds. The sky was now red with hellish flames, a stark contrast to the dark woods between her and the distant harbor. She looked back only once, hoping to see her brother watching them, but the archway that led back to the gardens and the palace beyond was empty except for firelight.

The dream she'd had so often of late proved to be prophetic that night as she and Pilar fled through the dark forest. The howls of men hungry for royal blood echoed all around them, and Anna and Pilar did not stop.

We must reach the water, she thought over and over again.

The water would save them. The water would carry them away. She prayed that her brother would survive. She had lost everything else. She could not lose him as well.

SEPTEMBER 1821
Scotland

Aiden Kincade kicked off his blankets as he struggled to wake. Old, painful memories of his tyrannical father left him quivering with fear and rage. He sat up and covered his face with his hands, letting out a shaky sigh before he dropped his hands and stared unseeing at the room around him.

How could a man long dead still strike such fear into his heart? Aiden was twenty-seven, long past the time when nightmares should frighten him. But it always seemed so real whenever his father appeared in his dreams. The scars his father Montgomery Kincade had given him, both physical and emotional, were ever present for him in a way that his siblings seemed to have escaped. Brock, Brodie, and Rosalind all shared his abusive history with their father, but his siblings had all have moved on with their lives, whereas Aiden couldn't manage to shake off the pain that lingered. It made him feel all the more alone for it.

His mother once said he was born with the wild spirit of her ancestors in his blood, the old warrior clans. That wild spirit had caught both his father's eye and his scorn. Montgomery had secretly helped the English government crush a Scottish rebellion years ago. He, more than most, despised the old ways. The clans, the lairds, the kilts. All of it. And so Aiden became a target for his father's venom.

Aiden climbed out of his bed and went to wash his face in the porcelain basin. The weak morning light was gray, and he could smell the rain upon the breeze that drifted in through the half-open window of his bedchamber. He washed his face, the cold water helping to banish the lingering murkiness of his dreams.

Something stirred in the corner of his room behind an old overstuffed armchair. Aiden clicked his teeth softly as a pine marten called out from beneath the legs of the chair and stretched, almost catlike. Its coat was a rich glossy brown that blended with the wood of the trees. Aiden had rescued the wee beastie when he had found its front paw caught in a hunter's snare.

It had taken him half a day to woo the marten into trusting him before he could release it from the snare without it biting him. Once he had freed it, he carried it home to treat its wounds. Thankfully, the paw had escaped infection, and the marten had been free to return to the wild after a few weeks, but like many of the creatures Aiden encountered and assisted, the marten seemed perfectly content to stay at Castle Kincade.

Along with the marten, there was also a female badger, Fiona, who enjoyed sleeping in his brother Brock's bed, which always amused Aiden because Brock's name actually meant badger. They also had a pair of river otters in the lake who sometimes came up to play in the garden fountains. There was even a small tawny owl.

He'd named the owl Honey because her black, brown, and gold speckled feathers reminded Aiden of the honeycombs of bees. Honey roosted in the castle's library, and Aiden had built a muslin flap entrance into one of the nearby windows where the owl could scuttle out onto a ledge on the outside of the castle and fly off to hunt when she needed to.

Aiden was lucky that neither of his brothers and their wives seemed to mind the comings and goings of the creatures. Even luckier for him, the two new occupants of Castle Kincade thought it was sweet how he nurtured the wee beasties. His sisters-in-law, Joanna and Lydia, seemed to enjoy the odd fox that sunned itself by his window, the doves that roosted in the hall, or the other various injured animals he brought home to heal. He wasn't sure how he'd gotten so lucky. His brothers had married English lasses who were compassionate and kind, especially considering that for most of their lives, his brothers hadn't been exactly predisposed to the English, by and large.

Aiden was secretly amused at his two older brothers having married into English families as they were both quite proud of their Scottish blood.

Even their younger sister, Rosalind, had married not one but *two* Englishmen. She had first married an older man with a kind heart years ago to escape their father, then as a wealthy widow had found her true match in her second husband, a powerful English baron.

Aiden's brothers had quite thoroughly mixed themselves into the lives of their wives' families, while Aiden had managed to escape this. He didn't mean to be apart from everyone else—it was just his way. His mother and siblings had understood that about him, but not his father.

He felt safest and most comfortable when he was alone

or with his animals. Distrusting other people was an issue he was constantly trying to overcome. His father had hurt him the most, and his brothers hadn't always been able to protect him, nor could his late mother. He'd often dreamed of running away to England or Wales or perhaps even farther, but he had stayed in Scotland because it was his home, and he loved his brothers and sister too much to leave.

Aiden dressed in a pair of buckskin trousers and a shirt, not bothering with a waistcoat. He left his bedchamber and walked down the hall, the pine marten trailing behind him as loyal as any hound. He came down the grand staircase and glanced up at the restored arched ceilings of the castle. Several months ago, the castle had partially burned in a fire that almost killed Brock and Joanna.

Despite how much work and money the repairs had required, the restoration of the castle had proved a positive experience for everyone. It felt like a new home now, one more welcoming, full of sunny memories rather than painful ones.

The marten wound herself through the gleaming wood spindles of the staircase before meandering off her own way to some other nest she had hidden in the castle. Sounds of laughter echoed down the hall from whatever it was that currently amused Brock and Joanna. No one would miss Aiden if he disappeared for an afternoon. No one ever did.

He headed to the kitchens, where their cook left out a bag of meats, cheeses, and fresh bread for him on the days she guessed he might go riding, which was usually every other day. He took the bag from the countertop while the plump cook had her back turned and slipped out the nearest door toward the stables. He was very good at going about unseen when he wished to, which, given his height, was an impressive skill.

The stable hands greeted Aiden and politely stepped back as he visited each of the horses in their stalls. The horses bumped his hands with their noses, eager for attention. He chuckled and stroked his fingertips down the bridges of each horse's nose and fed them clumps of sugar. When he reached his own horse, Thundir, named in Gaelic after the storm he was born in, Aiden put a harness on him, but no saddle. He rarely used them. He put a light blanket upon the horse's back and mounted up using a small footstool nearby. He rode Thundir out of the stables and toward the distant hills. Thick, building clouds towered above them in the sky, creating fast-moving shadows on the bright gold grass. The hills were adorned with hues of pink and purple heather blossoms.

He bent low over the beast's neck to whisper into his ear, "Chase the clouds." He had a strange feeling that he was not running away from but toward something for once. Whatever it was, he would find it. His heart was calling for him to find it. He sensed that when he did find it, the peace he had longed for all his life would finally be his.

CHAPTER 2

O*ne month later*
      The North Sea, off the coast of North
Berwick, Scotland

Anna and Pilar never saw the storm approach as their ship crossed the North Sea. Nor did the captain of the *Ruritanian Star* or his crew. A cold north wind rose up foul and fierce when they were almost all the way across the sea, headed toward England.

Under orders to stay below in their cabin, Anna and Pilar huddled together as the ship rose and fell upon mountainous white-capped waves. Pilar rushed over to a bucket in the corner to be sick, and Anna knelt beside her maid, holding her hair back from her face and sharing soothing words while she rubbed the other woman's back.

"That's it—take a breath and we'll be out of the storm soon," Anna said, but the words tasted like a lie. She had a terrible feeling that the storm would be the end of their voyage.

After several hours, she coaxed Pilar to lie in bed. Moments later, a sailor pounded a fist on their cabin door.

"My ladies, we're taking on water. We're abandoning the ship. You must come!" the man shouted.

"Abandoning the ship?" Anna frantically pulled Pilar up to her feet. They had slept in their clothes the last several days, so there was no need to worry about their state of dress.

They stumbled up the gangway and onto the deck. The captain was unfastening a lifeboat from the side of the ship. It was being lowered over the side when he saw Anna and her maid, and he waved them over frantically. Anna guided Pilar toward the boat first, despite her protest.

"My lady—Oh!" Anna pushed Pilar's back, and the captain's first mate caught her and settled her in the boat. The captain stepped in next, and Anna followed him over the side of the ship. The captain held out his hands to catch her, but just then a mighty wave rolled over the ship and his hands slipped. For a brief instant she hung in space, and the pit of her stomach dropped before she plunged into the waves far below.

She sucked in a breath before dark, gray water closed over her head. The icy water cut through her body like a knife. The weight of her skirts and boots pulled her down into the depths. Fatigue began to set in, weighing Anna's limbs down, but something deep within her was kindled to life, as weak as a small candle in a storm, but still a flame.

She remembered the man from the enchanted well in her dreams. He was racing toward her, the horse beneath him a dark, dappled gray. Shadows and light flickered upon his face as he rode and bent low over the horse. She somehow knew he was riding as fast as the wind itself, although the images were moving slowly.

"Trust me . . ." His words echoed inside her head.

That small flame grew brighter within her, and some latent strength returned to her. She kicked, clawed, and fought to reach the distant surface of the sea far above her. She was the daughter of kings and queens. She was descended from an ancient line of warriors. She would not let the sea claim her life.

Breaking the surface with a cry, she forced air into her searing lungs. She wiped seawater from her eyes but saw no sign of the lifeboat she'd hoped to find. There was nothing about her but the wreck of the *Ruritanian Star*. The ocean had torn the ship to pieces.

She swam toward the flotsam of timbers and planks, hoping to find something to catch hold of to stay above the water. A long, thick mast drifted past and she caught it, curling her arms around it just as a wave smashed into her. Holding her breath, she sank down and then bobbed back to the surface with the mast. She gasped for air and searched for any distant outline of land or the lifeboat that held the other survivors.

There was no sign of the boat, but she did spot the silhouette of land. It was so far away . . . too far away. And she was so very tired . . .

Anna bound her arms in the loose ropes that were attached to the mast to help keep herself above the water in case she passed out. Then she kicked toward the distant silhouette of land until her body surrendered to fatigue and she slipped into unconsciousness.

"Trust me . . ." The comforting words came to her some-

where between the waking world and one of her dreams. Pain became distant as the cold crept through her until she was too numb to stay in the land of the living . . .

Violent pain returned, smashing her head and chest. Then pressure on her lips, more pain and pressure. She wanted it to stop, but it didn't. It was rhythmic, and that flame within her kindled back to life. She coughed as seawater exploded from her mouth so hard that she gagged. When she was able to draw a steady breath, she realized she was in someone's arms and no longer in the sea. A man held her tenderly, his stormy gray-blue eyes searching her face as she gazed up at him.

Her lips parted in shock. It was him—the man from her dreams. Wet tendrils of rich dark-brown hair hung dripping above his eyes. She was confused and dazed as she struggled to remember how she knew him; she only knew that he must have pulled her into the world through the water. But why or how she didn't know. Her skull ached as though someone had struck it with a fire poker, and her thoughts, which had seemed so coherent before, were now tumbling over each other like the waves of the sea.

"*You*—it's you." Then the pain in her head grew so fierce that she slipped into darkness once more. The last thing she heard was his voice.

"Who are ye, lass?"

THE WOMAN WAS STILL UNCONSCIOUS AS AIDEN CRADLED her against his chest. He stood and carried her out of the water and toward the sandy beach. Her body was cold and limp now, and her beautiful face was as pale as alabaster. A second ago her warm brown eyes had held him completely still, utterly transfixed, before she sank into unconsciousness and broke the spell she'd cast. Aiden had to get her back to the village before she perished from exposure to the cold sea.

He whistled at Thundir, and his gelding trotted through the shallow rolling waves toward him. He was glad he had saddled Thundir this time because he'd need the firm saddle to hold him and the woman in place. He settled her carefully over the front of the saddle and then climbed up after her. Then he pulled one of her legs over so that she rode astride in front of him.

He then leaned the woman back against his chest and took the plaid blanket he always carried with him and wrapped it around her to secure her to him. The woman made a soft sound, almost a moan, and shuddered against his chest as though aware of the warmth that the blanket was giving her.

"That's it, lassie, hold on now," he murmured to her, hoping she could hear him. The sudden and fierce protectiveness that this woman drew forth surprised him, but he had no time to think on why that was—he only knew that he had to save her.

Then he dug his heels into Thundir's sides, and the horse sprinted forward. They rode hard along the beach until they reached a path that rose up the hillside toward the town of North Berwick. He pushed his horse to move as fast as he could without endangering them on the rocky trail up the cliffside. By the time they reached the bustling little port town, her wet gown had soaked the front of his own clothes clear through and he was shivering from the cold.

He rode straight to the inn where he had been staying the last few days as he waited for Brodie's ship to arrive from France. He earned odd looks along the way with an unconscious woman in his arms, but he cared little for the thoughts of others, especially strangers. If anyone thought he'd done the woman harm, he'd prove them wrong later, once she was out of danger. As if somehow aware of his thoughts, the woman's body began to tremble, and her lips, once the palest pink, were now turning a faint blue color. She made a soft sound again, a feminine whimper as if in pain, and the sound tore at his heart.

"Stay with me, lass," he pleaded. "*Stay with me.*"

When he reached the inn, a stable boy of around seven or eight rushed toward him and caught the reins Aiden threw him. He had to get the woman inside and away from the chill of the Scottish air before she perished.

"Stable my horse and fetch the best doctor ye have and send him directly to my room. I'll pay ye an extra shilling. Be quick—the lassie is deathly ill." He handed the boy the first shilling. The little boy's eyes grew as large as a hunter's moon as he held up the coin.

"Yes, sir!" the lad piped up.

Aiden slid out of the saddle and carefully caught the woman as she slipped off, limp, back into his arms. For a moment, Aiden stared at the woman's face, his world tilting wildly on its axis as he took in her features. He knew her face . . . He knew this beautiful creature from his dreams, and in that moment, he knew that if he lost her, he'd lose himself forever. It was a bloody miracle he'd been riding along the shore every morning for the last three days since he'd arrived here to wait for Brodie and his bride, Lydia to return from France. If he hadn't gone riding today . . . He dared not think what would have happened to her.

Aiden crossed the courtyard and shouldered his way into the taproom of the inn.

Molly Tanner spied him carrying the woman in his arms and was instantly firing questions at him.

"Ack, laddie, what's this now?" Molly, the innkeeper, was a formidable creature. A wiry figure in her late forties, with strong hands and hard eyes that softened a little when she realized it was Aiden.

"She washed up on the shore," he said before taking the stairs to his room. He heard Molly come up behind him as he realized with a curse that he'd need to set her down to find his key.

"Let me, laddie." Molly retrieved his key from his soaked coat pocket and unlocked the door for him. Once the door was open, he carried her into his room and gently laid her down on his bed.

Molly hovered next to him by the bed. "Washed ashore? There was a shipwreck, then?" Molly asked curiously. "Did ye see any cargo or—"

"Molly," he growled softly, not taking his eyes off the woman on his bed, "that was not my concern. But men should be sent to search for other survivors. When the doctor arrives, send him straight up." He fingered the hem of the woman's wet, icy clothes, which no doubt kept her skin at a dangerously cold temperature. "And bring me any extra nightgown ye have, until I can get her one of her own. I'll pay ye for it. She'll not survive if we dinna get her out of these wet clothes."

"She's verra pretty," Molly murmured.

Aiden sighed. "She's naught but a wounded creature who needs my help. Nothing more."

He knew Molly had seen his affinity for animals when he had rescued a horse the day before. The horse had been mad with pain after it sprained its front foreleg, and the rider, in his anger and haste, had wanted to put a bullet in the beast's head. Aiden bought the horse from the man and wrapped the injured leg. Molly had marveled at the way he'd tended to the horse and calmed it. It was a skill he'd had ever since he was a child, but he forgot that when he was among people who didn't know him, his way with animals tended to cause a great stir.

But this woman was not just another wounded creature. He had seen her before, *many* times in his dreams, the ones he had where the veil between dream and wakefulness was thinnest. In the dreams she was lost—always lost in a deep, dark forest, and he was always trying to reach her. As a boy, he had dreamt of a young girl, and now he dreamt of a grown woman. *This* woman. He'd never spoken to anyone of these dreams, not even his siblings.

How such a thing was possible, he didn't know.

"Ye need a nightgown, ye said?"

"Aye." He was barely aware of Molly leaving. His focus was almost entirely on the woman he'd rescued.

With tender hands, he removed her wet leather boots and rolled the stockings off her legs before he gently turned her over to undo the back laces of her gown and remove it. The clothes she wore were finely made, those of a highborn lady, and yet they were not overly extravagant.

He averted his eyes as best he could. It was impossible to ignore the beauty of her body as he revealed it, but his mind was focused on ridding her of the wet fabric. Then he peeled back the covers of his bed and tucked her naked body beneath the sheets and added a few logs to the fire to warm the room. He removed the soaked top blanket and retrieved another that was draped over the back of a nearby chair. He was used to the cold in Scotland, had spent his whole life in a drafty castle and often didn't need as many blankets to sleep at night, but this woman needed as much warmth as he could give her. The blue tint began to fade as her cheeks warmed, losing that fearful white cast to her skin. Her mouth moved as if she was trying to speak, and she stirred fretfully in the bed.

"Rest now. Ye're safe." He placed the backs of his fingers against her forehead, checking for any sign of a fever. He remained at her side, frowning slightly as he studied her features over and over, trying to understand how the woman of his dreams, whose name he didn't even know, was here with him now.

Molly came in once during the wait for the doctor and set a nightgown down on the bed and helped him hang the woman's clothes by the fire to dry.

A quarter of an hour into his silent vigil at her bedside, the doctor arrived with the stable lad on his heels. When the doctor set his black leather case down at the foot of the bed, Aiden tucked a shilling into the boy's open palm and ruffled his hair before sending him on his way.

The doctor was a younger man, perhaps only a few years older than Aiden. He offered his hand to Aiden.

"I'm Arthur MacDonald."

He shook the man's hand. "Aiden Kinkade."

"Now, tell me what's happened. I'll look her over while ye talk." The doctor reached for the sheets, about to pull them down, but Aiden caught his hand.

"I removed her clothes. She's as bare as a newborn bairn." He released the doctor's hand. "I found her washed up on the shore with water in her chest. I cleared much of the water out, but she was drenched and her lips were turning blue." He released Dr. MacDonald's hand.

"Dinna fret. I will endeavor to examine her carefully." The doctor lifted only parts of the sheet as he worked and kept his gaze averted whenever the woman had to be bared more openly for his examination.

"She has a nasty bruise on the back of her head. I see no other injuries except some bruises from a rope or some other binding on her arms. It's her lungs I am most concerned with. It will be easy for her to catch pneumonia. She must be kept warm and dry and sleep elevated with her chest up. Feed her hot broth for the first day or so, and if she's feeling better, she may have more substantial food. Avoid letting her have too much milk or cheese. They will make her cough worse when she starts to clear her lungs out. When she is feeling better, ye must get her up and walking. I've seen my patients do better when given exercise rather than staying in bed. The movement clears the lungs." The doctor stroked his short, dark beard thoughtfully. "Ye dinna ken who she is?"

"No," Aiden said quietly. "I was riding along the shore

when I noticed debris from a shipwreck washing in. That's when I spotted the lass in the shallows."

"A shipwreck, eh? Any other survivors?"

He shook his head. "If there were, I didna see them."

"Well, I'll leave ye to see to her when she wakes. I'm only a short distance away. My home is the last house at the end of this road. Dinna hesitate to summon me."

"Thank ye, Doctor." Aiden shook the man's hand again. Once Dr. MacDonald was gone, Aiden sat on the edge of the bed and stared at the beautiful woman from his dreams who had washed up on the shore. He couldn't help but wonder if she was a selkie princess. He smiled at the thought. No, she was a fae princess. Only the fairy folk could make a woman this beautiful.

"Who are ye, lass?" he asked again, but the woman slept on, oblivious to him and his concerns for her.

Color was continuing to return to her skin, and her breathing was deeper. Her face, which even in sleep had seemed so strained before, had eased and her lovely features softened. He traced her dark eyebrows with a fingertip and then touched her lips, wishing he could warm them with his own in a burning kiss. In his dreams, he was always reaching for her, wanting to hold her, to kiss her, to love her until the world ended and began again and new stars burst forth in the night sky. But it was madness. Surely a woman in his dreams whom he'd never met couldn't be real, couldn't be this woman. His brothers would have insisted it was a mere coincidence, but Aiden believed in things his brothers did not, things like fate and destiny. This woman . . . was both.

"Whoever ye are, I will protect ye, always," he vowed.

The woman gave a soft sigh, and her lips parted slightly as she murmured words too soft for him to hear.

❧

ANNA'S HEAD THROBBED. SHE WONDERED VAGUELY IF SHE had drunk too much wine at dinner. She moaned and rolled, then winced as she rotated her head on her pillow. The twist of her body released something in her lungs, and she coughed hard as she lay on her side. She tasted salty water in her mouth and licked her dry lips. When she moved again, the pain on the back of her head twinged again.

"Ouch!" she hissed, and her sore throat burned at the single exclamation of pain. *Sore throat?* Why did she have a sore throat?

"Easy, lass, ye'll hurt yerself." A deep, rich voice spoke softly from somewhere nearby. She flinched and opened her eyes. For a second her vision blurred, and then she realized she was in a strange room with a strange man. But this realization was worse when she didn't know what sort of room she *should* be in. The man was dark-haired, and his stormy blue-gray eyes were fixed on her in obvious concern.

"Who . . . who are you?" she demanded. She thought she had a vague memory of him and terrible, cold black water and then him again . . . in pale gray-blue water like the sky and how the sunlight had formed a ring of light around his head as he looked down at her.

"I canna understand ye, lass. Can you speak English?"

"Yes—yes, of course," she said in English. Had she been

speaking Danish? She knew the difference between the two languages and made the jump to English when he asked her.

"So ye speak more than one language," the man mused. "Do ye have a name, lass?"

"Anna. My name is Anna . . ." Her voice trailed off as her memory came up with nothing after *Anna*. Why couldn't she remember her own name?

"Anna what?"

A sudden fear rose in her so swiftly that her chest squeezed all the breath from her lungs.

"I don't know," she said with a gasp, then buried her face in her hands and wept. She felt out of control—she didn't know who she was or where she was. It was *terrifying*.

"There now, lass. Dinna cry." The man's hand touched her shoulder, and his warm palm felt good on her bare skin. Bare skin? She lowered her hands from her face to see that her upper body was naked, but mostly concealed by sheets.

"Why am I naked?" she asked in a whisper.

The bedclothes covering her were warm but scratchier than she was used to, and she felt too warm and the air in this small room too stifling. She thought she remembered gentle fingers sliding cold, wet clothes from her skin. Had that been him? Had this man touched her? She should have been terrified, but somehow seeing his face, the kindness mixed with desire, made her blood stir in a way she didn't fully understand.

"Yer clothes were soaked with seawater, and ye were freezing to death." The man removed his hand from her shoulder and stepped back to hold up a nightgown. It was a plain cotton one, but it looked very comfortable.

"Is that for me?" she asked. She should have been afraid of this man. He was impossibly tall, his shoulders broad, and the outline of his muscled physique was clear in the way his waistcoat hugged his waist and the trousers he wore clung to his powerful thighs. But she felt no fear, only confusion.

The man's face reddened. "Aye. Do ye want to put it on now?"

"Yes." She accepted the nightgown, and he turned his back while she stepped out of bed, wobbling a little as her legs felt too weak to hold her up. She had only a moment to pull it over her head and let it slip down her body before a wave of dizziness swamped her.

Strong arms caught her and lowered her onto the bed. His deep, subtle scent reminded her of old forests with trees so ancient they had seen more centuries than men had on earth. She buried her head against the man's throat, wanting to take in more of it. It was a scent that felt familiar, comforting in all the strangeness around her.

"You're so warm," she whispered. If she hadn't been so dizzy and hurting she would have questioned his motives, but right then she took the comfort that she needed from him.

A rich chuckle rumbled from his chest.

"The room is still cold. I'll add more logs to the fire." He tucked her beneath the covers, then turned away to tend to the crackling fire. She had a moment to admire the lean, muscular form of him. He was truly *beautiful*. He wore dark-brown trousers and a simple waistcoat with no fine embroidery, yet he carried himself with a quiet confidence that spoke of a noble spirit. She wasn't sure how she knew that, except to say that she felt oddly in tune with this stranger.

A delicious fire burned in her belly as he crouched in front of the flames. He reached for two logs and placed them with care on the fire, whereas other men would have tossed them in carelessly. That was something she had noticed about him. Everything the man did was careful and controlled. It made her feel safe somehow, though she couldn't say why.

She cuddled deeper beneath the warm bedding. "Who are you to me?" she asked.

"I dinna ken," he replied, and his words only added to her confusion. Wouldn't he know if he knew her? She tried a different question.

"Do you have a name?"

"Aye, lass," he replied, still with his back to her as he used a poker to nudge the logs.

"Will you tell me what it is?" She waited expectantly for the man to answer.

He straightened, placed the poker back in the metal stand, and faced her. Dark hair fell into his stormy blue-gray eyes. They reminded her of the sea. Full of mysteries that would never be solved.

"Aiden Kincade." He made a courtly bow that prompted her to smile.

"And how did we meet, Aiden Kincade?" She remembered him mentioning she'd been found freezing to death in seawater-drenched clothing.

"I found ye drifting toward the beach on the waves. Ye washed up from a shipwreck."

"Shipwreck?" She mouthed the word, baffled.

"Aye, lass. Whatever poor souls sailed with ye must have perished. I didna see anyone else among the wreckage as ye washed in."

A shipwreck and no memories and . . . She touched the back of her head and winced again.

"Careful." He moved toward her but halted inches from touching her, as if remembering they were strangers and he shouldn't touch her. Something about that filled her with tenderness, that he cared about her enough to breach whatever rules of society he followed here in his land.

"The doctor said ye must've struck yer head on something. Ye have bruises too. Ye canna remember anything that happened?"

She closed her eyes, trying to remember. She thought she remembered the ocean . . . and fighting for air. But perhaps that was her imagination trying to fill in the blank spaces. All she truly remembered was his face . . . both through a dark pool of water and again in the pale sea as he rescued her.

"Ye also seemed to ken me," Aiden said as he sat on the edge of her bed, close to her.

Rather than be frightened by his proximity, she was comforted. "Ken?"

"Know," he enunciated.

"Did I?"

"Aye, ye did. Ye said, 'You—it's you.'" He spoke the words in a more English accent than his own.

Anna twisted her fingers in the covers, crumpling them in her lap.

"It's strange, but I feel as if I do know you," she said after a moment. "Not that I could say how." The fire crackled, and her skin felt too warm now.

Aiden studied her face, and the intensity of his eyes on her only heated her more. The familiarity, that connection to him she couldn't explain, tugged at her mind again—as if she should know this man anywhere. He swallowed and shifted closer on the bed, his lips parting as he continued to look upon her. His male beauty took her breath away. It was as though his features had been carved by angels.

Someone knocked on the door. He went to answer it. A woman stood there with a worried look on her face as she peered around Aiden to look at Anna. She was middle-aged and had a fierce expression on her face that softened slightly as she saw Anna sitting up.

"I hate to bother ye, but ye'd best come out and check on that horse with the bad leg. That fool McPherson said he wants it back now. I can watch over yer lassie."

Aiden's eyes darkened. He looked back at Anna. "Dinna move from this bed, lass. I must go, but ye need your rest. I'll be back with food." And just like that, the tall Scottish stranger was gone. That was something she'd recognized in the last few minutes. His accent was *Scottish*, as well as the woman's who had knocked at the door.

Was she lost in Scotland?

CHAPTER 3

"How is the lass?" Molly asked Aiden as he stepped into the hallway.

Aiden was still trying to come to terms with the situation of having found a beautiful half-drowned woman whom he'd seen in his dreams almost all his life, and he didn't hear Molly's question at first until she repeated it.

"Weary, but awake." He followed the innkeeper back down the stairs. "She says her name is Anna, but she seems to have no memory of anything but her first name. She speaks English, but she also speaks . . . Danish, I think, if I recognized it correctly."

"What?" Molly blinked as they reached the bottom of the stairs. The taproom was full of customers, mostly men who worked on the docks, along with the occasional traveler who stayed at the inn. Her exclamation drew a few curious looks, and Aiden kept his voice down as he responded.

"Dr. MacDonald found a wound on her head. I suspect she's lost a bit of her memory until the injury heals itself." He had seen something like this once with an old collie he'd had as a wee lad. His father had struck the dog's head with a cane in a moment of anger, and for three weeks the dog hadn't seemed to know Aiden at all. It got lost in the castle more than once, whereas before it had always known its way about. Aiden had to win the dog's trust all over again. Eventually the wound on its skull healed, and the dog, over time, reverted back to its old habits and mannerisms. Perhaps it would be the same with his mystery woman.

"The poor dear," Molly said with surprising sweetness. "I'll check on her while you handle that bastard McPherson."

Aiden crossed the taproom and exited the front of the inn toward the stables. The stable lad who had fetched the doctor for him before was shouting at a rotund man wearing a top hat whom Aiden recognized.

"McPherson," he growled at the man an instant before McPherson raised a hand to cuff the boy. Aiden caught the man's arm, easily holding it away from the child's face.

"*Manners*, McPherson, or else people will start to think ye hit wee bairns rather than men your own size."

"Take yer hands off me, Kincade! The whelp deserves to have his ears boxed." McPherson brushed imaginary dust off his coat sleeves and scowled.

"Does he, now?" Aiden shot the boy a pretend scowl, and the boy caught on, looking down at the ground bashfully.

"Off with ye," Aiden barked at the boy, who took the

hint and fled from sight. Aiden turned his attention back to the man. "Now, what's this I hear about ye wanting yer horse back?"

McPherson's mustache twitched and his beady dark eyes narrowed as he seemed to anticipate Aiden's displeasure at his next words.

"I want my horse back; I've sold it to the butcher down the street. He pays handsomely for horseflesh."

Aiden's blood boiled with sudden rage, but he held in the flames.

"*The butcher?* Ye mean to sell it to be slaughtered? Have ye lost yer mind?"

McPherson bristled. "It's my horse. I can do as I wish with it."

"Ye sold it to me first, if ye'll recall," Aiden growled.

"And I found a better price. I want it back." McPherson thrust out the bag of coins that Aiden had given him. Aiden made no move to accept the bag. He kept his hands at his sides, clenched into fists.

"We had a deal, McPherson. I willna take back any money for the beast. The horse is mine. I dinna care how much the butcher gave ye. Ye can sort it out with him."

McPherson grabbed Aiden's arm when Aiden made to pass by him to go to the stables. "How dare ye—"

Aiden whirled, his fist connecting with McPherson's nose. The man hit the ground on his back, crying out in pain as he clutched his bloody nose.

Cold fury rippled beneath his skin, but he kept a rein on it as he'd always done. Aiden had never struck a man who didn't deserve it, but this bastard certainly deserved it.

"Come here again and it will be more than yer nose I

break," Aiden said. His icy tone sparked fear in the man's eyes. Aiden walked past him and went into the stables. The scent of hay and horses soothed the furious beast that paced inside Aiden. Abuse of others, especially the weak and helpless, was one of the few things in this world that could arouse his fury. McPherson was lucky, luckier than he knew, to be walking away with only a bloody nose.

"Ye drew his cork!" the stable boy crowed with glee, and Aiden glanced toward the loft, where the boy peered over the ledge at him.

"Aye," Aiden agreed solemnly.

"Ye shoulda killed him." The boy climbed down the ladder near him and jumped the last step with the rambunctious energy only children ever possessed.

"No, lad, he's not worth the blood I'd spill if I did." Aiden ruffled his hand through the lad's hair and noticed the boy flinched at his touch and then relaxed. His heart sank as he recognized the signs of a beaten child. He'd once been just like this boy, flinching at every touch, good or bad.

"How are the horses?" Aiden asked.

"Thundir's good. Bob's doing much better."

"Bob?" Aiden asked as the boy kept pace with him. They walked down toward Thundir's stall.

"Bob's the one with the bad leg. I think he looks like a Bob, so I named him Bob."

Aiden smiled. "Bob it is, then. But there's just one problem."

The little boy's eyes widened. "What's that?"

"Bob's a *lass*."

"Oh . . ." The boy's smile faded. "Bob's a lass?"

"Aye, lad, afraid so. Ye dinna ken the difference between a male and female horse?" Aiden studied the little sandy-haired boy. He was thin, likely malnourished, but his eyes were bright with a keen intelligence.

"I guess not. I've only been here a week," the boy admitted.

"Then I'm happy to teach ye all that I ken about horses. Yer first lesson is this: mares like Bob are stronger than ye might expect. They may not be as large as some of the stallions or geldings, but they can run longer and are tougher than ye'd expect. Never underestimate a female, no matter the species." He couldn't help but think of Anna as he said this. She'd survived a shipwreck and had nearly drowned but was already recovering. If that wasn't strength, he didn't know what was.

"Like the pretty lady ye brought to the inn? The one they're saying ye found in the sea?" The boy climbed up on a nearby barrel to better look at Thundir while the gelding ate his oats. Thundir poked his head out of the stall, chewing contentedly.

"Aye, she's very strong, just like Bob," Aiden agreed sagely. "Let's go check on her, eh?" He lifted the lad down from the barrel, and they moved to the next stall, where the mare was being kept.

Aiden's mind returned to the mystery woman lying in his bed. He wondered if anyone else had survived the shipwreck. When he'd found her, she'd been drifting near a broken mast, with ropes lightly wound around her as though at one point she'd been tied to it. She was strong, of that he had no doubt. He only wished he knew who she was so he could better help her.

It was clear she was from the Continent. She had spoken in a language he thought he recognized as Danish, but she'd also spoken English as well as any Englishwoman when he'd asked her if she could. Once he was done checking on the horses, he would pay a call on the doctor and see what he thought of the woman's memory loss.

Bob was in the stall on the opposite side of Thundir, and the horse eyed Aiden warily as he approached. She lifted her head a little, drawing back, her eyes full of suspicion.

"Easy, lassie. That fat fool is gone. He willna take ye anywhere." Aiden curled his hand in a loose fist as he extended it toward the mare. Bob took her time and eventually came to him and ate the lump of sugar he had hidden in his curved palm when he turned his hand over to her exploring nose.

"Will ye let me look at yer leg?" he asked.

She huffed and backed up from the door so he could enter the stall.

"She understands ye?" the boy asked from behind him.

"Aye. Animals mayna know all of our words, but they hear our tone and see our body language. They can tell better than us when someone is lying."

"How do they do that?"

"Yer body betrays ye. Ye might be speaking sweet words, but if she sees yer eyes dart to a riding crop, she'll know yer thinking about striking her. Ye should always be honest about yer intentions with animals. 'Tis the only way ye'll earn their trust."

He examined Bob's foreleg and changed the bindings. Then he carefully brushed out the horse's coat and combed tangles from her mane. That care earned Bob's trust more than anything else, and by the time he finished she was nuzzling his shoulder and nibbling at his shirtsleeve.

Aiden exited the stall and gave the stable lad instructions to feed her and bring fresh water, and then he left and headed for the doctor's home. He'd taken care of one injured female—now he needed to see to the one lying upstairs in his bed.

⚜

ANNA COULDN'T STAY IN BED, NO MATTER HOW TIRED she was. After Aiden left the room, she walked to the small window. She leaned against the frame and gazed upon the little village below her. She glimpsed Aiden speaking to a man in the courtyard of the inn. Although she couldn't hear what was being said, Aiden's body language was taut and angry. Anna pressed her nose to the glass, trying to get a better few of the encounter—or rather, of Aiden. The man said something, and then Aiden threw a punch, felling the man to the ground. Anna gasped, but despite the show of violence, she wasn't afraid of Aiden.

At first, she was shocked by his behavior. Aiden stood tall, strong, and fearless over the other man, but he did no further harm when he easily could have. As much as Anna knew she was a mystery to herself, her quiet, handsome, strong rescuer was a mystery too.

The thought sent a little flutter through her chest. She expected few other men would have been as honorable with her as he had been. He could have taken advantage of her, but hadn't. When he disappeared into the stables by the inn, she looked toward the small houses and beyond to the blue-gray sea on the horizon.

Her heart panged with a deep ache that had no explanation as she gazed out at the endless sea. With a sigh, she abandoned the window and approached the cheval mirror that sat atop the washstand. She could tell she wasn't a pale-faced creature, but pale from her ordeal rather than pale by nature. She could see the hint of sun in her skin that would gleam once she felt better. Her hair was a mess of dark waves that turned russet as they dried.

Bruises shadowed her wrists and forearms. She drew her fingertips along them and had a flash of memory—tying the ropes of a broken mast around her arms. *She* had made these marks herself . . . She flinched at the flashes of memory that were there, but murky as though half sunk beneath the waters that had nearly killed her.

Anna couldn't deny her relief at remembering at least that much. There was something terrifying about waking up bruised and injured while having no memory of how she'd come to be that way. At least it hadn't been done to her by another person.

Someone knocked on the door, breaking through her meandering thoughts. A woman's voice came through the door. "Miss Anna?"

She crossed the room and braced herself against one of the bedposts to rest. "Yes?"

"Mr. Kincade sent up some food for ye," the woman said.

Anna opened the door and let the woman inside. She was a spry creature with sharp features and gray-streaked hair pulled back into a loose knot on top of her head. Anna had the sense this was not a woman one should cross but that she could be kind and fair in her dealings.

The woman saw Anna half hidden behind the open door. "Ah, there ye are. Come and sit down before ye faint, lassie." She set the tray down on the small table and motioned Anna over. "Come and eat—ye're too thin. 'Tis making *my* bones ache jes to look at ye. My name is Molly, an' this is my inn. If ye need anything, ask for me, ye ken?"

"Thank you, Molly. I'm Anna." She followed Molly to the edge of the bed and sat. "Could I ask you what may sound like a rather silly question?"

The innkeeper tilted her head curiously. "Ask, dearie."

"Where . . . am I? Is this Scotland?"

At this Molly chuckled. "'Tis indeed. You're in North Berwick on the east coast of Scotland."

"Ah . . ." Anna sighed, relieved to realize she could picture Scotland's coastline in her head and where North Berwick was.

Molly put her hands on her hips and frowned. "Ye look as weak as a kitten," she muttered. "Ye shouldna be alone, not until Mr. Kincade returns." She picked up a bowl of soup and handed it to Anna, along with a spoon. "Eat up, now. I'll sit with ye."

Anna accepted the food gratefully. Her stomach felt like a bottomless pit.

"Now, Anna, how did ye end up wrecked as ye were? What ship were ye sailing on?"

Anna ate a few spoonfuls before she answered. "I don't remember . . ."

Molly's brows rose. "Ye canna remember?"

"No. I remember nothing else about who I am or how I

arrived in Scotland." The admission depressed her more than she wished. Not knowing oneself was an odd and unsettling feeling. It felt silly too, like she should simply be able to just remember. But she couldn't, no matter how hard she tried.

"Perhaps we had better fetch Dr. MacDonald back to tend to ye again?"

"Dr. MacDonald?"

"Aye, lassie. Mr. Aiden had him look ye over straight-away when he brought ye here."

So she was even more indebted to Aiden than she realized.

"Ye truly canna remember a thing?" Molly asked. "Nothing at all?"

"Only that I tied myself to a broken mast while I was at sea so I wouldn't drown." She showed Molly the bruises on her arms caused by the ropes. "But I only remembered that a few minutes ago."

The innkeeper tapped her chin. "Maybe yer memory will return in pieces."

Anna hoped it would. "Do you know Mr. Kincade very well?" she asked.

"No, not well. He's been here a few days. He's waiting on a ship from France to arrive, and one can never guess exactly when a ship will come into port. Running an inn, ye see every sort of person, ye ken. The good and the bad. Mr. Kincade is one of the good ones. He is kind, respectful, and makes no trouble."

"But he just struck a man outside. I saw him do it from up here through the window."

Molly grimaced. "The bastard he hit deserved far worse

than he got. Mr. Kincade bought the man's injured horse, fair and honest-like. Then the man comes back this morning, saying he sold it to a butcher. Now Mr. Kincade won't hear of an animal being killed, especially one he can help."

Anna relaxed, and Molly smiled at her. "Dinna worry, lass. If I thought he wasna a good man, I wouldna let him keep ye here. But that does remind me—ye need proper clothes for when ye're feeling more like yerself. I'll have one of my dresses brought up for ye to try on. Ye have more curves than I do, but I can let out the seams and get it to fit."

Molly's kindness was such a relief that Anna felt much of the tension still inside her fade. "Thank you, Molly. I am in your debt."

"Ye owe me no debt," Molly insisted. "Womenfolk have to help each other wherever we can. Now finish yer supper and I'll come back to check on ye."

Anna finished her soup and then found herself exhausted again. She crept back between the sheets of Aiden's bed to sleep. She felt safe knowing that he and Molly were nearby. She had been blessed to wash ashore here and not somewhere else.

A hesitant smile tugged at her lips as she thought of Aiden and the way his gaze burned through her. He made her feel like she was the only person on earth. She couldn't explain why that mattered, but it made her feel safe and cared for . . . and it made her want to care for him the same way. He'd suffered much, she could see that so clearly in his eyes, and she wished she could heal him the way he was healing her. Something about them together felt right . . . And she knew that sounded mad, given that she remembered nothing of her past. She could only trust her instincts, and her instincts told her to stay with Aiden.

❦

AIDEN RAPPED HIS KNUCKLES ON THE QUAINT HOME THAT belonged to Dr. MacDonald. An elderly housekeeper answered and looked him up and down from behind her spectacles.

"Ye dinna look sick," the woman said bluntly. She was a plump creature with gray hair and a short nose, which her spectacles perched precariously on. Aiden could tell she was a brusque woman who responded best to politeness and honesty.

Aiden smiled at her. "I didna know that was a requirement. I'm not a patient, but I have one I need to speak to Dr. MacDonald about."

The housekeeper beckoned him inside. "He's in his surgery, but 'tis empty. Ye can go on back."

Aiden passed by a bedroom and a kitchen before he found the room, which had a sign that read "Surgery" in gold painted letters. The door was partially open. MacDonald was at a desk behind an operating table with his back to the door.

Aiden cleared his throat. "Dr. MacDonald?"

The doctor turned around. "Ah, Mr. Kincade. How is our young patient?"

"She is awake but doesna seem to remember a thing other than that her first name is Anna." Anna's beautiful honey-brown eyes flashed across his mind at the mention of her name. She'd looked so frightened when she'd realized that she couldn't remember anything. He'd wanted to pull her onto his lap and cuddle her and kiss away the worries. He'd also wanted to do more than that, but he couldn't take advantage of her like that.

"She doesn't remember the shipwreck?" The doctor's eyebrows rose as he set aside the papers he'd been making notes in.

"Not the wreck or anything else. I fear she's lost her memories," Aiden said. "I know it can happen sometimes. Ye mentioned she'd struck her head. Perhaps that's what did it."

The doctor pursed his lips in thought, then stood and reached for a large book on his desk.

"Do ye happen to know much about the country Ruritania, Mr. Kincade?"

Unsure of where Dr. MacDonald was going with this question, Aiden shrugged. "Isna it some country on the Continent?" He'd heard the name tossed about . . . mainly by his sister, Rosalind, whose shipping company did business with Ruritanian ports. He usually got distracted when she started talking about business, and now he wished he had listened more.

"It's on the coast. Prussia surrounds it everywhere but on the sea." The doctor opened the book he held to a page he had marked and handed it to Aiden.

Aiden saw what the doctor meant as he examined the map.

"What does Ruritania have to do with Anna?"

"Possibly everything." The doctor's eyes gleamed with excitement. "I was planning to visit ye and Miss Anna this evening. I heard this afternoon the name of our wrecked mystery ship that we believe Anna was on. One of the local fishermen found a piece of the vessel that was painted with the words *Ruritanian Star* in Danish and English. I made some inquiries, and it seems that it's a royal merchant ship from Ruritania."

Aiden frowned as he imagined Anna being tossed from the ship into the icy water. How strong she was to have survived to reach the shore when it seemed others, at least so far, hadn't.

"Do they speak a different language there than English?" Aiden asked.

"Yes, they speak primarily Danish, but also French and German. The country is small but quite wealthy. It's possible Anna came from that ship."

"She first spoke to me in a tongue I didna recognize, but I thought it might be Danish. If she is from Ruritania, that would explain it. But she speaks English."

"That's not so surprising. England is one of Ruritania's trade partners. Many of their countrymen would likely learn English. I ken a bit of Danish myself." When Aiden sent him a surprised look, the doctor chuckled. "I studied medicine at the University of Edinburgh, but I have a passion for languages."

That was a relief to Aiden. Although Anna seemed to understand him just fine, he wondered if hearing Danish spoken to her might bring back some of her memories.

"Would ye come see her now?" Aiden asked.

"Yes, I shall. I would very much like to examine her head again, and also try my hand at speaking her language, if I am right." The doctor retrieved his bag. "I'll follow ye."

Aiden was glad he'd connected one more piece to the

puzzle, but if she came from another land, it would make it even harder to find out who she really was.

❦

ALEXEI ZELENSKY, CROWN PRINCE OF RURITANIA AND second of his name, crouched in the underbrush of the vast ancient area of woods known as the Dark Forest, which lay north of the ruins of the royal Summer Palace. At his back stood William, who had been elected as the new captain of the now renegade royal guards that had stood with Alexei. William was his most trusted friend. They had fled the Summer Palace as it burned. The gutted remains of his former home were all that was left of one of Europe's finest jewels of royal homes. The last few moments he'd spent there on the once beautiful grounds had been marred with sweat, blood, and tears as he'd been forced to flee with his men.

It had been two long weeks since the palace had fallen and he'd sent Anna toward the harbor to sail to England. Two weeks of his men living in the woods and eating whatever they could catch in snares or shoot with longbows.

Alexei knew that his uncle's top priority would be finding him and his rebel men in the woods. No heirs to the throne could be left, and no challenge could be made if Alexei was dead. The thought of his uncle filled Alexei with fresh rage. He tightened his hand on the sword that he held ready.

"The caravan will be coming soon," William whispered behind him. William had been born in England, but his parents had moved here for trade when he'd been a lad. He and Alexei had been friends since they'd been old enough to run about the castle unsupervised. Alexei wouldn't have trusted any other man with the fate of his country.

Alexei nodded. "We attack on my signal." William passed the order along to the other loyal guards waiting in the woods using hand signals.

Between the guards and servants who'd escaped the massacre at the palace, Alexei had managed to bring a hundred and fifty others with him. His uncle's followers had killed every man, woman, and child they could find, along with Alexei's parents. Ruritania's three hundred years of peace had been overturned by one man who believed Alexei's father was weak and that Ruritania needed to conquer its neighbors in order to survive. Alexei had never trusted his uncle, but he would never have foreseen that the man would take so many innocent lives to become king.

At least Anna was safe in England. If she was here, he'd be terrified for her safety at every turn, even though she had trained alongside him all these years in the arts of sword and pistols, even arrows. But it only took one lucky shot by the enemy to kill someone, and he couldn't risk his twin. Once he defeated his uncle and restored peace to the land, he would send for her to come home.

Ahead of them, a caravan of soldiers in bloodred uniforms marched down the road through the woods. Alexei knew the wagons would be heavy with gold and food, and he aimed to take both. Already in a short time, his uncle had raised taxes and confiscated livestock and crops all over the country. Alexei's people were starving. He couldn't let them suffer much longer.

A number of guards bearing the Red Wolf on their uniforms passed by on horseback. Two wagons came after them, and a rear guard followed behind. Alexei raised his hand slightly and then pointed forward. The signal given, they then leapt from their hiding spots and charged the caravan. The cries of his men shouting, *"The White Lion forever!"* buoyed his spirits. Shots rang out as men fired pistols and rifles before turning to swords. Alexei and his men fought his uncle's soldiers in a clash of violence and steel.

The first wagon bolted through the chaos. Alexei climbed up on a free horse and chased the wagon down, climbing onto it and stopping the driver with a blade to the man's throat.

"You shall go no farther," Alexei warned, and gestured for the man to abandon his seat. The man got down to the ground, arms raised.

"Tell my uncle I'm coming for him. His days as a pretender to the throne are coming to an end. The White Lion will roar once more." The man nodded frantically, eyes wide with terror as he ran off into the woods. He would either become lost or find his way back. Alexei cared not which.

Alexei's men broke into a cheer behind him as the last guard was subdued and the wagons were taken off the main road.

When they met up once more at their camp hidden deep in the forest, William came to greet him. "What are your orders, my king?"

Alexei flinched at the title. *King* . . . He didn't feel like a king. He felt like a young man who'd been forced into a role he hadn't planned to take on for another twenty years or more. Now he was carrying the weight of a crown and the hopes and dreams of a people that were being threatened by his uncle. He would have given anything to go back and save his parents, stop his uncle, and return to the life he'd had before . . . a life of innocence. He wished Anna was there. She always knew what to do in difficult situations.

He drew in a breath, calming himself as he planned his next move.

"Set aside enough food for the men for the next few months and as much coin as we need to secure better equipment. Then distribute the rest to the people, starting with those most in need."

"I'll see it done," William vowed and left. Alexei joined the rest of his men at the fireside while they sang songs and shared stories of the old days. He said nothing himself, but raised his mug of ale and drank whenever they toasted.

He kept a brave face for his men, but deep inside, he was a broken man, a man who'd seen his parents murdered, and he'd had to send his twin into exile. He knew very well he might never see Anna again.

He bid his men good night. A thousand fears plagued him as he pushed the flap of his small tent back and stretched out on the blankets on the forest floor.

He lay awake until the fires turned white with ash and the smoke faded into the predawn sky. His last thoughts before sleep claimed him were of his sister and whether she'd reached England safely.

CHAPTER 4

Anna sat by the fire, staring at the flames. Small flashes of fear and pain kept darting across her mind like shadowy wraiths. The small fire in the hearth didn't scare her, but she remembered a great fear of fire. Her body remembered it more than her mind. It was a strange thing for one's body to carry memories that one's mind could not remember.

Made restless by her memory failing her, she got up to splash cold water on her face. As she looked into the porcelain basin, the surface rippled when she saw . . . No, what she saw was impossible. It was as though she was looking through the inside of a wishing well and seeing the canopy of a dark forest stretching over the tops of smooth, water-worn stones. She knew that place, didn't she? Anna blinked, and the strange vision was suddenly gone.

"*Trust me, lass . . . ,*" Aiden's voice whispered in her mind. Anna dipped her fingers into the water, and the knot of tension within her bled away.

"Stop being such a ninny," she chided herself.

She washed her face and grimaced at the sight of her russet hair all in tangles. She searched Aiden's travel case and found a brush and, with some effort, she finally managed to tease the knots from her hair. The brush was coarse, the bristles reminding her of a boar's hairs. She ran her thumb over them and smiled a little as she thought of the brush's owner. She returned the item to his case and tried to ignore the urge to examine the clothes inside the valise.

Anna gathered the long, wavy mass of her hair at the nape of her neck and bound it with a leather strap she'd found in Aiden's valise. Once that was done, she settled by the window to watch the townsfolk below. All the while, she secretly hoped she'd get a glimpse of Aiden. As a stranger in this land, he was the only person she really felt like she knew. Whenever he was near, she felt warm and safe. She pulled her hair over her shoulder and played with a strand of it while she observed the people below. It was drawing close to dusk when she was startled by a knock.

"Anna, it's Aiden. I brought Dr. MacDonald to see you."

"Come in." Anna rose from the chair to greet them. But more than that, she sought the comfort of Aiden's face. He was the one person she trusted in this strange land.

"Ye're looking better," he observed. His eyes softened a little, and his lips formed a hint of a smile. That single expression made her belly quiver with excitement.

"I feel better," she confessed in a slightly roughened voice. The seawater she'd swallowed had made her a little hoarse at first, but she was feeling so much better. "Molly brought me some food."

"That's good to hear." The doctor followed Aiden into the room and closed the door behind him. "Miss Anna, I am Dr. MacDonald. I am the physician Mr. Kincade summoned to examine you. May I see how ye are doing now?"

She nodded and sat patiently while the doctor examined her. He was younger than she'd expected. Older than her—at least she thought so, given how she looked in the cheval mirror—but he wasn't a gruff old man with a temper. She had vague memories of such a doctor treating her when she'd broken her arm.

"I broke my arm," she blurted out in sudden excitement and shared a smile with Aiden. She was remembering things, and even if they seemed small and unimportant, they were at least memories.

"No, ye didna, lass. It was only a bit of bruising," Aiden reassured her as he came to stand beside the doctor.

"No, no, what I mean is I *remember* I broke my arm long ago. I was thinking about how nice Dr. MacDonald is and not at all like this doctor who once treated me when I broke my arm. I must have been a child then. I remember feeling so very small."

"Her memory is coming back," Dr. MacDonald said. "This is good. Things she does or sees in the next few weeks may bring back even more memories if we're lucky. It's possible the trauma of the shipwreck caused her mind to hide from those memories. The mind sometimes does that when an event causes enough trauma."

The doctor then lifted Anna's chin and studied her eyes while moving a finger back and forth as he instructed her to follow it with her gaze. Then he spoke haltingly in Danish. It was a relief to hear a language that was as familiar as English to her, perhaps even a little more so. It also explained why her own English when she spoke had a hint of an accent—it was a Danish accent. She still answered his questions, despite being rather confused as to why he was speaking Danish and not English.

"Excellent. Well, we've established this for certain, Miss Anna." Dr. MacDonald winked at her teasingly like an older brother might. "Ye are from Ruritania, *or* ye have extensive knowledge of speaking Danish."

"I'm Ruritanian?" Aiden had mentioned that she had spoken another language to him, but he hadn't known what she'd said. Now she had an answer. But what did it mean?

"Do not fret, my dear," Dr. MacDonald soothed. "The memories will come with time. The more anxious ye are, the more energy it will require for yer mind to fetch them from where they've been buried."

Anna tried to calm herself, but it wasn't easy.

"Let's see yer scalp and yer arms." He gently touched her head and looked over her arms. The bruises had turned a dark purple in the last few hours. "Once yer feeling well enough, I suggest ye walk a little, with Mr. Kincade, of course. Not alone, lest ye become dizzy. I dinna wish ye to fall."

Walking did sound nice. Anna was tired, but she was far more tired of being cooped up in this little room. She hadn't even been here a full day and already she was wanting to get up and move about.

"How are ye feeling overall? Any other aches or pains?" Dr. MacDonald asked her.

"No, not really. It just feels as if I was battered about on the sea, and my body must need time to recover from that."

"It certainly does. Have ye been coughing?"

"No, not at all."

"That's good." Dr. MacDonald shot a glance at Aiden, and she saw Aiden's relief at whatever the doctor's silent look had told him.

"Well, Miss Anna, continue to rest. Eat whatever ye want for now, but avoid cheese and milk if ye start coughing." The doctor closed his bag after setting a small bottle on the washstand. "Take two drops of this if ye have any pain." To Aiden, he added, "Be strict with the dose. 'Tis morphine and must be given with care."

"I understand," Aiden promised. After the doctor left, Aiden's gaze returned to Anna.

She was alone with him now. Her mind told her that was dangerously scandalous. But her heart trusted this quiet, solemn stranger beyond all rationality. He represented warmth, strength, and safety to her, yet he also awakened other feelings in her, ones she had trouble recognizing. Ones that made her skin flush and her breath catch when he came too close to her.

"Are ye hungry?" he asked.

Strangely, she was. "Yes, I'm rather famished."

"I'll fetch some dinner for us." He offered her a reassuring smile and then left her alone once more.

Anna was going to wait in bed until he returned, but then she decided she wanted to feel *normal* and not like some invalid. She moved the two armchairs by the fire until they faced each other, and then she set a small side table between them so they might use it for their plates. She was moving her hands over the blankets of the bed after setting the sheets back in place when he returned. Aiden carried a tray of meat and some freshly baked bread, along with a plate of boiled potatoes. It was hearty fare and simple food, yet it smelled wonderfully divine.

Aiden's gaze swept over her little arrangements to create a dining area for them.

"I thought it might be nice to . . ." She faltered at his silence. If only she knew what he was thinking. She examined him in the brief silence, taking in his height and broad chest. His dark hair fell into his eyes, and Lord, those eyes . . . They blazed in the half-light of twilight. It made her all the more aware of his closeness, his size compared to hers, and the wealth of unsaid words in his gaze.

"That's a lovely idea, lass. I'm sorry I didna think of it myself." He set the food down and poured them each a glass of wine, and then they sat down in their chairs so very properly despite being in such a tiny little room.

"Mr. Kincade . . . ," she began uncertainly.

"Aiden, lass, call me *Aiden*."

"Oh, but I feel I shouldn't." She longed to call him Aiden, but it seemed she had been drilled on the proper way to address a person she didn't know.

"Ye should. I can only call ye Anna, after all. 'Tis only fair."

She laughed softly. "I can't argue with that logic, I suppose." She was silent a long moment before finding the nerve to speak again. "Aiden?"

"Yes?" He broke off a piece of bread and took a bite. His gaze never left hers, and it was strange to feel the intensity of his focus, yet exciting too.

"I'm sorry. I don't know much about myself to provide decent conversation. So I was hoping you might perhaps tell me about yourself instead?"

He swallowed and looked at her a long moment, his expression still unreadable. "Ask me anything ye wish." His voice was impossibly soft, and yet there was a hint of roughness to it, as though he didn't speak often, which made this conversation, however casual, seem all the more important.

"I'm a stranger to ye, and ye have put yerself into my safekeeping," he continued. "'Tis yer right to know me."

To know him . . . How those words filled her with a deep ache that had no explanation.

"For which I am grateful," she was quick to add. "I will repay you once I discover who I am."

"Do not trouble yerself over that. I seek no repayment of any kind."

She blushed at the quiet, elegantly put assurance that he would make no scandalous demands of her.

"I'm the third child of the last of Kincade clan who still remain in Scotland after Culloden."

"Culloden?" The word sounded familiar to her.

"It was the last major battle we Scots fought against the English, almost eighty years ago. We lost. Bitterly." Aiden spoke with a well of sorrow in his eyes, and it ripped something soft inside of her. His voice was so deep and sad, resonating in her chest. "Everything in my country was destroyed. Clans were broken, lairds killed, homes burned to the ground, and property taken from my people and given to the English."

"That's horrible," Anna breathed, the horror of it branding itself on her soul.

Aiden's eyes flicked to her, full of fire and misery. "They called it the clearances—because my people were cleared off their land."

Something niggled in the back of her mind, fire and war and betrayal, but before she could grasp it, it was gone. Hesitantly, she continued her interrogation. "And your family, they survived Culloden?"

He answered with a sad smile. "Oh yes, our ancestors were clever and won the trust of an English lord, and he let them have their castle back. Our mother was the last true Kincade. Her people had been in Scotland since the beginning of our country. My father was but a distant cousin but was the only male heir left. To keep the land in my mother's family, she agreed to marry him, but he wasna a good man."

Anna swallowed past the sadness that engulfed the room, waiting for him to continue.

"They had four children—my older brothers, Brock and Brodie, and my wee baby sister, Rosalind—not so wee now, actually. You look about her age, perhaps a few years younger." He gestured slightly to Anna, and Anna felt an absurd blush crawl up her cheeks. She didn't know why, but this man's attention made her warm.

She cleared her throat and refocused on his words. "And your parents, they are—"

"Dead. Both are dead and gone." Aiden's voice was wooden and quiet.

"Oh, I'm so sorry," she replied in a voice as soft as his. A sudden flash of blood and smoke, pain and grief, stabbed her heart so violently that she held her breath and rubbed at her chest to erase the feeling. And just as quickly as it had struck, it faded away.

"'Tis the past," he said. "'Tis over and done."

"We say that, don't we?" she mused. "But the past and future echo forward and backward in time endlessly." She'd heard someone tell her that once, but she couldn't remember who.

Aiden sipped his wine. "That is more true than I care to admit. My father was a brutal man, and my mother, rest her soul, was unable to protect her children. She was a warmhearted woman, kind and gentle, not made to be married to a cruel, cunning creature like my father. A broken heart drove her to an early grave. My father's hate still lingers, even though he's dead and buried."

"I'm sorry." As she said that, Anna had a sudden memory, as clear as the sun breaking through a bank of clouds. She had clung to that broken ship mast in the vast and stormy sea, and she had cursed someone. Screamed a name over and over and wished the cruelest of fates upon the man's head. A name that was ruthless, a name that meant betrayal of the deepest kind.

Aiden leaned forward. "What is it? Ye've gone pale."

"It's a name, the name of someone who drew my deepest hate . . . When you spoke of your father and his brutality, a name came to me, one that made me feel an unspeakable rage."

"What name?"

"Yuri." She wished she could remember why that name

came to mean something so violent in her mind. It was terrifying to come again and again to a blank void in her mind where everything that mattered should be clear, but wasn't.

"Yuri . . ." Aiden repeated the name as if he hoped it would mean something to him.

They ate in silence for a few minutes before she worked up the courage to ask another question.

"What are your brothers and sister like?" She finished her wine and basked in the comforting warmth that filled her body.

Aiden smiled broadly. "My brothers are trouble, ye ken. But one canna help but love them. Brock is responsible, but he has a strong temper—mind ye, one he would never vent on innocent people or animals. But he can become cross, like the badger he is named after. Brodie, well, he can charm a snake, and before he married Lydia he bedded far too many lassies. And Rosalind, my sister, is a darling. A very smart and clever and beautiful lass. All three of my siblings are married to English bloodlines."

"Oh?"

"Brock married a lass named Joanna Lennox. And Joanna's older brother, Ashton, married our sister, Rosalind."

"Really?" Anna giggled at the tangled web of his family tree.

"Brodie married an English lassie too, but thankfully she wasna a Lennox. That would have been too strange for my liking."

"And you . . . are not married?" She'd seen no evidence of a wife, but that was easy enough to hide, and the customs here for such things were unfamiliar to her.

"No, not me," he replied. "I was once told that my path to love would come at a great and terrible price."

"Someone told you that as a child?" Anna was horrified at the thought of someone putting such a great weight of the soul upon a little boy's shoulders.

"Aye. When I was a wee lad, a band of Romani, Travellers, came to our lands while my father was in Edinburgh for business. My brothers and I let them stay for three weeks while my father was gone. I used to sneak out of the castle at night, lured by their fires burning bright in the dark.

"Women in bright skirts wearing golden bangles on their hands and ankles would dance around the fires. Men would play tunes on pan flutes, and I would join the children in their dancing. The embers would catch upon the breeze and lift in the air, swirling like fireflies all around us. It was magical. The last night the Travellers stayed with us, an old woman, the ruling grandmother of their clan, called me to sit before her next to the fire. She took my palm and read my fate in the fire's glow."

Anna leaned forward, spellbound by his words.

"She told me that I could have the greatest love I'd ever know, but it would come at a terrible price. She said I was never fully a part of my world. That I was of the water and my love would be of the air. That I would have to give up my very soul to be with her. Ever since that night, I have dreamed of one person. I kenned the dreams weren't *just* dreams. I saw a girl at first in these dreams, but as I grew into a man, she grew into a woman . . . I never expected to meet her."

"Have you? Met her, I mean." Anna's heart was filled

with an intense ache of loneliness. She had foolishly begun to hope that Aiden might come to desire her someday, as she was starting to desire him, but it seemed this other woman was his destiny.

"Ye truly wish to ken?" he asked, his eyes catching the glow of the firelight.

"Yes, tell me." She would pretend to be happy for him and hide her disappointment.

"I met this woman this morning when I rescued her from the ocean."

For a long moment, she didn't breathe. He was talking about *her*.

"Aiden . . ." Her voice faltered because she wasn't quite sure what she wanted to say.

"It was ye, Anna. I have seen ye in my dreams for more than twenty years, and now here ye are. How that is possible, I dinna ken."

"Me?"

"And what's more, ye seemed to ken who I was as well. When I found ye in the waves, ye opened yer eyes and said, 'You—it's you.'"

Anna remembered him telling her that when she'd first awakened, but she didn't know why she had said it.

"That is why I will guard ye, Anna. I will be with ye at yer side until ye tell me to leave." Something about the way he said that made her feel as if he'd made a claim upon her. The thought created a well of complicated feelings within her that she couldn't begin to sort out.

"We are bound, ye and I. It seems we have always been. I ken that may frighten ye, since we've only just met, but 'tis the truth."

Her arms broke out in goosebumps at his words, and even though she had no memories of him now or how she should know him, she *believed* what he said. Perhaps that was why she felt so safe around him and drawn to him. Her body *remembered* him, even if her mind could not. The vision she'd thought she'd seen in the washbasin came back to her and she trembled. She'd heard his voice, but perhaps that had been an overactive imagination? Despite that being more possible, her very bones argued that what he said was true.

With all these sudden revelations, her limbs felt heavy. She stifled a yawn with a fist.

"Ye've eaten, and now ye should sleep. Rest, Anna, lass. I'll still be here in the morning."

She rose from her chair and moved toward the bed, her steps dragging. She pulled back the covers and crawled into the bed.

"Where will you sleep?"

He chuckled and came over to her. He pulled the sheets up to her collarbone, tucking her in as though she were a child.

"I'll be here in a chair beside you."

"Oh, that must be uncomfortable."

He reached out and brushed the backs of his knuckles over her cheek and flashed her a roguish smile that stirred her body with a desire she'd never felt before.

"Perhaps, but I'm a gentleman, and it's better than the floor."

AIDEN HAD TOLD HER THE TRUTH. SHE WAS THE WOMAN from his dreams, the one the Romani woman had warned him about. He had not sought her out, yet she had found her way to him, as fate determined she would. He would not turn his back on her, however, no matter the price. Now that he'd seen her, held her in his arms, he felt the peace he had searched for all his life when he was near her. And she didn't even know who she was.

That was just like fate, wasn't it? To deliver to him a beautiful woman who clearly was brave and strong, yet when she looked at him, she had the most trusting eyes he'd ever seen and the sweetest innocence on her face as she slept. He couldn't deny wanting her, couldn't deny wanting to protect her, to give everything he had to her in whatever way she needed. Yes, this was a woman he would give his life for . . . just as fate had wished him to.

For most of his life, that Romani prophecy had hung over him like an invisible shroud. He'd never told his siblings, never told anyone. It was a weight that he alone must carry. As the years passed and he'd lived in the world as a grown man, his fear of finding the woman who would hold his heart faded. He'd dallied with maids here and there, finding passion in the dark and giving passion to those women in return, but nothing had touched his heart and soul.

Nothing like the way he'd felt when he'd first touched Anna. Even the cold water rushing around their bodies hadn't dimmed the sudden heated desire or the ancient sense of "knowing" this woman as his in that moment he first saw her face clearly. The threat of dying still held a weight on him, but now he was ready to carry the burden because he'd seen and held the reason for his existence. This woman was everything to him. And what man wouldn't die for that?

Anna lay asleep in his bed, as trusting and innocent as a wee bairn. His chest ached just to look at her, and despite that ache, he smiled as he settled down into a chair to sleep next to her. That peace, that sense of rightness, was so strong that for the first time in years he knew he'd sleep without dreaming about his father.

"Ye have me now, lass," he promised her, and closed his eyes.

Several hours later, he woke to the sound of crying. The candle on the table beside him burned low. Wax pooled at the base of the candleholder. Only a faint flame's glow, aided by moonlight, showed Anna on the bed. She was curled up tight, her body racked with sobs, her face contorted in pain.

"Anna, Anna, my wee darling, wake up." He shook her shoulder as she continued to softly weep in her sleep.

It took a moment before she could shake off the nightmare. "Aiden!" She threw herself into his arms, and he nearly fell off the side of the bed.

"I'm here, lass. I've got you." He moved himself to the center of the bed and pulled her onto his lap so he could hold her better. "What were ye dreaming about?" he asked when her hitched breathing calmed.

"Fire . . . fire everywhere. Someone I love died. I can't remember. I can't—" She buried her face against his throat. "Oh, it was too awful."

Aiden tightened his arms around her, wishing he could take her pain and carry it himself.

"Well, ye're safe now. Whatever happened before, ye're safe now." He kissed the crown of her hair. It seemed such a natural thing to do. But when she lifted her head up to see him, her lips brushed innocently against his cheek, and he felt his body harden with desire.

"Are we truly destined for each other?" she asked.

He gazed at her face in the moonlight. He remembered the Romani woman's eyes as she'd spoken. *"You will die for her . . ."* And he knew it was true. She was his, this mysterious stranger, and he would do anything for her, even give his life.

"Do ye ken what selkies are?"

She shook her head.

"They are people of the water who live in a seal's skin but can shed that skin to become human for a time. When ye washed up before me, I thought at first ye might be a selkie princess." He smiled softly, hoping the change of subject would distract her.

"A selkie princess?" She smiled drowsily. "That sounds rather nice." She yawned again and laid her head on his shoulder. "Will you hold me a little while longer? I think I might not have any more nightmares if you do."

"Aye. I will hold ye all night if ye wish."

"Thank you." She pressed a kiss to his throat and, after a moment, he felt her body completely relax. She slept on, clutching him like a favorite child's toy. He didn't mind.

Somehow he managed to doze off in that position until after dawn, when a surprised feminine screech sent him bolting awake.

"*Aiden Kincade!* What do you think you're doing?"

His eyes flew open. He tensed at the sight of two people hovering in the open doorway of his room.

CHAPTER 5

Aiden shot out of bed. He put his body between Anna and whatever threat had entered their room, but he relaxed as the sleep left him and he realized who it was.

"Easy, brother. The innkeeper said ye were in this room so we thought to see ye first before we saw to our own room. We didna ken ye were entertaining a lassie." Brodie's laugh made Aiden lower his fists. Lydia, the Englishwoman Brodie had recently married, stood next to him, her eyes wide in scandalized shock. She was the one who had yelled at him.

"What are you doing, Aiden?" Lydia asked, clearly stunned. "And who is that with you?"

"Aiden?" Anna's anxious voice grabbed his attention. She had the covers pulled up to her chin, not in fear, but shame and worry.

"'Tis only my brother Brodie and his wife, Lydia. Give

me a minute to talk with them, lass." He braced a hand on the headboard as he leaned forward and kissed Anna's forehead, and then he shooed his brother and sister-in-law back out into the hall, where he closed the door. Lydia was still flabbergasted, but Brodie was holding in a laugh.

"I'm glad to see ye enjoying yerself for a change, little brother." Brodie grinned wickedly until his petite wife jabbed a sharp elbow into his stomach. "Oof!" He doubled over as air whooshed out of his lungs. Then Lydia rounded on Aiden again.

"Really, Aiden, bringing a woman of the night to *your* room . . . I never thought you might take after Brodie and would sleep with just *anyone*." She shot a pointed look at her roguish husband.

"Have a care, wife—that's yer husband ye're talking about," Brodie warned, but his eyes promised only sensual punishment. "Also, yer making a wee bit of an assumption there, arna ye? A lot may have happened since we left. Mayhap my brother has found a bride!" Brodie's tone was full of teasing, as if the idea of Aiden marrying anyone was a lark.

"My bonnie Lydia," Aiden greeted magnanimously and pulled the prickly woman into his arms until her disapproval softened and she hugged him back. "Honeymooning has suited ye well. Ye look happy." He meant it too. Lydia had carried many burdens after her mother died. Marrying a bounder like Brodie who loved to tease and spoil her rotten had been good for her spirit and her heart.

Lydia blushed. "It was wonderful, wasn't it?" she asked Brodie. Her husband leaned down and kissed her cheek, his hard features softening.

"It was." Then Brodie cleared his throat. "Now, tell us who's the wench in yer bed?"

"She's no wench, brother," Aiden said, his tone quiet. They were in an open corridor, and he didn't want anyone to overhear them.

"Not a wench?" Brodie echoed, and got another elbow from Lydia. "*Oi*, wife, stop that," he growled.

"Or what?" Lydia tilted her chin back in defiance.

"Or I'll carry ye off to bed and when I'm done, ye will be half dead from pleasure and willna have any energy to jab me with your pretty elbows, *that's* what," he said in warning.

Lydia's eyes darkened as she shot him a seductive look. "Well, in that case . . ." She pulled her elbow back to strike him again.

"Ye two arna tired of tupping yet?" Aiden asked with an aggrieved sigh.

"No," they replied in unison.

"Well, kindly restrain yerselves in front of Anna," he ordered. "I'll not have her thinking we are savages."

"And *who* is Anna?" Lydia asked, her gaze straying to the closed door.

"Aye, who is she?" Brodie asked, understandably curious. Aiden took women to bed far less than his brothers. He had been with women, of course, and knew how to pleasure them, but he wasn't like Brodie. When he mated his body to a woman's, it was also a mating of the heart and soul.

That those past relationships hadn't turned into something more was his own fault. His heart always held back, telling him there was something more. And now here was

Anna, and there was an intensity of connection he felt with her he'd never felt with anyone else.

He wasn't about to rush her into bed. He wanted to savor every moment he had with her.

He didn't dare tell Brodie that; his brother would mock him for falling in love at first sight. But he knew that destiny was at play, that he was meant to love Anna, and had loved her since he was a boy, even if only in his dreams. That was something his brother would understand far less than love at first sight.

"I found her," he said, still considering how to approach this.

Brodie and Lydia shared a concerned look.

"Aiden, dear," Lydia began in her most motherly tone, "what do you mean you *found* her? Women aren't like half-drowned kittens you find in a rainstorm that need fussing over and cuddling."

"Well, now, just wait a moment, wife," Brodie cut in. "*Ye* like a good cuddle."

"That's *not* what I meant."

"I found her on the shore. She washed up from a shipwreck and was *half-drowned*," Aiden clarified.

"A shipwreck?" This captured his brother's interest. "I see. We were riding the tail of that storm. Which ship? How many others survived?"

"She's the only survivor, as far as I know. Apparently, it was the *Ruritanian Star*. She has no memory beyond her first name, which is Anna."

Lydia covered her mouth with her hands. "Oh, that's awful . . ."

"She's been weak as a kitten," he added. "And to not ken who she is, that's left her frightened and vulnerable. She has only her first name and the clothes she wore when she washed up on shore. She had a nightmare last night, and I fell asleep comforting her. Nothing more happened."

"Oh . . ." Lydia's already beautiful face transformed with compassion. "We must help her."

Brodie rolled his eyes. "Now ye're wanting to help the kitten too?"

"Of course, and so will you," she said firmly. "You and Aiden will let another room—I will stay with her."

"What? Now hold on a minute, wife." Brodie put an arm around Lydia's waist, keeping her where she was. "I want to sleep with *ye*, not my brother."

"It's not proper for Aiden to stay with her alone," Lydia insisted. "Even though we don't know who she is, we must still treat her properly."

"Since when do Kincade men care about propriety?" Brodie asked. "I kidnapped ye and carried ye off into the night, remember? I wasna proper then."

At this, Lydia was the one who rolled her eyes. "This is different. This poor woman has no one to look out for her. You Kincade men are far more honorable than you pretend to be, and I simply want to help Aiden take care of this woman."

Brodie seemed horrified at the thought of being considered *honorable*, and his face scrunched in displeasure at the notion. He had worked hard to earn his reputation, only to suddenly turn into an honorable man.

Aiden bit his lip to keep from laughing at his brother's

face. "Ye are both forgetting whose opinion actually matters. *Anna* will decide who she wants in her room," Aiden said. "Ye may offer to stay with her, but if she wants me, then she'll have me. She's been through too much for me to leave her frightened." He understood as well as Lydia about propriety, but he also knew that Anna was his woman, his destiny, and he would only leave her side if she told him to.

Lydia acquiesced. "Very well, but I wish to buy her some proper clothing today. There is a decent dressmaker not far from here. When she's ready, I'll take her over and purchase some gowns for her."

"I'll speak with the innkeeper about a second room." Brodie kissed Lydia's temple, and with a bemused smile, he left Aiden and Lydia to settle the matter of who would be sleeping with whom.

"Well, shouldn't you introduce us to her?" Lydia asked.

"I suppose I must. Give me a moment." He slipped back into the room and closed the door, giving him one more minute alone with Anna.

ANNA'S HEART WAS STILL RACING WHEN AIDEN CAME back into the room. She'd woken in a nightmare and then slept peacefully through the rest of the night because Aiden was with her. His body had been warm, hard, and strong, and she'd felt safe and a little excited to have him so near, but the rude awakening this morning had left her discombobulated and wishing she could go back to the drowsy early morning when she was still in his arms.

Had that really been his family at the door? She was utterly mortified. She might not remember her past, but she knew that to be caught in bed with a man, especially one she wasn't married to, was incredibly inappropriate. What if his family thought her to be a woman of ill-repute? They may demand he leave her alone, and then she'd be in an even worse situation than she already was.

Aiden slipped back into the room and closed the door behind him, giving them privacy.

"Lydia is outside waiting to meet ye. Is that all right?" he asked.

Swallowing back a wave of panic, she tried to keep calm. "Yes, but, oh heavens, I have to put some clothes on —I couldn't possibly meet her in a nightgown."

"I'll help ye put it on." Aiden found a brown wool dress that Molly had also brought up yesterday that she'd draped over one of the chairs. He held it out to Anna before he turned his back to let her remove Molly's borrowed nightgown. Then Anna stepped into the brown wool dress and pulled it up before tucking her arms through the sleeves. Then Aiden laced up the back, and she slipped her feet into the slightly oversized boots that Molly had also left for her.

She tugged on Aiden's sleeve as he came around to stand in front of her. "Do I look all right?"

"Ye look fine, lass. Besides, Lydia is anxious to take ye shopping."

"Shopping?"

"Aye, for all the things that lasses like you need. Dresses, bonnets, gloves . . . the lacy things you wear beneath your gowns that frustrate a man." He winked at her.

She laughed at his scandalous suggestion. From another man, it might have caused a ripple of concern, but with Aiden, his teasing was exciting and strangely delightful. "Frustrate you?"

"Aye, and a frustrated man has less time to give a woman the pleasure she deserves." He arched a brow. "Now, enough tempting me, lassie—I must be on my best behavior. Lydia wouldna like me talking about lacy underpinnings." He approached the door. "Shall I let her in?"

"Very well." Anna stood in her most poised position, ready to greet Aiden's sister-in-law.

He opened the door, and a lovely blonde woman about her own age came into the room. She wore a pale-blue walking dress, and her hair was done up fashionably with matching ribbons. A white shawl was draped loosely over her shoulders. She looked effortlessly graceful.

"This is Lydia," Aiden said. "Lydia, this is Anna."

Lydia beamed at her. "It's so lovely to meet you. I'm terribly sorry if I startled you a moment ago. I forgot that Aiden isn't like his brother." At this, Anna glanced worriedly at Aiden.

"She means it as a compliment, lass," Aiden said. "My brother is a wicked charmer, remember. She kens I'm not like that."

"I don't know about that," Anna said to herself. She thought Aiden was very charming, and the heat in his eyes when he looked at her was very wicked indeed, but she liked that.

"It's lovely to meet you," Anna said to Lydia as the other woman approached her. There was something about Lydia's voice that tugged at her memories. Well, perhaps not so much her voice as her accent. She was English, not Scottish, and something about that continued to nudge her mind, but she couldn't quite remember why.

"It's lovely to meet you too. My husband will be back shortly. He's getting a second room." Lydia smiled reassuringly. "Aiden told us a bit about the shipwreck and how you haven't a thing to wear. I'd love to take you to the local dressmaker here, if you'd like?"

"I would," Anna admitted. "This woolen gown itches quite terribly."

"Wonderful. We'll go now, if you feel up to it." Lydia linked her arm in Anna's, not waiting for an answer. "Aiden, if we go shopping now, you should hire a coach to take us to Castle Kinkade tomorrow. I'm assuming we will take her back with us?"

"Aye," Aiden agreed instantly. "Her memory is coming back in bits and pieces, but she canna stay here alone."

"That's all right with you, isn't it?" Lydia asked Anna.

Anna looked to Aiden, strangely needing his reassurance that he wanted her to go where he went. He smiled at her, the soft expression full of sensual promise, and yet his eyes held such a tender compassion that she knew she would be safe with him.

"I suppose . . . I don't know where my ship was bound or what I'm to do, so I have no idea where I should go." She also didn't want to be parted from Aiden, but she wasn't about to tell Lydia that. What existed between the two of them was something they didn't understand, so how could anyone else?

"It's settled, then," said Aiden. "I will meet with Dr. MacDonald and tell him where ye will be should he learn of any news of your ship."

Anna brightened with the hope of that idea. "Perhaps more survivors will be found and someone will know me."

"That's an excellent idea," Lydia said to Aiden. "Come along, Anna. I have a purse full of coins that need spending on pretty clothes." She winked at Anna, and Anna found herself smiling.

Anna let Lydia take the lead, and they were met on the stairs by Aiden's dashing dark-haired brother.

"Brodie, this is Anna. We're off to the dressmaker's."

Brodie smiled. "It's a pleasure, Miss Anna. I hope my brother has been treating ye well."

"Very well," Anna assured him. "He's been quite the hero."

"Aye, that sounds like my brother." Brodie chuckled as he walked past the ladies, and Lydia let out a little shriek and jumped.

"What's wrong?" Anna asked, but even as she said it she heard Brodie snickering behind them.

"Pinching my bottom—honestly, the nerve," Lydia muttered, although she was grinning. "Let's go before those two decide to tag along on our hunt. The last thing we need is men underfoot when we have so much to do."

"WELL?" BRODIE ASKED AS HE AND AIDEN CROSSED THE courtyard of the inn and headed toward the stables. "What *really* happened with you and Anna?"

"Everything I told ye was true. She washed up on the shore like some half-drowned selkie who'd had her skin stolen. She lost her memories when she hurt her head."

"Ye found no other survivors?"

Aiden shook his head.

"No other bodies?" Brodie pressed.

Again, Aiden shook his head.

"That doesna sound right to me. Unless they were far from shore? I suppose sharks could've . . . disposed of all the bodies save one? Ye see how mad that sounds?"

"I ken how that sounds, but that isna what happened. She was the only one I saw wash up on the shore. You ken as well as I do that shipwreck debris can travel far. It's possible other survivors could be farther up or down the coast or still out at sea. She truly doesna remember what happened when the ship wrecked."

Brodie slapped his leather gloves on his thigh. "Christ, Aiden, this sounds like one of those novels Joanna likes to read about drafty castles, evil lords, and other such nonsense."

Aiden kept his thoughts to himself, knowing his brother wouldn't understand if he tried to tell him that he'd been dreaming of Anna since he was a boy. They entered the stables, where Aiden began checking on Thundir and Bob. His mind was already preoccupied with thoughts of taking Anna home. He had so much to show her, so much to experience with her now that he'd found her.

"I ken what it sounds like, but that's the truth." Aiden stroked Bob's nose.

Brodie leaned against the stall. "I canna believe I'm asking this of ye of all people, but what are yer intentions toward this woman?"

"My intentions?" Aiden wasn't sure himself. He only knew that he wanted to be with her in whatever way fate would let him.

"Are ye going to bring the wee lassie home and marry her?" Brodie's brusque tone sounded far more commanding, more like Brock. Normally, Brodie was the brother encouraging him to tup every woman in sight.

Aiden couldn't help but tease his brother for his sudden sense of propriety, which was quite uncharacteristic of him. "I canna speak for the lady, but 'twas my plan to topple her into the nearest haystack and have my wicked way with her."

Brodie scowled, and it made him look so much like their eldest brother, Brock, that Aiden burst out laughing.

"What is so amusing?" Brodie crossed his arms, which only deepen the similarity between him and Brock.

"Ye've turned into a mother hen, just like Brock. 'Ack, laddie, ye'd better marry that woman if'n ye ken what's good for ye,'" he mimicked in a bossy, motherly voice.

"Ye take that back." Brodie grabbed Aiden's shirtfront, and Aiden responded in kind. Moments later, the pair were scuffling like boys, both struggling to get an arm around the other's neck. They tossed each other against the sides of the stalls as they tussled.

"Oi! Leave my friend alone!" The small cry came from the loft above. Brodie yelped and fell back onto a pile of hay as the little stable lad leaped on his back and started punching him.

"Easy, laddie, 'tis only my brother," Aiden said with a chuckle as he pulled the lad off Brodie.

Brodie arched a brow as he sat up. "Have an army of wee bairns fighting yer battles now?"

"I'm no bairn!" the little boy growled at Brodie.

"An army? It was just one lad," Aiden argued.

"He fought with the strength of twelve lads," Brodie grumbled.

Aiden ignored the remark and set the boy on his feet. "What's yer name?"

The boy beamed at Aiden with pride. "Cameron MacLeod."

Brodie climbed to his feet and smacked his trousers to rid them of hay and dust. "Christ, he's a bloody MacLeod."

"Well, Cameron, how are Thundir and Bob doing?" Aiden asked.

"Who the devil is Bob?" Brodie asked.

"Our mare," Cameron announced.

"*Our mare?*" Brodie mouthed the words to Aiden over the top of the boy's head.

"Aye, I brought her from an ill-tempered oaf who, after laming the poor beast and selling her to me, then tried to sell her to the butcher. I reminded him that the sale to me was valid and he could sod off. So Cameron and I are taking care of her."

"Dinna tell me ye've adopted the boy too? We have enough bloody orphans running about the castle."

Aiden put his hands on his hips and studied the child thoughtfully. "Yer not an orphan, are ye, lad?"

"No, but I wish I was. My pa isna a nice man," the lad grumbled and glanced at the ground.

"And yer mother?"

"She died when I was born," Cameron said. "Pa said I was the one who killed her."

Brodie looked at Aiden with clear regret for bringing up the subject.

"Does yer father hit ye?" Aiden asked in a low tone. The boy's reluctance to answer was answer enough.

"Cameron, we'll be leaving tomorrow—"

"So soon?" The child's eyes filled with tears, and he brushed them away.

"Aye, but if ye want to come with us, ye can. I could use a spare set of hands to tend to Bob while I take care of Miss Anna."

Cameron wiped his eyes and raised his chin. "I'd like to, but my pa won't let me."

"We'll handle him," Brodie said flatly.

"Where is yer father?" Aiden asked.

"At the smithy." Cameron's face was pale. "Be careful. He's mean and strong."

Aiden clapped a hand on the lad's shoulder. "So are we. Stay here and watch the horses."

Brodie fell in step beside Aiden as they left the stables.

"We arna going to chat with this father of his, are we?" his brother asked.

"No."

"Good. I wasna in the mood to be polite anyway," Brodie replied, and rolled up his sleeves.

"We'll make sure the father understands things, then

Cameron will join us at Castle Kinkade and the lad can learn to tend to the horses in our stables."

He had a sense that he would need all the help he could get. Something in his bones told him that the danger he'd been warned of by the old Romani woman was drawing closer. He had to do whatever he could to protect Anna. This was his fate, after all, and he would do all within his power to protect her.

CHAPTER 6

Despite her embarrassing first meeting with Lydia, Anna quickly came to love the beautiful Englishwoman. Lydia was sweet and quick-witted, and once she grew comfortable around Anna, she became quite entertaining. As they stood in the dress shop, she regaled Anna with tales of the Kincade brothers until both of them were laughing so hard they had to wipe tears from their eyes.

It filled Anna's heart with a quiet, brightly burning joy to hear tales of Aiden and his brothers and the adventures and often amusing *trouble* they found themselves in. These were stories she hoped to hear Aiden tell her someday as they learned more about each other.

"They destroyed a taproom during a brawl?" Anna asked as Lydia began another story. She stood on a small dais surrounded by mirrors, trying to ignore her reflection and how bedraggled she looked while the modiste took her measurements.

"It was a matter of honor, apparently, and funnily enough, the same 'English louts' they beat up were the very friends of Brock's future brother-in-law."

"That would be Ashton Lennox?" she asked Lydia. There were so many names she'd learned in the last few hours that she could barely keep it all straight.

"Oh yes, Ashton and his entire so-called League of Rogues."

Anna frowned. "Rogues? Does that mean they are very wicked?"

Lydia smiled. "Yes and no. Surely they are dangerous, but they are far less wicked than I hear they used to be—after all, most of them are leg-shackled now, except for Charles. But it's only a matter of time—the Duchess of Essex, one of Ashton's friends, is quite determined to find Charles a bride."

"Leg-shackled?" Anna wasn't familiar with the term, but since English wasn't her native language, it seemed, that wasn't too much of a surprise.

"Oh, it's a term men use for marriage—I have no idea why they say that, though, since the members of the League made good marriages with excellent women and they seem quite happy in their capacity as married men. One wouldn't be happy if one's marriage felt like a set of chains and a lead ball, yet they tease each other mercilessly about it." Her eyes sparkled with a mixture of love and amusement. "Love is a funny thing, isn't it?"

"It certainly is," Anna agreed as she thought of Aiden and how she felt so in tune with him. "Is Aiden a member of this . . . League of Rogues?" She still didn't quite understand who these men were.

"No, not quite. The League are all Englishmen, and they are Ashton's friends from his years studying at Cambridge. They got into a bit of trouble back then and sort of banded together and have been quite inseparable ever since." Lydia leaned in to whisper her next words. "I heard there was some delicious scandal with how the duke of the group courted his wife, Emily, something about kidnapping, and Ashton and the others were all involved in the entire affair." She chuckled. "Emily won't tell me the full story whenever I ask her about it. She just smiles and gives me a little wink."

"Emily is a duchess now?" Anna asked.

"Yes. There's the duke, Godric, and his wife, Emily. Then there's Lucien, the Marquess of Rochester, who married Viscount Sheridan's little sister, which of course caused a duel over Christmas . . ."

Anna just stared at Lydia, completely a loss for words.

"But of course Cedric, Viscount Sheridan, was distracted by his own marriage to Anne Chessley, and then his youngest sister married Godric's younger brother— Lord, imagine what their family dinners must be like." Lydia chuckled. "Do you think you've ever been in love?"

"I don't think so." Even without her memories, Anna was sure that her heart would have felt as if it already belonged to someone if she had ever been in love. The longing and envy she felt when she watched Lydia and Brodie together seemed to be proof of that.

Lydia sat on a nearby settee, her gentle gaze full of concern.

"You truly don't remember anything?"

"Only small things," Anna admitted. "It's coming back

in little memories here and there, like a puzzle, only I haven't been able to put any pieces together." She closed her eyes as the seamstress tugged on the ready-made dress that was to be adjusted for her so she could wear it out of the shop. Another memory, one as small as the others, came back.

"I had a lot of dress fittings . . . I remember that. I recall the last gown I had made . . . a cream-and-red velvet one." She touched her waist. "A gold sash studded with pearls and gold trimming and more pearls along the edges of the red velvet." She could see the red-and-cream gown with a long train, perhaps eight feet behind her. Where would she have worn such a gown?

"Cream and red velvet with pearls?" Lydia tapped her chin. "That sounds lovely and rather expensive. You must have been very well off if you had so many fittings for gowns like that."

"Perhaps I was," Anna agreed.

She also remembered wearing jewels, extravagant ones that weighed heavily upon her skin, but she hadn't cared much for them. She didn't mention them to Lydia. It felt somehow wrong to discuss fine gowns and jewels when she was in a tiny Scottish village where it was apparent that most people struggled hard to earn a living. The last thing she wanted to do was put on airs or seem snobbish in any way. It might put distance between her and Aiden, and that was the very last thing she wanted.

"I'm sure once you spend time with us at Castle Kincade, you'll regain more of your memories. There is something healing about the Kincade lands. I lived most of my life in London, but *home* to me is the castle." Lydia's smile softened as she spoke. "You'll feel as if you belong to it right away, I promise."

"I should like to see it." Anna longed for a place to belong the way Lydia seemed to at the castle.

Lydia perused some hair ornaments. There was a lovely band that would wind around one's hair. It was made of red ribbon and had glittering jeweled stars on it. The jewels were likely paste, but they looked very pretty. Lydia studied the piece, then eyed Anna again. She nodded to herself and added it to the pile of gloves and other accessories she'd already chosen. "If you continue to spend time with Aiden, you'll have to be a lover of animals."

"Oh? Does he have pets?" That intrigued Anna. She'd heard of Aiden's compassion for animals from Molly, but that had been only a brief story about the injured horse in the stables.

"Oh yes," Lydia chuckled. "He has an affinity with practically all animals. As a result, the castle is *full* of creatures. Owls in the library, otters in the lake, hedgehogs in the halls, kestrels in the kitchen, a pine marten who nests in Aiden's bedchamber, and even a badger named Fiona who insists on sleeping in Brock's bedroom. Aiden finds injured creatures and brings them home to tend to them. Some of them choose to stay once they are healed. I think it's because they like being around Aiden. He's so calm and gentle, and when he sings in that voice of his . . . it's almost hypnotic."

Anna warmed at the thought of so many creatures living with Aiden in his castle and how his musical voice could cast a spell over wounded creatures.

"It sounds magical." She couldn't help but wonder if she could get Aiden to sing for her.

"It is, in a way," Lydia agreed. "Although it can be upsetting to guests who aren't prepared for hedgehogs trundling along the halls. If you bump into one wearing only slippers, you'll find it stings a bit. And if you are reading in the library, you'd best remember to check your hair in a mirror before dinner. I once sat through an entire meal while my husband and his brothers giggled like little boys and only later found a number of downy feathers resting on my head. If Joanna, Brock's wife, hadn't been in London visiting her family, she would have told me, but as it was, I was at the mercy of Brodie and his brothers. They didn't bother to tell me about the feathers, of course. They apparently had a wager to see how long it would take me to notice."

Anna couldn't help but laugh. "And how long was that?"

"When Brodie and I were in our room later that night, he plucked one out of my hair and gently blew it off his palm in front of me toward my face to tease me."

"You love him, don't you?" Anna asked, though she was certain of the answer.

Lydia seemed momentarily lost in thoughts of herself and Brodie. "*Madly*. Not at first, mind you. But love came when I saw who he really was beneath his rakish exterior."

Anna had seen hints of charm from Aiden. He was so vastly different from Brodie. There was a sorrow in his eyes that wasn't found in his brother's.

"Lydia, may I ask you something about Aiden? I do not wish to pry, but . . ."

"When it comes to Aiden, you deserve to know whatever you wish." Lydia came to Anna where she stood on the dais and took her hands. "What's your question?"

"Aiden told me about his father, and it explains much of his sadness, but then I see Brodie and he seems unburdened by the past, at least compared to Aiden. Why is there such a difference between the two brothers?" Anna relaxed as the dressmaker finished her pinning and measurements and jotted down some notes. Lydia helped her down from the dais, and she went behind the changing screen to remove the ready-made gown. Then Lydia helped Anna put on another one that had already been fitted for her so that she would be able to wear it out of the shop.

"Aiden is one of the kindest men I've ever met. He's not hard as stone like Brock, nor is he able to distract himself with amusements like Brodie. Rosalind, their sister, once told me that she sees them like this: Brock as the mind, Brodie as the body, and Aiden as the heart. He is different than his brothers. They were more the sons their father expected to have. But Aiden . . . Aiden was a man all his own in a way their father couldn't understand. Evil always seeks to destroy something that is entirely good and pure, doesn't it? I think that's why their father seemed driven to hurt Aiden far deeper than the others. He wanted to break Aiden in body and spirit. Having a parent neglect you is difficult, but having a parent bent on destroying all that you are . . . That's a devastation few people ever know."

Anna's heart stopped at the thought of anyone hurting Aiden. He seemed to have an infinite supply of compassion. How could anyone want to hurt someone who only ever helped people?

Lydia cleared her throat and continued. "Hate, especially from a parent, can leave a deep and lasting scar." Lydia helped Anna fasten the laces of the gown. "But I noticed he smiles when he talks about you. I think you chase his sorrows away."

"He smiles when he talks about me?" Anna felt silly that such a thing should send her head spinning with girlish joy.

"Yes, at first I was worried that he saw you as simply another creature to care for, but now I don't think that is the case. His eyes light up when he speaks about you. It's a side of him I've never seen before, nor has Brodie."

Aiden could have only had a brief discussion with Lydia and Brodie about her earlier in the hallway outside Aiden's room—there wasn't time for an in-depth conversation. But Anna still clung to the hope that Lydia's observations were true. Aiden had said he'd dreamed of her for years, that she was the woman destined to be his. Others might dismiss it as a foolish flight of fancy or a transparent attempt at seduction. But after everything Anna had been through and feeling so deeply connected to Aiden so quickly, she couldn't deny that what he said might be true.

Last night, she had been trapped in a nightmare. Of endless fire burning all around her and running through the woods toward a wishing well. She'd dreamt of peering down into the well and seeing Aiden's face. It would have been easy to dismiss that as a dream stemming from meeting him, but she *knew* that she had dreamed of this many times before, at least part of it. They were connected, but neither of them knew how or why. She knew only that she wanted to stay with him.

"There we are." The modiste packaged a few gowns

that needed no further alterations, and Lydia added gloves, stockings, and several chemises to the pile, along with slippers, boots, and a shawl.

"That should be sufficient for now." Lydia nodded in approval and paid the dressmaker.

Anna was humbled and grateful for the woman's help, both emotionally and financially. "Thank you, Lydia, I will find a way to repay you." It was a comfort to have another woman she could talk to.

"Nonsense. It is a gift. Now, let's get back to the inn and get you bathed and changed. I want to fix your hair for dinner." Lydia gave her shoulders a sisterly squeeze.

"Thank you, it is an awful mess."

"Not to worry—I can handle it," Lydia assured her. "Besides, I can't wait to see how Aiden reacts when he sees how beautiful you look."

Anna couldn't either. If she could make him smile, that would be a wonderful victory against the sorrow he carried in his heart.

◈

YURI STRAVONOV, HALF BROTHER TO THE FORMER KING of Ruritania, leaned over the large table covered with maps of the surrounding countryside close to the Summer Palace. He frowned as he studied the series of maps that he'd recovered from the palace library before he'd burned it to the ground. He hadn't bothered to salvage anything else from the library. Those books and records belonged to Ruritania's past, and Yuri believed only in the future he planned to create. Soon he would have libraries full of new books about the grand changes he'd made to the country and his wealth and power as he spread his control over the rest of Europe.

"We've tracked the rebel camp to the Dark Forest, but we can't seem to find where they are sleeping." Yuri's captain of the guard, Radovan Fain, pointed to several places on the map that had been marked with a set of small black stones. "There have been signs of camps, but nothing recent."

Fain was a tall man with bricklike shoulders, a square jaw, and cold blue eyes. Both he and Yuri were in their forties, but Fain had the strength and agility of a man ten years younger. It had proved a valuable attribute when he'd led the attack on the palace and killed King Alfred.

"They must be moving every night," Yuri muttered. His nephew was a more cunning adversary than he'd expected. Fain had been in charge of the king and queen's security detail, and he'd been the one to kill them in their beds as they slept.

Alexei had been the next threat. Unfortunately, one of the young guardsmen had woken the prince as the attack began. The two men had sought a retreat with the remaining guards still loyal to Yuri's half brother, and now the little pest was playing hide-and-seek in the woods and stealing food and money bound for Yuri's treasury and larder.

"What of the princess?" Yuri asked. Yuri knew his captain was most interested in Anna, and before the coup Yuri had promised Fain that the princess would be spared and given to the captain as his bride in payment for the man's loyalty.

"We found witnesses at the harbor who say she and her maid boarded a royal merchant vessel bound for England," Fain informed him. "If she reaches London, she could appeal to King George, and he might send troops," Fain warned. "We should send someone after her and bring her back."

Yuri did not believe a woman, even a princess, could convince the English king to go to war. George was a man who enjoyed his pleasures and entertainments. He was not a warrior. Ruritania was also not necessarily an ally of England, even though an English-born queen had sat on the throne.

"She's just a woman, Fain. My envoy is already in London convincing the king and his advisors that this transition of power is in the best interests of Ruritania and her trade partners. He will spread the story that I came into power after my beloved half brother died at the hands of rebels. No one listens to women in matters of politics."

No one save his elder half brother, Alfred. His older brother had married an Englishwoman named Isadora. Isadora, once she became queen had dared to attend the council meetings and voice her opinions on matters of state, and his brother had actually heeded her advice. It was just one of many ways his brother had shown himself to be unfit to lead. Women had no place in politics. They belonged to the realm of giving men pleasure and providing heirs, nothing more.

"Your Highness, allow me to send a small group of men to retrieve her," Fain insisted.

Of course, his captain's true motive was to reclaim his escaped prize. Yuri wasn't fooled by his request.

"Very well, send some men." Yuri waved a hand to dismiss the subject. He didn't care about his niece. She had no power, she had no armies at her back, and because she was not a male, she had no claim to the throne, unless of course she gave birth to a child, but that was something he could control if she married Fain. She was just a woman he would use to control the loyalty of his captain and—

"Wait . . ." Yuri grinned as a new plan formed in his mind. "Fain, when they find her, have her brought to me first. I will use her to lure Alexei into surrendering."

Faint halted in the doorway of Yuri's private study.

"She was promised to me," the captain said firmly.

"And still shall be. But if we send word that she is to be executed unless Alexei surrenders, he will. I know my dear nephew." Alexei adored his sister and would do anything to save her life. "When we have the prince, we'll execute him, and you may have the girl as I promised."

Satisfied with this, Fain left the room to assemble a group of men to send to England. Yuri turned his focus back to the maps and stared at the vast outline of the forest.

"Where are you hiding, princeling?" he murmured, his gaze cold as he plotted his nephew's death.

☙❧

IT WAS NEARLY TIME FOR DINNER WHEN LYDIA PUT THE finishing touches on Anna's coiffure.

"There, now you look better," Lydia said. "Not that you looked bad before . . ."

"I looked like I'd been tossed about in a ship," Anna

said with a laugh and put a hand on Lydia's where it rested on her shoulder. "Thank you, truly."

Lydia grinned. "You look stunning. Aiden won't recognize you." Lydia tugged a few more loose curls into place at the nape of Anna's neck.

"Let's go down to the taproom and see if we can find the men." Lydia collected their shawls and gave Anna hers. They left the room and proceeded downstairs toward the sound of boisterous laughter and singing.

Lydia, who went ahead, halted abruptly at the bottom of the stairs. "Oh goodness. What on earth?"

Anna paused a few steps above Lydia and bent a little to peer over her shoulder and get a better look at the chaos in the taproom.

Brodie and Aiden each held a mug of ale, singing and swaying and encouraging the men around them to join in. Anna guessed it to be a Gaelic song, and from the kind of laughter they elicited, it had to be a bawdy one.

Lydia shook her head and looked heavenward, as if seeking divine help. "I swear, you can never leave a Scot alone for a minute without him getting into trouble. It looks like they've been fighting."

"Who?"

"Given the lack of unconscious people in the room, they probably tussled with each other. Brothers, as I understand it, are like that, always trying to put each other in a headlock or toss each other to the ground. It makes me rather glad I only had to deal with a sister growing up, and she was dreadfully difficult to keep out of trouble. I couldn't imagine having brothers," Lydia said matter-of-factly.

Anna gasped when she saw the bruises on Aiden and Brodie. Brodie's nose was bloody, and Aiden's lower lip was puffy with a bit of dried blood on his chin. With a growl, Lydia lifted her skirts and strode toward her husband.

"Ah, lassie!" Brodie set his tankard of ale down and picked his wife up by the waist, whirling her around, then shouted to a man by the fire who had a violin resting on his lap, "Give us a tune!" The man picked it up and started a lively jig.

"Put me down!" Lydia demanded, but her husband just grinned up at her. "We haven't had dinner yet, Brodie."

"Ye like dancing, wife. Dance with me! We can have a private dinner in our room later." He set her down on her feet, and Lydia's stern expression vanished.

"Oh, all right." She started to dance with Brodie. "If it will keep you from throwing any more punches."

"All the punches are thrown, lass. Now is the time for dancing!" Brodie teased.

Anna's heart was full of joy for her friend, but she also felt an ache underneath. She wanted that same carefree happiness Lydia and Brodie had, but with Aiden.

As if summoned, Aiden stepped away from the men he was speaking to and halted in front of her. His eyes went wide. "Anna! Ye look . . . ye look . . ."

"How do I look?" she asked, her heart pounding.

"Ye look magnificent." Coming from him, the compliment was somehow much more meaningful. He nodded at the others behind him and held a hand out to her. "Ye fancy a dance?"

"I'd love to, but I don't know the steps," she admitted.

Aiden's face split in a wide, delighted grin that warmed Anna to her very toes.

"Dance to yer own steps, lassie. I promise I can keep up with ye."

His words, or perhaps the way he said them, seemed to sink deep into her very bones as she somehow knew that if she danced with him, he would match her step for step, as if they'd danced a thousand times before in a dream within a dream. Perhaps they had . . . and it was only that she couldn't remember her dreams.

Aiden's charming smile had her blushing and smiling shyly back as she took his hand. She knew one sort of jig. Her muscle memory had retained the familiar pattern. She danced across the floor, her slippered feet moving about with ease. Aiden curled an arm around her waist as his feet matched hers in the complicated pattern. For all his size and strength, he moved lightly and elegantly. He adapted easily to every step she made as if he knew where she intended to go, how she intended to move.

Anna smiled and relaxed as she realized he was right about keeping up with her. Soon she forgot all about her worries and was simply *dancing*, carefree and wild, with the handsome Scotsman holding her as though she were a precious treasure. The more they danced, the more the shadows behind his eyes faded. The chiseled features of his handsome face were touched by an inner light of joy that softened that warrior's edge to him.

They danced until her feet ached, and even then, Aiden merely lifted her up in the cradle of his arms, spinning around while she laughed. When the violin player finally had to rest, Anna saw that Brodie and Lydia were sneaking away up the stairs, no doubt to continue the festivities in the privacy of their own room.

Aiden set her down by one of the empty tables and collected two fresh mugs of ale from Molly and a plate of food to share. She took one of the mugs, liked the taste of the ale, and then began to gulp it down greedily. She hadn't realized how thirsty she was until after they'd stopped dancing. Aiden sat down beside her, grinning from ear to ear.

"Dinna forget to eat something, lass. Ye must be starving."

He was right, she was quite hungry, and only after she'd had several bites did he begin to eat. Even in something so small, he thought of her first, and the thought pricked her heart with a bittersweet ache as she wondered if anyone had ever stopped and cared for him the way he cared for others.

He wiped at his lip with his fingertips, and a bit of blood came away on his skin. Anna suddenly remembered that he and Brodie had been in a fight.

"Let me have a look at you," she said, and motioned for him to come closer.

She took a cloth napkin and wet it in a cup of water, then gently grasped his chin and turned his face to her. He held still, his eyes locked with hers as she wiped away the dried blood.

"What happened?"

As she finished cleaning the wound, he reached up and caught her wrist before she could lower her hand. His knuckles were dark purple with bruises.

"I started a fight with the blacksmith."

"The blacksmith? Why?" she asked. "Do you make a habit of starting fights with tradesmen?"

The shadows crept back into his eyes. "Only with ones who hit children or animals."

"Oh. Well, good." She didn't know what else to say to that. If she'd met a man who struck a child, she would have hit him too.

"Ye don't mind that I'm a brute?" Aiden asked.

She lifted her chin almost defiantly. "Defending someone who is defenseless is not being a brute. I think it's rather heroic."

Aiden still held her wrist, and he moved his fingers up until he held her hand instead. Then he slowly pressed his lips to her knuckles.

A hot flush swept through her as she drew in a sharp breath.

"Is it madness to want to kiss ye, lass?" His low, husky voice did funny, wonderful things to her lower belly.

"Kiss me?" she echoed as her gaze fell to his lips.

"Aye. Have ye been kissed before?" Aiden pressed his mouth to her fingers again, which only made it harder to think.

"I . . . Once, I think . . . But I was young."

"Ye're still young," he teased.

She laughed. "I mean, I think I was perhaps fourteen or fifteen? It was with a young stable hand. I remember the smell of hay and . . ." She looked up into his eyes. "Have you kissed someone?"

"A few someones, but not many." His eyes held hers. "Will ye let me kiss ye now, Anna?"

"Yes, but what if I am terrible at it?" A sudden fear of her own inadequacy made the rising desire within her dim.

Aiden cupped her cheek in his other hand. "If that is the case, then it will be my pleasurable duty to tutor ye. I've never met a woman yet who canna kiss better than a man. I believe women were born for kissing and it's the men who need lessons." Well, when he put it like that, she worried a little less. Lessons from him would be *most* welcome. He gave her a little wink, and she found her worries vanishing. He had the most wonderful way of doing that to her.

"All right . . ." She leaned in, perhaps in too much haste, because the next thing she knew their foreheads had collided.

"Ouch!" She drew back and covered her forehead with a hand. Aiden rubbed a similar spot on his own head.

"Let me come to ye, lass. That's the first lesson. Ye lean in just a little, and then ye let me come the rest of the way."

"Oh, I see." They returned to their positions. This time she leaned in an inch and closed her eyes.

There was a moment of nothing but her own hungry anticipation, the sounds of the room fading as her ears homed in on the soft exhale of Aiden's breath. His fingers fluttered against her jaw, the touch hot and tingly, and then his lips pressed against hers, velvety caresses that pulled a sigh of delight from her. Aiden moved his lips back and forth over hers, and soon she learned to move with him. It was somewhat like dancing, only these were new steps she was learning, and Aiden was a masterful teacher. Anna wasn't sure how long they kissed—it seemed to go on forever, and yet it ended far too soon.

When their lips parted, he had a hand cupping the back of her neck while their foreheads rested against each other.

"Good?" he asked her.

"Very good," she replied between deep breaths. "Was I?"

"Like a dream, lass." He gave her a dreamy smile, and her heart fluttered in response.

"'Tis late. We should go to bed. I'll take the chair again while ye take the bed." He stood and clasped her hand in his and then led her back up the stairs.

She paused when they reached the door to their room. "And if I have more bad dreams?" she asked, suddenly anxious that her nightmares might return.

Aiden's eyes glowed in the dim light of the corridor. "Then I'll be right there to chase them away."

CHAPTER 7

A iden kept his promise, and no dreams haunted his beautiful lass that night. He slept lightly, stirring to wakefulness each time she moved on the bed, just in case she needed him. She looked better this morning. Her tawny brown eyes were bright, and shadows no longer darkened her face. Her tempting mouth curved up in an enchanting smile when she saw him. She and Lydia met him and Brodie outside the inn, ready for the journey ahead. Anna wore a dark hunter-green carriage dress that had sleeves embroidered with acorns and oak leaves. She was like a woodland sprite or a tree nymph come to life.

She came toward him, her movements elegant and careful as a queen. He had the wild urge to set her free, like removing a falcon's hood and setting the bird loose upon the wind.

"Is our coach ready?" Anna asked him.

"Aye. And I have my horses ready to travel. And the lad, of course."

"Cameron?" She glanced about, looking for the little boy he had told her about before she fell asleep the previous night. It had been so sweet to sit beside her while she lay in bed and tell her about the child he'd taken under his wing. She'd watched him with drowsy amusement, and he knew his voice had put her to sleep, which was what he'd intended. Lydia often teased him about how his voice was soothing.

"Cam, lad, time to leave," Aiden hollered toward the stables. The boy marched out to meet them, an overstuffed burlap sack slung over his small shoulder. Cameron had slept in the stables the night before, even though his father had been in no condition to harm the boy after the thrashing he'd received from Aiden and Brodie. Cam halted when he saw Anna, his face turning red as he attempted a courtly bow. The bag fell off his shoulder, and he had to heft it back up all over again.

Anna took the boy's greeting in stride and dipped into a low curtsy.

"Master Cameron, I presume?" she asked him.

He nodded proudly. "Mistress Anna," he greeted.

Brodie stepped up beside Aiden and chuckled. "He may have been born a MacLeod, but I reckon the lad is a Kincade now."

On that, Aiden agreed. Brodie was right. The Kincades did have a soft spot for orphans and children in need.

"Pack yer bag in the top trunk, Cameron, and then we'll be off."

The boy climbed onto the back of the waiting coach and set his sack inside the trunk Aiden had left open for him. Aiden checked on Thundir and Bob one last time.

Anna followed him to the back of the coach. She looked between the tall dappled-gray gelding and the smaller bay mare.

"Is this the injured one?" Anna gently stroked Bob's nose and neck. Her lack of hesitancy told him she was comfortable with horses.

"Aye, she is doing much better. We'll travel slow. The ride to Kincade lands is but a day, and we will eat lunch to give Bob here time to rest her leg. She and Thundir will follow behind the coach."

"Bob?" Anna giggled. "That's her name?"

"Cameron thought she was male. The name stuck." Aiden grinned.

"Well, Bob, you are a beauty." Anna gave the mare a cuddle, then stepped back and watched Aiden check the leads connected to the back of the coach.

Lydia and Brodie were already inside. Aiden and Anna took the seat opposite them, with Cameron wedged between. The little boy talked everyone's ears off for the next few hours until he wore himself out and fell asleep against Anna's shoulder.

"He's such a little darling." Anna brushed sandy hair back from the boy's eyes while he slept.

"We'll introduce him to Isla when she and Rafe come to visit," Lydia said. "They would make good playmates."

"Who are they?" Anna asked.

"Remember how I told ye about our oldest brother marrying Joanna Lennox? And Joanna's brother Ashton married our sister, Rosalind? Well, Joanna's other brother, Rafe, took in a orphan. A wee lass close to Cameron in age. Her name is Isla."

"Ah. More Lennoxes, I see."

"Rafe is the wild one," Brodie added with a chuckle. "He's our favorite Lennox."

"That's because he's trouble like you." Lydia poked a finger in Brodie's chest. "When you lot kidnapped me, he knew you had the wrong sister and didn't say anything. He thought it was all an amusing lark."

"That is why I like him best," Brodie reiterated. Lydia rolled her eyes.

Anna laughed, and Aiden relished the soft, delightful sound. He was glad to see her so happy. By the time they stopped at a coaching inn to eat, Cameron was awake and full of boundless energy. Aiden and Anna laughed as he ran about the meadow near the inn and played with a dog that belonged to the innkeeper.

They dined at the inn and rested the horses before continuing on toward Castle Kinkade. Aiden invited young Cameron to ride up with the driver to keep the boy entertained, and then he untethered Thundir from the back of the coach and mounted him to take some time to stretch the gelding's legs. A few minutes into his ride, he decided that he would travel farther ahead and reach the castle before the others.

As he rode around the nearest bit of forest, he reached the bottom of the hill that sloped upward to the gray stone Castle Kincade. The sight used to cause him fear, but now . . . so much had changed. Ever since their father had died and Brock had married Joanna, the castle had managed to change from a grim tower of stone to a majestic edifice. Aiden smiled a little at the thought of showing Anna all the nooks and crannies and introducing her to his wee beasties. He kicked his horse's sides, and Thundir galloped faster up the hill toward Aiden's home.

A groom took his horse to the castle stables, and Aiden headed inside to inform his brother of their arriving guests.

"Brock!" Aiden bellowed his brother's name.

"What?" Brock bellowed from down the hall. Aiden peered down the corridor, waiting for his brother to come out of his study.

"Really, Aiden, must you yell a wounded bear?" His sister-in-law appeared at the top of the stairs, a stack of books in her hands, no doubt bound for the library.

"We have visitors," Aiden announced.

"Visitors? Oh heavens!" Joanna rushed downstairs toward him. "How many? Who is it?" Then she was the one bellowing as she called for the butler.

"Brodie and Lydia are coming—they'll be here soon."

"Oh, is that all?" Joanna laughed with relief. She and Brock had known that Aiden had gone to wait for Brodie and Lydia's ship to arrive, but they had no way of knowing about Anna and Cameron.

"But we do have two guests. A wee lad named Cameron who will be helping out around here, and a lady."

Joanna placed her stack of books on the end of the banister and stared at him. "A lady? What sort of lady?"

"Well . . . I found her. She's the survivor of a shipwreck."

"You found a *shipwrecked* woman?" Joanna asked, as if trying to puzzle out the meaning of what he'd said.

"Aye. Her name is Anna, and she doesna remember much. She was injured . . ."

Joanna pressed her thumb and index finger against her closed eyelids.

"Aiden, you must stop teasing me."

"I'm not," he insisted. He did enjoy teasing her, but he wouldn't tease her about something like this.

She gasped as another possibility occurred to her. "It wasn't Brodie's ship, was it?"

"No, their ship was fine."

"Oh, thank goodness."

"Joanna? Where are ye?" Brock's voice came from nearby.

"We're by the stairs," she called out to her husband just as he appeared in the entry way.

Brock, the eldest of their family, shared Aiden's dark hair and stormy eyes. He was a bit taller and a little broader, but Aiden had won his share of wrestling matches against Brock.

Brock embraced him in a fierce hug. "I trust ye brought Brodie and Lydia with ye?"

"They'll arrive in a few minutes," Aiden explained. "I rode out ahead to let ye know we've got some other guests coming."

"Your brother says he found a shipwrecked woman and brought her home," Joanna told Brock.

Brock's smile faded. "Ye did what now?"

"I found a lass washed ashore on the coast of North Berwick."

His brother believed him more easily than Joanna had. "Is she all right?"

"She seems to be, but she took a blow to her head. Her memory is a bit muddled."

Brock nodded. "And ye brought her here to care for her?"

"Aye. She was all alone and had no way to care for herself. I thought perhaps we could let her stay here while she heals."

"Aiden, she's a woman, not a wild animal. She must have a family or people who need to find her."

"If she does, I'll reunite her with them the moment she has her memory again. But 'tis likely her family lives on the Continent far away from here."

Joanna shot Brock a clearly concerned look. It didn't escape Aiden's notice that Brodie and Lydia had reacted similarly to his story. Why did they all think that he saw her as a wounded creature like one of his many animals? She was infinitely more than that. Aiden was all too aware that Anna was a woman. And more importantly, she was *his* woman. But that was something he could not explain to anyone but Anna.

"Of course, she is welcome here for as long as she wishes to stay," Brock said.

"Yes," Joanna echoed, but clearly her English way of thinking was making it more difficult for her to understand that Aiden had taken responsibility for Anna. He would care for her until she no longer wished him to. It was a Scotsman's way.

A moment later, the butler announced that a coach was coming up the drive.

Aiden grinned. "They're here."

BROCK PUT AN ARM AROUND JOANNA'S SHOULDERS AS they followed behind Aiden at a short distance.

"Brock, I'm worried about him," Joanna confessed. "I know he's had his brief romances, but that is it—they always end because he seems forever trapped in his solitude and melancholy. But something tells me this girl might be different. I wish for Aiden to be happy, but what if he loses this one too?"

"I ken ye're worried, Joanna, but maybe this will be good for him. Perhaps the lass is bonnie. It would do him good to practice courting, and mayhap he will leave his melancholy behind."

The coach rolled to a stop, and a young boy leapt off the driver's seat into Aiden's arms. Aiden caught the boy and set him down. Then the lad sprinted up toward Brock and Joanna, who stood at the top of the steps to the castle's entrance.

"Are ye the mighty laird of this castle?" the boy asked him with wide eyes.

"Aye, laddie. My name is Brock Kincade."

"I'm Cameron MacLeod." The boy held out a hand, and Brock shook it with a chuckle and glanced at Aiden. They'd tangled with plenty of MacLeods in the past, but unlike Brodie, Brock clearly thought taking in a MacLeod was amusing rather than a cause for grumbling.

"Welcome, Cameron. This is my wife, Joanna. The mistress of this castle."

"Ye're verra pretty," Cameron said. Joanna blushed and laughed softly.

"Just what we need in this house, another charmer."

The boy rushed back to the carriage to help the driver

unload the trunks and travel cases. Brodie assisted Lydia out of the coach, and Aiden took his place at the open door after they moved out of the way.

A feminine hand extended from the coach door, and Aiden gently took it. The mysterious female Aiden had rescued from the sea emerged from the vehicle. As she stepped down to the ground and turned to look up at Aiden, Brock saw something that made his throat tighten. The woman looked at Aiden as though she were under an enchantment. And he looked at her with the same bespelled expression.

An old fear, one Brock had thought long buried, dug its icy claws into his chest.

Brock had been a young man, barely in his teens, when a Romani tribe had visited his home years ago. He had been welcoming to them during his father's absence, and the matriarch of the band had warned him upon their parting that his deepest fear would come true. He would see his youngest brother lost, and it would start with a beautiful stranger from another land who would capture his brother's heart.

Was this the woman whose mere presence heralded his brother's doom?

"Brock, what's the matter?" Joanna whispered. His wife leaned against his arm, her eyes wide with worry.

"Nothing—it's nothing."

Joanna turned her focus back to Aiden and the stranger. "She's very beautiful. Look at the way she moves," Joanna said. "They look like they like each other, don't they? Maybe I was silly to worry about him. Perhaps he's finally found the woman of his heart who will help him find happiness, the way you and Brodie found yours."

Brock said nothing. That was the very thing he dreaded.

"You will try to save him, but will not succeed. It is the only way to set him free."

He shook his head to rid himself of the memory of the old woman as she'd whispered her warning. Brock painted a smile upon his face and led his wife over to meet Aiden's guest.

ANNA HELD TIGHTLY TO AIDEN'S ARM, LIKE HE WAS THE mast she had clung to before he'd found her. No matter how beautiful the landscape here was, she was all too aware that she was a stranger in a strange land.

The massive castle in front of her was a daunting gray stone edifice at the top of an emerald-green hill, over-looking a picturesque lake. She'd marveled at the beauty of the landscape from the window of the coach, but to stand here with Aiden's home all around her, she was both nervous and excited. The air was clean, and a heavy fragrance of flowers from the nearby gardens perfumed the breeze. Purple heather bloomed on the distant fields. Everything here was rich in color and stunning to behold.

"Dinna worry," Aiden said. "My brother may growl a wee bit, but he has a soft heart."

She looked up at the imposing lord of the castle and his English wife. The resemblance between Aiden and Brock was clear, just as it was with Brodie. The brothers were all so alike, and yet different too. Brodie had a bit of mischief in his face, whereas Brock was far more solemn, and Aiden's face held a depth of compassion.

"Anna, this is my brother Brock and his wife, Joanna."

Brock nodded politely. "Welcome, Anna." There was a hint of shadow in his eyes, but he still welcomed her with a warm smile.

"Come inside, Anna." Joanna gently pried Aiden away from her and led Anna away, with Lydia eagerly trailing behind them. "The three of us should have tea," Joanna suggested.

Anna glanced back to see Brock speaking quietly to Aiden, his expression rather serious.

"I hope my presence is not a burden to you," she said to Joanna.

"Burden? No, of course not." Joanna's honest reply relieved some of the tension that had been building in Anna. Perhaps the brothers had other matters to discuss that had nothing to do with her.

Joanna led her to a sunny drawing room and waved for her to sit in one of the welcoming chairs.

"Careful!" Lydia cried out. Anna froze, her bottom hovering slightly above the nearest chair. "You must always check behind the cushions," she explained. Anna moved the pillows at the back of the chair. A hedgehog was curled up, fast asleep, half concealed by the pillow. Anna might have squished it if she sat down.

"See?" Lydia was still laughing. "Aiden's *wee beasties* are everywhere," she said, feigning a Scottish accent.

"She's right. I always forget and am forever startling all manner of creatures," Joanna said. "Just this morning, I was helping an upstairs maid collect fresh linens for one of the bedrooms, and we found a nest of rabbits in the sheets. Baby bunnies were running all about the room. It took us ages to trap them all along with their mother and take them down to the gardens."

Anna couldn't help but giggle at the image Joanna painted.

"Don't forget the time you found that Scottish wildcat hunting mice in the kitchens," Lydia said, then turned to explain to Anna. "Aiden found it with a paw full of thistles and treated it. Then it decided it liked living here in the castle, but it hissed at everyone. He was such a grumpy creature and so ill-tempered. The cook, was forever chasing it about with a soup ladle, trying to get it to leave."

Joanna nodded, still giggling. "It was a good mouser—even Mrs. Tate had to admit that."

Anna turned her attention to the little spiky creature on the chair. Without hesitation, she scooped the hedgehog into her hands, then sat down and placed it on her lap rather than on the floor. She didn't want it to be trampled if it wished to continue sleeping.

"No wonder Aiden likes you," Joanna said with an approving smile. "You seem to be just as comfortable with animals as he is."

Anna stroked a fingertip over the nose of the hedgehog. It snuffled and rubbed its little snout with one paw but continued to sleep.

"I do like them," she agreed.

"Anna, I heard you were shipwrecked. Is that true?" Joanna leaned over and pulled a bell cord near the wall to ring for a tea service.

"Yes. Aiden rescued me. My memory is still a bit . . ."

"Aiden mentioned you don't remember much."

"She's remembering things in bits and pieces now," Lydia interjected. "The doctor believes it will all come back to her at some point."

"Well, that's good," Joanna said. "It must be very frightening not to remember who you are."

"It is," Anna admitted. "But Aiden has made me feel safe, and I owe him much for that."

Joanna and Lydia shared a glance at that. Anna couldn't help but feel a little outnumbered here. These two women were in tune with each other and shared a history through their husbands. She was but a stranger. It shouldn't surprise her that they would be curious as to her feelings for their brother-in-law.

"You seem to like him, don't you?" said Joanna.

"I confess, I do like him very much."

The sitting room door opened. A maid brought in a tea tray and set it down beside Joanna's chair. Joanna poured three cups and handed one to Anna and one to Lydia.

"It seems I've missed quite a tale. Would you tell me everything?" Joanna asked.

Over the next half hour, Anna told Joanna all that she remembered. Some new memories had come back during the coach ride too, which added to what she could share.

"I remember traveling with my parents by coach all over the countryside, visiting people. I wish I could remember more about my parents. My father had dark hair, and my mother, she looked like me in coloring. And there was a little boy . . . He . . ." Suddenly her mind filled with joy at the new kernel of knowledge. "He was my *twin brother*." She strained but remembered nothing more.

Lydia patted her knee. "Don't fret, Anna. It will come back."

"I hope so." She thought of the smiling faces of her parents and the mischievous grin of her brother. The memories held such happiness, even though she couldn't recall much more than brief images.

I have a family . . .

Somewhere out there, she had people who loved her. Anna would find a way back to them. She had to, because at the back of her mind was a growing sense of terrible dread that had no explanation.

CHAPTER 8

"Shall we walk?" Brock asked Aiden.

Aiden knew by his brother's tone that he wanted to do more than simply walk with him.

Brodie joined them as they left the castle and stepped out into the sunlight. The three brothers moved toward the loch. Despite the fact that Aiden knew a lecture or a warning was likely coming, he took the time to enjoy being with his brothers. They'd made a home of these lands now that their father was dead, and so much had changed for the better. None of them spoke until they reached the water's edge.

"Speak yer mind, brother." Aiden could almost feel the weight of his brother's thoughts on his shoulders.

Brock looked out over the water of the loch. "This woman . . . What is she to ye? Another wounded creature ye need to heal? Or is she something more?"

Aiden rolled up the sleeves of his shirt and crouched by the water's edge to pick up a smooth skipping stone. After quiet contemplation of the water's surface, he artfully tossed the stone. It bounced as light as air upon the water several times before dropping beneath the surface and vanishing.

Neither Brock nor Brodie pushed him for an answer. They had been together too long for them to ever pressure one another into giving answers before they were ready. He knew that once he spoke, he would be telling them that Anna was his, and he expected they would push back, arguing that it was too soon to know that about a woman he'd just met.

"Anna is my fate. I canna explain to ye how I ken this, but it's true."

Brock placed a hand on his shoulder. "I ken that ye've always been gifted in ways Brodie and I are not."

"Ye mean ye think I'm different," Aiden replied, trying to ignore the sting of those words.

"Ye were too young to remember our mother sharing stories of our grandmother," Brock said. "Even Brodie might not remember that."

Aiden waited for Brock to continue. It wasn't often that Brock spoke of those old days when their mother and grandmother had still been alive. Aiden often wished he could have known what it was like to have a sense of his family, of the generations upon generations living closely together and sharing their lives. His father had been a master at isolating them from his mother's family and the tenants who lived on the land.

Brock's smile was wistful, and his gaze turned distant. "Our grandmother was of the old ways. She wore silver to ward off the vengeful and jealous eyes of the old gods. They say animals of every kind came to her when she called and that she wasn't ever fully a part of this world. She was gifted. Different. And *different* was good. She healed the livestock of our clan, could sense when the weather would change, and inspired compassion and understanding in everyone she met. She was a beacon of fire lit in the dark for all those who became lost." Brock squeezed Aiden's shoulder. "I worry that ye may mistake a lost woman's need for light in the dark as love. That is all."

Had Aiden never heard the Romani Traveller's prophecy or had those dreams about Anna, he might have been tempted to agree with Brock. It was easy to confuse caring and compassion with affection, but he felt so much more for Anna.

"I understand, Brock, I do. But sometimes the light in the dark *is* love." As he said this, an ancient pain glimmered in Brock's eyes. It was a look of loss and heartbreak, but Aiden couldn't understand why.

"Very well, then. Just promise me ye will court the lass properly if ye care about her. Show her the countryside and our people. Show her yer true self. She deserves to love ye as we do."

Aiden smiled. He would do that. He would show Anna everything he loved and let down the barriers he'd always kept up to protect himself.

"And if ye marry her, we'll hold the ceremony in the old kirk. Mother would have wanted that. I missed my chance, and so did Brodie."

"Aye, brother." Aiden chuckled at Brock's mother-henning.

Brock lightly pushed Aiden's shoulder. "Well, off with

ye, then. Go rescue yer woman from our wives before she has her ears talked off."

"I think I'll take her riding," he called over his shoulder at his brothers before he sprinted up the hill toward the castle.

৩%ঃ

"W HAT'S THE MATTER?" B RODIE PRESSED B ROCK WHEN Aiden was well out of earshot. He could tell from the look on his brother's face that something was still bothering him.

"Ye wouldna believe me," Brock muttered. "I'm not even sure *I* believe it. Yet it has me worried."

"Tell me, brother," Brodie said.

"Do ye remember when the Romani visited us for a time when you were but a lad?"

Brodie grinned. "I'd never kissed so many pretty Romani lassies before—"

"Brodie," Brock growled.

Brodie sighed. "Aye, I remember them. What of it?"

"The old woman who led their clan gave me a warning about Aiden."

"About Aiden?" Brodie's dark brows arched.

Brock crossed his arms as he looked at the castle up the hill. "She said that he will be lost to us when he meets a woman from a faraway land who will steal his heart."

"What?"

"At the time, I didn't think much of it. I mean, it sounded foolish, ye ken. But now . . . ?"

Brodie gazed at the castle, his own heart now full of an echoing dread.

"That's why ye asked him about her, and about love."

"Aye. If he never loves her, he might be safe." Brock dragged a hand through his hair, his face weary. "We never protected him enough, and now we canna stop him from falling in love."

"He canna die if we protect him," Brodie said.

Brock was silent a moment, as if considering it, then shook his head. "No, we must let him choose his path. The old woman made that clear too. Every man's destiny is his own. No matter how much we wish to interfere, we must not."

The brothers stared at the castle as they each contemplated what it might mean to them to lose Aiden.

৩%৬

THE HEDGEHOG WAS STILL ON ANNA'S LAP WHEN SHE finished her tea. After Joanna and Lydia's round of questions, weariness had settled in Anna's limbs and her head was aching. Then Aiden appeared in the doorway, making her forget all about those things simply by smiling at her.

"I see ye found Prissy." His face lit up with delight as he joined her, Lydia, and Joanna in the sitting room.

"Prissy?"

"The hedgehog." He came over to her and with delicate hands removed the sleeping hedgehog from her lap. The creature woke up and made small chirping noises as it recognized him.

Anna rose to her feet and leaned into Aiden as he held

the hedgehog in one of his hands. "What do you think she wants?"

"She's hoping I have treats," he said, then reached into the pocket of his waistcoat. He held up some seeds for Prissy. Prissy examined the offering closely before taking a few seeds in her mouth and munching away.

"She's a prissy little thing," Aiden said with a chuckle and then set her down on the ground. She scurried off into a corner and curled up into a ball again.

Aiden turned to the others. "Ladies, I am stealing Anna for a ride. We'll be back later."

"For dinner?" Joanna asked.

"Aye, we'll be back for dinner." His bemused expression softened to one of tenderness as he offered his arm to Anna. She smiled up at him as she tucked her arm in his.

"Be careful, Aiden," Lydia called out after them as they left the sitting room.

"Are we truly going riding, or did you think I needed rescuing from your sisters-in-law?" She dearly hoped so. She remembered now that she loved to ride. It seemed to go hand in hand with her love of horses.

"I wish to show ye my home and our lands. I also need to visit some of the tenants and their livestock. I hope ye won't mind accompanying me."

"Not at all. It sounds lovely."

As they exited the castle, a groom stood waiting with Thundir and a mare saddled. They approached the horses, and then Aiden assisted her onto the other horse. There was no sidesaddle, so she swung her leg over to the other side and set her booted feet into the stirrups.

Her skirts rose up, exposing her stocking-covered legs

up to her knees. Aiden noticed and blinked a few times at the sight of her legs before he cleared his throat. His face reddened, and Anna felt her own skin heating at the realization that he was noticing her legs, scandalously exposed, and she was all too aware of how much she liked him noticing.

"This horse is Nevis. She's named after one of our mountains here in Scotland." Aiden gave the mare a solid pat on her neck. "I didna think about a sidesaddle since Nevis is calm, but if ye want one—"

"No, I don't mind," she assured him. "It actually is easier to ride this way. Sidesaddles twist my back."

He smiled at her as if relieved. Then he mounted Thundir, and Anna took hold of Nevis's reins.

"You remember how to ride?" he asked.

"I think so. It's like the dancing—my body remembers."

"Good. Yer muscles have memories too, the way minds do." He suddenly shot her a playful smirk. "Try to keep up, lass!" Then he gave a cry to his horse, and Thundir took off at a gallop.

Laughing, Anna mimicked him, and the roan mare chased after them. They raced down the hill toward the lake, then up another hill and through the fields of heather. Clouds towered over them in endless shapes of brilliant white, set against the deep-blue sky.

The wind whipped through her hair as she rode, and something tight and dark in her chest began to fade away. She was able to breathe deeply, taking in the aroma of the heather and wildflowers. A sudden flash of memory streaked like a shooting star across the night sky of her mind. She had ridden before, wildly just like this, with a young man beside her, his laughter ringing through the hills. His face was a match to her own, but masculine.

"Alexei . . ." The name formed on her lips, and with it came a flood of tenderness and love.

This was her brother. *Her twin.* Tears filled her eyes, and the wind blew them from her cheeks as she urged her horse to catch up to Aiden's. They galloped side by side to a small forest glen. Aiden slowed Thundir's pace, and she did the same with her mare. They walked their horses in a cooldown and entered the woods. Tall, thick-trunked, green-leafed trees arched over the forest paths, letting the sun dapple the ground with shimmers of light. It was a beautiful glen.

If she closed her eyes, she could almost hear the trees talking to each other. The breeze and the leaves, the crack and pop of roots and branches, all formed a natural symphony. She and Aiden continued through the forest without speaking. Words weren't needed in a place like this. It was an old forest, like the one she remembered dreaming about, but this wasn't *her* forest. It was Aiden's.

His handsome face glowed with the soft gold light that filtered down from the canopy. The shadows that haunted him were gone here in this sacred place. There was only peace in his eyes as he studied the trees. He slowed his horse to a stop. With barely a sound, he dismounted and came to help her slide off her horse. They stared at each other a moment, him close to her, and then he slowly reached out his arms, indicating he was ready to catch her when she dismounted. Anna's breath caught at the intensity of his stormy eyes. Aiden caught her, letting her move slowly down his body until her toes touched the ground.

The way he carried her weight with such ease showed the immensity of his strength.

As he held her, their bodies pressed chest to chest, she thought for a moment he might kiss her, and she desperately wished he would. But instead, he pressed a finger to his lips, and she nodded, understanding that he wished for them both to be quiet.

They left the horses alone to graze. Aiden curled his fingers around hers as they walked toward a distant patch of light where the canopy opened above them. Once they reached it, they stepped out onto the edge of a sunny spread of grass and wildflowers. He faced the forest ahead of them, patient, silent, and unmoving. Anna watched him as he watched the trees. He was waiting for something, but who or what?

A moment later she had her answer. A mighty stag stepped into the light, his impressive crown of antlers rising high above him. She held her breath as the deer moved in graceful steps to stand fully in the sunlight, like a king coming to greet his subjects. He bowed his head and began to eat the tops of the wildflowers that flourished around his hooves.

Aiden still held her hand, and he pulled her close to whisper in her ear. "'Tis the monarch of the glen."

Aiden's warm breath on her neck caused her body to shiver with sudden longing. She wanted to turn and wrap her arms around his neck and kiss him.

"There, you see his crown?" he asked.

She refocused on the stag, though her body was still aware of the heat of Aiden beside her.

"He's beautiful. The most beautiful thing I've ever

seen," she whispered in return, her gaze flitting to him and back to the stag.

Aiden's lips brushed her ear. "Aye. He is beautiful, but ye are far more so." Then he rose and faced the stag.

The stag lifted his head and slowly turned to look at them. Aiden took a step toward the prince of the forest and led Anna with him. The deer's quiet gaze moved between Aiden and Anna before staying on her.

"Why isn't he running?" she whispered.

"Because he kens he has nothing to fear from us," Aiden replied, his voice just as soft as hers.

The stag bowed his head to them, and with solemn, almost ethereal grace, he walked away, vanishing into the woods beyond. For a moment the spell of the monarch of the glen lingered like a golden haze over Anna and Aiden, and then finally it faded as all magic does from time to time.

"Whoever ye are, lass, ye must have a royal heart. The monarch sees ye as his equal."

Anna wanted to wave the notion away and argue that stags simply did not go about bowing to people in forests. But this was Aiden's glen, and a kind of magic hung heavy in the air, making it feel like she was in a wonderful dream where anything was possible and not simply in a forest like any other. In this place, it was possible that a kingly deer might bow his head.

"I can feel it—the magic," she told him. "I'm not dreaming, am I?"

Aiden pulled her into his arms and cupped her cheeks as their eyes met.

"I feel it too. 'Tis stronger now than before, because of

ye." The desire in his eyes wasn't merely physical. She could see the heat there in his gaze, but also something softer, infinitely deeper like the depths of the ocean that he'd rescued her from.

He lowered his head toward hers, and their lips met in a spark of glorious fire. She was captive to the burning sweetness of Aiden's mouth. He curled an arm around her waist, and she clutched his shoulders, feeling the heat and strength of him beneath the white lawn fabric. A flame kindled to life within her, warming her as she parted her lips beneath his tongue. It felt wicked, wanton, and yet utterly perfect to let her tongue entwine with his.

She had never known kissing could be equal parts fire and tenderness. A delicious ache in her lower belly made her clench her thighs together. Aiden's strong hand pressed into the hollow of her lower back, pulling her tight to him. He was so tall, yet she didn't mind standing up on her toes to kiss him. His hand moved down and cupped her bottom, which he clenched hard. A groan escaped her at the sudden throb between her thighs.

"Aiden," she breathed urgently against him.

"Aye?" he murmured back before stealing another kiss that made her toes curl.

"I need . . . I . . ." She wasn't sure what she needed; she only hoped that he would understand.

His hand moved on her bottom as he started to pull up her skirts along one hip.

"What are you doing?" She didn't pull away; she was too excited by the fresh spark of passion that rippled beneath her skin. Then his mouth was on hers, and she gasped in surprise as his warm fingers delved through her underpinnings to touch her bare skin. She dug her nails into his shoulders as he reached the sensitive folds of her sex and began to stroke. She was fairly certain she'd never been touched down there by anyone other than herself.

"Easy now." Aiden flicked his tongue in her ear. He slid a finger inside her, and she felt a rush of wetness in response to his touch. She tried to close her thighs in embarrassment.

"Open for me, Anna. Trust me to give ye what ye need." He nipped her earlobe, tugging on it in a way that sent a thrill from the tips of her breasts down to where he touched her. She arched into him, allowing his finger to push deeper, panting against him as he withdrew the finger and thrust it back in. He continued the motion over and over, changing positions and pace each time she gave a little startled cry. Then he inserted another finger, stretching her a little more as his penetration quickened. All the while his mouth was gently exploring her neck, her ears, or her lips. She was lost to him in this sensual but oh so lovely assault on her senses.

Something inside her was racing toward a high peak. She grew desperate for more, more frantic as she gasped and begged him to move faster, to give her what she needed. And then it happened. Something exquisite blinded her, obliterating all her thoughts.

For a brief few seconds, she felt as though she contained the sun itself within her body. She cried out Aiden's name, and when she opened her eyes, she found him staring at her in wonder and reverence. He withdrew his hand from between her legs, and after a soft kiss to her lips, he used a handkerchief to clean his hand, then reached up beneath her skirts and wiped between her legs. She clung to his arms, her legs trembling too hard for her to trust herself to stand.

"That was yer first time?" he asked. His voice held a hint of roughness to it, as though he was just as affected by what had happened as she was.

"Y-yes . . . What was that?"

"Ye dinna know? How are ye as innocent as a bairn?" He sat down on the bed of wildflowers and pulled her close to him so that she sat between his legs and leaned back against him in the sunlight.

"Is that what women feel when they lie with men?"

"Aye, but it doesna always feel like that. It's better when yer heart is involved, ye ken."

"Like love . . ."

"Like love."

"But you didn't—"

"No, but it wasna my turn. Someday we will share it together. Today was yer time to experience it, and I assure you, it was my truest pleasure to watch ye." He stroked his hands down her arms, soothing her.

"Oh . . ." She was a little disappointed at that. She wanted him to feel that glorious rush too. He cupped her chin and tilted her face up to his so he could kiss her again. She giggled and relaxed, sated in ways she never knew she could be. He held her as the clouds passed overhead.

"Aiden . . . I remembered something while I was riding with you today."

"What did ye remember?"

"I remembered how my twin, Alexei, and I used to ride like that, wild and free."

"That's wonderful, lassie." Aiden hugged her from behind. "The more ye remember, the sooner we can find yer family."

A sudden terrible thought struck her, and she covered her mouth. "Aiden, what if my family was on the ship with me? What if they all perished?"

She buried her cheek against his shoulder as she fought off a wave of panic that threatened to drown her. To have hope only to see it wrecked just like the ship she'd been on . . . It was unbearable to think about.

"Easy, Anna. Ye canna be sure of that. Not yet. Ye must have hope. And even if ye find out the worst, ye arna alone. *Ye have me.* And ye are a strong, brave woman."

Her breathing slowly steadied itself. He was right. She was strong and brave, and she wasn't alone. She looked up at him. "It was fortunate that *you* were the one to find me on the beach."

Aiden smiled at her as a cluster of clouds parted above them and sunlight illuminated the clearing.

"Maybe it wasn't luck," said Aiden. "Maybe it was destiny."

ARTHUR MACDONALD WAS SITTING IN HIS SURGERY, reading over the latest medical treatises from London, when his housekeeper's cry alerted him to trouble. He nearly knocked over his chair as he raced toward the front door.

"Doctor! They found more people from the shipwreck." The old housekeeper was nearly bowled over as a young man pushed his way into the home.

"Ye must come, Doctor. They're barely alive."

"Let me fetch my bag." Arthur returned to his surgery, frantically shoving anything he thought he might need into his black bag before he returned to the door. "Lead the way." He followed the man as they jogged toward the distant shoreline.

When they reached the cliffs, Arthur saw a lifeboat being pulled onto the sand by several fishermen far below on the shore. Bodies layered the interior of the tiny vessel. This must have been the majority of the ship's crew.

Thankfully, the narrow path that zigzagged down to the beach was one Arthur knew well, and he was able to move quickly. He and the young man sprinted down until they hit the thick, heavy sand, then they made their way to the lifeboat. The fishermen were waiting for him by the time he reached the vessel.

"We saw 'em drifting in a short while ago, Doctor." An older man with a grizzled beard pointed to a part of the sea that was heavy with a rocky outcropping. "We swam out and caught 'em before the boat broke on the rocks."

"Well done," Arthur praised. "Let me see them." He moved from body to body. Nearly all of them were sailors. Their blue short pants, red scarves, and white shirts were uniforms of merchant ship sailors he'd seen so often before. Unfortunately, all but a few were deceased.

A single woman at the tip of the boat was still breathing faintly, along with two other men. Her clothes were simple in design but well tailored and made from costly fabrics. She was highborn, or close to it, if he had to guess. He removed a wooden cylinder called a stethoscope from his bag. It was a revolutionary new invention, and he found it worked better to hear a heartbeat than pressing his ear to a patient's chest. This proved extremely useful with female patients so that he didn't create distress by putting his face directly against their breasts. He pressed the end of the cylinder to the woman's bosom and his ear to the other end. A weak thumping sound came back to him.

"They must've been at sea without food or water," the older fishermen said. "Look at their lips."

Arthur had noted the parched, chapped lips of the sailors. But the woman seemed less dehydrated than the men.

"They must've given the woman their share of the water they had," another sailor guessed as he pointed to an empty water bucket at the woman's feet.

Arthur put his hand on her chin, raising her head to check her breathing. Her eyelids fluttered.

"Help," the woman whispered in Danish. "Help us . . ."

"We will help ye," Arthur replied in her tongue. These might be other survivors of the *Ruritanian Star*. It had been almost a week since Miss Anna had washed up on the shore.

"Must . . . find my lady . . . ," the woman murmured.

"Does anyone have any water?" Arthur asked the fishermen. The oldest among the group produced a flask of water.

He took the water and pressed the round opening of the flask against the woman's parted lips. "Drink," he urged as he trickled the water down her throat. She drank, coughed weakly, and trembled.

"Miss Anna . . . must find Miss Anna," she tried again. "My lady . . . lost in the water . . ."

"Anna is yer lady?" he asked the woman. He feared pushing her to speak, but he also feared she might not survive, and he needed to get whatever information he could while she was able to talk.

"Must get to London . . . Her brother will come for her . . ." The woman lifted a hand, grasping Arthur's wrist as her weary eyes pleaded with him. "Matter of life and death . . ." The woman closed her eyes and passed out.

"Help me carry these two men and the woman to my home," he directed several of the sailors. "If the rest of ye can please take the ones who didn't survive up to the kirk graveyard and see them buried, I will pay ye for yer trouble."

By the time they reached his house, the woman's skin was cold to the touch and she was shivering. The two men were doing a little better. He instructed his housekeeper to put the woman in his bed and the two men in the beds in his surgery. The fisherman saw to the two men, while Arthur and his housekeeper focused on the woman. His bedroom blankets were thicker than the ones in his surgery and would help her temperature rise. They stripped her of her wet clothes before they tucked her under the sheets. They would have to warm her up slowly—too fast and she could die. Arthur heated several stones in the fireplace and then tucked them under the woman's feet and back beneath the sheets.

"Is she one of them foreign ladies, like the one that

handsome young lad found?" his housekeeper asked in a whisper.

"Aye." Arthur sank down onto the nearest chair, exhausted. "And I think this woman knows Mr. Kincade's foundling girl."

His housekeeper bustled about the room, tutting softly and muttering about strange women washing up on shore. She gently tucked the sheets around the woman and touched her forehead, then turned her focus on Arthur.

"Can I get ye some tea while ye wait for her to wake, Doctor?" the housekeeper offered.

"Yes, thank ye, and bring me some paper. I must write an urgent missive. If what this woman said was true, then I must tell Mr. Kincade to take Anna to London to find her brother. It sounded quite urgent."

He would have a message taken to Castle Kincade as swiftly as possible. Then he would do his best to care for the woman now lying in his bed.

CHAPTER 9

A full week had passed since Aiden had rescued Anna from the ocean, and in those seven days Anna had grown far more confident and, he suspected, more like herself, even though she still lacked so many memories. Aiden was delighted to find that Anna was amusing, intelligent, and adventurous. And her love for animals was almost as strong as his own.

He worried each time he asked to take her out on horseback that she'd say no, but she seemed to thrive on the time they spent together out in the country. He'd always felt that nature was healing for one's body and soul, and it seemed Anna agreed. It helped that they often ended up tumbled in the grass, kissing each other beneath the late-autumn sun and losing track of time altogether. Kissing Anna had to be one of life's greatest pleasures. He adored the way she'd gaze up at him, dreamy-eyed and soft, and he'd feel like a blessed man. Everything she did fascinated him—the way she talked, the thoughts that ran like quicksilver in her mind. Being with her filled that hollow-ness inside him that he'd always tried to pretend he didn't feel. With her . . . he felt whole. He felt no weight upon his shoulders and no burden upon his soul.

They rode everywhere together and stayed up late after dinner talking in the library while he tended to his tawny owl, Honey. The previous night, he'd shown Anna the nest where Honey was roosting on her eggs. They'd climbed a ladder to the top of the corner shelf where the owl had made her home. Honey had eyed them with half-closed eyes and was entirely unruffled when Aiden stroked her feathery breast and even allowed Anna to do the same. His wee beasties seemed to adore her as much as they adored him, which delighted Anna to no end and pleased him far more than he could ever say. It was as if she was always meant to be here with him.

He was enjoying every moment of watching her come out of her shell and become the woman she'd been before the shipwreck. She seemed to enjoy teaching him Danish, and he was rather surprised he was picking it up quickly. It helped that each time he successfully mastered a word, she rewarded him in kisses.

They were becoming closer each day, but he had not dared to touch her intimately again the way he had in the meadow. He wanted more than anything to take her to bed, but he didn't want to rush something so important to both of them. He still stole plenty of kisses in all sorts of places that made her giggle afterward with a sensual delight that proved to be the best kind of torture for him. The haunted look that he had once seen in her eyes had faded beneath her natural joy.

Now he stood in an alcove, watching her in a huddle with his sisters-in-law. They were all dressed in day gowns that were the height of London's latest fashions, which he only knew because Joanna and Lydia constantly spoke of clothing, when not discussing politics or social issues. Anna stood out from the other two women in her cream-and-blue satin gown. Her dark-russet hair was pulled up in a loose Grecian fashion, and a blue ribbon studded with star-shaped jewels was wound over her hair like a headband. She looked regal. No doubt that had been Lydia's intention when she'd purchased the clothes and other items in North Berwick.

Anna said something, and the other two women laughed. Aiden's heart swelled with such joy as he knew he was glimpsing a possible future. If he married Anna some-day, this could be something he would see every day. She could have friendships with Lydia and Joanna. She could live here and give his home light and hope. And in return, he would give her everything she could possibly desire. He would be whatever she needed him to be for her to be happy. He didn't let himself think past the bright and glittering future they could have together.

He decided that whatever the old Romani woman had seen, he wouldn't let it cast storm clouds upon his and Anna's horizon. If that day came, he would do whatever he had to in order to protect her, but until then, he wanted to live a life of joy with her for however long they might have.

The three women broke apart when he stepped out of the alcove and walked toward them.

"Afternoon, Aiden," Lydia and Joanna said before giggling behind their hands like schoolgirls. Anna flushed but smiled at him, and it made him feel like he could do anything in the world so long as he had that smile to carry in his memories.

"I thought ye might wish to visit the mews with me?" he asked her. "I have a few birds to take out hunting."

"Yes, of course. I'd love to." She winked at Lydia and Joanna before coming toward him. As he had done so often of late, he took her into his arms and kissed her without a care as to who was watching. Anna smiled against his lips, and they both laughed as their mouths broke apart.

"You really shouldn't do that in front of them," Anna whispered, as if scandalized. "They keep waiting for you to behave."

"Do *ye* want me to behave?" he asked.

"No," she replied without hesitation. "I just wonder . . . is it like this for other people? We just ran straight into each other's arms and haven't looked back since." She nibbled her bottom lip. "Is it because we both think this is destiny? What if it's not? What if we're wrong and this is all . . . I don't know . . . just a shared dream?"

Her words created a hole of dread in his chest. "Are ye having second thoughts about me? If ye are, that's all right, lass. We did rush things," he admitted. But it had felt so right to him the moment he'd taken her in his arms that day on the beach. Why would he ignore what his instincts told him was the right thing to do?

"No, but that's what I mean, Aiden. Shouldn't I be second-guessing all of this? I keep wondering if something went wrong inside me when I hit my head. I . . ." She paused, then frowned. "Am I being silly?"

Aiden tipped her chin back to see her tawny brown eyes. "Do ye trust me?" he asked.

She curled her fingers around his wrist, holding on to him. "I trust you in a way I don't think I've ever trusted anyone else. I shouldn't know that for certain, but I feel it's true."

He stroked his thumb over her bottom lip as he gazed at her. "If ye ever change yer mind, I will understand," he promised. "I dinna wish to force ye to do anything ye dinna wish to do."

"Thank you."

She rocked up on her tiptoes and kissed him sweetly in the way that made him feel both homesick and as if he had just come home at the same time. It was . . . bittersweet.

"Take me to see your falcons," she said when they stepped apart.

"With pleasure." He led her outside to the mews behind the stables. The tall structure had places for the birds of prey to exit and return easily. While they could go hunting on their own at any time, he liked to take them out every so often. He had a mated pair of ospreys, a golden eagle, and his favorite, a small merlin.

He opened the door to the darkened mews and listened to the clicks and chirps of the birds recognizing he was there. The flutter of wings and a dusting of downy feathers drifted down from above as the birds settled down.

Aiden clicked his tongue and slid a long leather glove over his right arm. He raised his wrist, and a small merlin descended toward him. Many people confused merlins with kestrels, but merlins were smaller, and their wings were short, pointed, and broad, which gave them incredible agility in flight. They were also a grayish-blue color with a white-and-brown speckled breast and a brown tail, whereas kestrels were more brown and gold. Like other birds of prey, they thrived in the vast woodlands, mountains, and coastlines of his country.

As Aiden emerged from the mews, the merlin saw Anna and let out an excited chirp that sounded like the bird was stuttering.

"Oh, he is so beautiful," Anna said.

"Here, put this on." Aiden offered her a glove of her own, which she slid up her arm. Then he carefully urged the merlin to tiptoe from his wrist to hers.

The merlin's feathers were puffed and a bit out of place. Then the little raptor suddenly shook his entire body, and his feathers gently drifted back down, sleek and smooth against his back and breast.

Anna's eyes went wide, and her face glowed with fascination. "Heavens! What did he do that for?"

"That's called rousing. It clears the plumage of dirt, debris, and excess water. They often do it when they're content as well," Aiden explained. He used his gloved finger to stroke the bird's chest.

"He likes me, then?" she asked.

"He must." Aiden chuckled. "Let's take him down to the lake."

They walked down the hill to the water, and Aiden raised his arm with the glove.

"Do what I do, and ye can cast him off." He then pumped his fist into the air.

"Like this?" She waited until the merlin crept to her

closed fist on the glove, and then she propelled him into flight.

The merlin swept up over the landscape. He was not the most graceful flyer, but his speed and agility were unmatched. Aiden turned to watch Anna as the bird flew high above them. Something caught in his throat as the sun lit up her face. He knew in that moment he'd found her—the woman who would forever hold his heart.

🙰

THEY WATCHED THE MERLIN TAIL-CHASE A FEW SPARROWS in the distance before it caught a small one and landed in a tree some yards in the water to eat it.

"Poor little bird," Anna said.

"Aye, but 'tis the way of life. I love all animals, ye ken, but to love them means to respect the hierarchy of both predator and prey when in nature. I help what animals I can when I feel there is a lack of balance."

"I suppose you're right." Her voice suddenly hardened with a rage. "But not all predators maintain the balance of nature."

"Nature has a way of keeping balance on its own, given time. But when men are added to the mix, they can throw it off without thinking."

Anna smiled. "That's what I mean. Some men deliberately kill . . ."

Her head suddenly exploded with pain. She cried out, sinking to her knees. Aiden caught her in his arms before she fell over.

"Anna?" He held her close to his chest. "What's the matter?"

"My head . . . it hurts." She could barely think. All she saw in her head were fleeting, painful images of a village burning, children screaming, and death . . . such needless death. She held on to Aiden, breathing through the pain until the nightmarish vision faded.

"I saw things," she whispered as she turned in his arms. "I saw terrible things."

"Can ye tell me what things?" He pressed his lips comfortingly to her forehead.

"A village was burning . . . People were being slaughtered as if they did not matter." She shuddered as the vision poured through her mind, blood and sorrow tainting every image.

"Was it before ye got on the ship? Was it long ago?"

As the pain faded, Anna regained some clarity, enough that she could actually tell that this wasn't a memory.

"No, I don't think it has happened yet."

Aiden's eyes were dark as he gazed at her. "Ye mean it will happen in the future? How can ye be sure?"

"I just am. Something terrible is going to happen," she insisted. It was different to how her returning memories felt. A clear sense not of things that were, but would be. "You believe me, don't you?"

"Aye, lass, I do." Aiden brushed a lock of hair from her face and tucked it behind her ear. "Can ye stand?"

"Y-yes. The pain is almost gone." She climbed to her feet with his help. Then he gave a sharp whistle and raised his arm. The merlin streaked back to earth and landed on Aiden's fist. He chirped, his cheery tone indicating he was quite pleased with himself for having caught his meal.

"Let's go back. Ye should have some tea and rest."

Anna didn't want to admit to being tired, but she felt hollow now that the images had faded. Hollow and weary beyond her years.

"I'm sorry if I ruined our outing." She turned away from him, walking more quickly up the hill to hide her embarrassment.

Reaching out, he caught her arm and gently turned her to face him. "Caring about someone does not mean the days are always sunny and the air full of laughter. It means weathering the storms too, the winter chill and the stifling heat. Ye ride out these things together, good or bad." His gray-blue eyes were so deep, Anna could have gazed into their depths and lost herself forever . . . or perhaps found herself.

She was falling in love with him, and had been since the day he'd pulled her from the water. It was a love that would grow so fierce that it would have the power to tear the world apart or put it back together. It was a love born of destiny, as he once put it, and now more than ever, she *believed* it.

And the stronger her feelings grew, the more that knot of dread grew inside her, and her fears fed it hour by hour as she worried about what was yet to come.

YURI AND FAIN, ALONG WITH A CONTINGENT OF ONE hundred men, surrounded the little village of Vasler just before dawn. They waited in the shadows of the wood as they watched the fires burn low and the village guards, who were no more than a few farmers with pitiful pitchforks, drift to sleep at their posts.

"Your orders, my king?" Fane whispered. The horses shifted restlessly beneath them.

"Take the men captive. Round up the women and children and lock them in the church. I want them to see what their loyalty to the rebel princeling has cost them."

Vasler was one of many villages that Yuri had learned were receiving food and coin from the wagons that his nephew and his men had looted en route to Yuri's camp. He couldn't afford to keep his small army of guards happy if he didn't have money to pay them or food to feed them. His ability to maintain control of the country was hanging by a thread, and as much as he wanted to deny it, he couldn't, at least not to himself. His men couldn't know how close he was to losing his hold on everything. That damned brat of a prince was going to destroy him.

He dares to steal from me, so I will show him the price of his rebellion.

Fain and the armed soldiers charged the village, throwing torches onto the roofs of homes and trampling those who stood in their way. Screams tore through the air as their pitiful resistance was quelled. When it was over, Yuri walked in front of the captured men of the village, who were all on their knees, their hands bound behind them. The women and children were forced into the small church, and Yuri's men closed the door, dropping a heavy timber into place to seal the door from the outside.

"You accepted food and coin from those who oppose

me and my claim to these lands. Now you pay the price for that betrayal." He turned to Fain, who handed him a torch. He walked toward the church. Behind him, the men of Vasler began to shout, plead, and beg for mercy. But Yuri heard only the glorious sound of subjugation by force as he threw the torch onto the church's roof.

He let the village men drown in the screams of their wives and children. And then, when the embers burned in the collapsed chapel and no life remained within its blackened walls, Fain gave the signal and his men raised their swords, hacking the surviving men down. When Alexei came to check on this village, he would find every last man, woman, and child dead. And he would know who had done it.

Yuri mounted his horse and surveyed the chaos he had sown and was pleased. This land was his, because he alone had the will to take it. He would take everything Ruritania had to give, and then, when he'd sated himself on the riches of this land, he would turn his gaze to Prussia. Such was the way of things. The way of those with the might to take what they wanted.

CHAPTER 10

Anna bit her lip to keep from laughing. She sat across from Aiden at the dining room table as they ate breakfast. Prissy, Aiden's hedgehog, was slowly meandering down the length of the table toward Brock and his plate of half-eaten kippers, berries, and nuts. Brock had the morning post spread out in front of him and was completely unaware of the approaching creature.

Brock was at the far end of the table, while Joanna, Lydia, and Brodie were seated at chairs in the middle of the long table. As Anna fought to hide her laughter, she and Aiden both kept shooting looks at each other, then back at the hedgehog.

Anna had no idea how the hedgehog had gotten onto the table, but she hadn't bothered to stop Prissy because she was too busy trying not to giggle. If there was one thing she'd learned about the animals Aiden healed, it was that they lost all fear of people in general, including the other members of Aiden's family.

Prissy paused at Brodie's plate, sniffed at the crumbs he'd left, and then continued on down the line, checking each plate as she went. But the closer she got to Brock's plate, the more the tip of her little snout quivered in anticipation.

Brodie, having now noticed the hedgehog, leaned forward and grinned down at the creature. Lydia and Joanna were both engrossed in talking about the latest political developments in France and hadn't noticed the hedgehog. Prissy perused their empty plates, then continued on, unnoticed by the two women who were deep in discussion.

With a ruffle of his paper, Brock reached for his plate to grasp a slice of apple, but he didn't see that the hedgehog had now perched halfway onto his plate and was nibbling at one. His large hand landed heavily right on top of the prickly creature.

"Bloody hell!" Brock leapt up from his chair, clutching his hand.

The newspaper dropped, covering the hedgehog entirely. Brock peeled up one corner of the paper to reveal Prissy still eating. She paused when she realized Brock was glaring down at her. She snuffled loudly, then sneezed on the kippers.

"Aiden," Brock growled, "remove this beastie now!"

Aiden was already moving to rescue Prissy from the Highland lord.

"I told ye no beasts on the table," Brock warned him.

Aiden grinned, as if knowing full well this wouldn't be the last time a creature ended up on the dining room table. "I dinna ken how she got up there. She has such wee stubby legs." Aiden shot Anna a wink, and she bit her lip to keep from laughing.

Brock, still fuming, lifted up his reddened hand, rubbing his palm gingerly. Joanna came to her husband's rescue, gently taking his wounded hand and pressing a kiss to his palm.

"Feel better?" she asked in a sweet voice.

Brock's eyes softened and heated. "Aye, 'tis much better. Perhaps ye had better attend me in our chambers." Brock, no longer concerned about his hand, scooped Joanna up into his arms and carried her off. Their laughter still echoed down the hall as Aiden removed Brock's breakfast plate and set it on the floor next to Prissy, where the hedgehog could eat in peace.

Anna rose from her chair and bid the others a good day before she and Aiden left the breakfast room and burst into giggles.

"Are ye up for another adventure?" he asked her.

"With you? *Always*," she said honestly.

"Good. I have a special place to show ye. Dress in yer warmest riding gown."

Anna went upstairs to change with the help of one of the housemaids and came back down wearing a hunter-green riding habit, riding boots, and a little green hat perched jauntily on her head.

Aiden's eyes widened at the sight of her, and she blushed at the desire she saw in his eyes.

"Ye look quite fetching," he said as he caught her in his arms at the bottom of the stairs.

"As do you." She ran her hands over his gold-and-black embroidered waistcoat. His eyes lit up, and her whole body simmered with the heat he always caused within her. It was almost dangerous to be around him. It felt as though they were just a kiss away from setting the world ablaze around them.

Anna loved knowing that he desired her the same way she desired him. Ever since he'd touched her that day in the meadow, she'd wanted nothing more than to experience that pleasure again, only this time she wanted to share it with him.

The horses were outside, and she was delighted to see Bob saddled and waiting beside Thundir this time instead of one of the other horses from the castle stables. She'd been watching the mare's healing over the last several days, and it was a good sign as to her condition if Aiden thought she was ready to take a rider. Draped over Thundir's back was a folded plaid that looked big enough to act as a blanket for both of them.

"Are we having a picnic?" she asked hopefully.

Aiden chuckled. "Aye." They walked down toward the horses together.

"Is Bob healed now?" Anna came over to coo at the beautiful horse. Bob brushed her nose gracefully against Anna's shoulder.

"She is, and anxious to be running in the countryside, from what I can tell." Aiden helped Anna up into the saddle before he mounted Thundir. "Cameron has taken his stable lessons seriously and has become Bob's personal caretaker," Aiden said, and Anna heard the pride in his voice about Cameron.

"Cameron is doing well, then?" She'd seen the boy

running about the house, but the Kincade brothers had taken his youthful mischief in stride.

"Quite well. The boy simply needed a safe place to learn and grow without fear of the strap," Aiden said, and his gaze turned sorrowful.

Anna regretted bringing it up. "Oh, Aiden, I didn't mean to . . ."

He shook his head, a rueful glint in his eyes. "I am glad that Cameron will suffer far less than I did."

They rode far to the west across new lands she had not seen before during her frequent rides with him. Rain clouds gathered and thunder rumbled in the distance by the low mountain wreathed with fog, but all around them a bright early autumn sun burnished the fields in heavy gold glow. They came across a small creek and allowed the horses to drink before following it upstream into a set of foothills.

"We'll leave the horses here." He removed the folded plaid from the back of his saddle and slung it over his shoulder. Then he nodded at a nearby copse of trees, where they tied the reins of the horses to a pair of low-hanging branches. The horses would have plenty of slack in their reins to feed on the nearby grasses.

"Follow me, and be mindful of yer steps," Aiden said.

Anna placed her hand in his, following him through a narrow outcropping of rocks as they stepped carefully across the stream, which was pouring out of fissure in the rocks ahead of them. Anna braced herself against the tall gray stones that had been smoothed by centuries of rain. A low hum began in her head as they passed through the narrow chasm in the rocks, and she gasped.

In front of her were half a dozen pools of water. Each was a different size, and each one had a mirrorlike surface that rippled with rainbows of colors. The bigger pools fed into a larger pool at the base of a cluster of waterfalls that formed below a small hill that tapered away on the other side of a forest. The rocks beneath the water, rather than being brown or gray like most stones, were a brilliant blue or a rich emerald green. It didn't seem possible. They stood side by side to admire the view.

"What is this place?"

"These, lass, are the fairy pools. I have never shown anyone this place before." He knelt by the water, and she joined him as they sat on the rounded surface of a large stone by the biggest pool beneath the falls.

"Not even your brothers?"

"No, not even them." He looked out over the water. "When my father first beat me, I ran on foot for days, thinking I would never come back. I was bleeding and hurting, and somehow, after five days on my small feet, I stumbled upon this place. Desperate for water, I drank from the pool just over there."

He pointed to a spot by the edge of the water where they sat. Anna leaned against his shoulder and curled her arms around his, holding on to him as he spoke.

"The water felt good upon my battered skin. I swam and bathed here for a few hours and fell asleep on the shore. When I woke, my wounds were gone. The blood, the open flesh, all healed. Most people dinna believe in magic, that the old ways of the Scots are but nonsense and should be forgotten. But *something* here in these waters took pity on an injured child."

His blue-gray eyes were bright, and Anna sucked in a breath at the sight of his face. The hard lines softened, and his eyes were full of a glowing warmth when he spoke of the magic of the fairy pools. He was more beautiful to her now than ever before. Beautiful because he had bared his soul fully and completely to her.

"Most people would say it was a pretty story, but they wouldna truly believe me, but I think ye do." He placed his palm over hers on his arm.

Anna nodded and scooted closer, her eyes searching his. For what she wasn't sure, but she stroked her fingers over his cheek, her heart clenching as tears burned the corners of her eyes.

"I wish . . . I wish I knew who I was. I want you to know me as you have let me know you. I want to give you all of myself the way you've done for me." They might not have been the most eloquent words, but they came straight from her heart.

Aiden cupped her hand against his cheek, keeping her cold fingers pressed to his warm skin.

"I know who ye are, from yer favorite color, which is green, to the way ye hold yerself verra still when unsure of yerself. Ye are smart and brave and ye aren't afraid to explore things. Ye have a heart that could love every creature on this earth and still have room for more. Whatever else ye may one day remember about yerself, those will be just extra things for me to ken and love ye for."

"You love me?" She still didn't know how it was possible that they could feel so connected and so in tune with each other that *love* seemed like the only word strong enough to match what they felt.

"Aye, lassie." Aiden's soft words were so full of emotion that she held her breath. "I love ye more than the breath in my own body. I love ye as if we were born under the same blanket of stars a thousand years before and loved each other in another life. Ye and I . . . we are the same. Two pieces of the earth once separated, brought back together." He swallowed, and his voice grew rougher as he struggled to speak. "Ye dinna ken how lost I've been, Anna. Finding ye that day on the shore . . . it was as if I'd stumbled upon the fairy pools a second time and was healed. Now I wish to heal ye." He nodded toward the pool.

She followed his gaze toward the water where rainbows rippled across its misty surface. The humming grew deeper this time, so deep her bones seemed to vibrate with it.

They stood and moved toward the water together, as if it was always meant to be this way. She paused at the edge and removed the hat pins from her hair so she could set her hat on the ground.

Her heart beat wildly as she spoke. "Would you help me undress?" She lifted her skirts to show her boots.

He looked her up and down, as if sizing up her clothes and what it would mean to undress her. Then his sensual lips kicked up into a devilish grin that stole her breath.

"Aye, I'll help ye, lass." Aiden knelt at her feet, and she braced her hands on his shoulders as he unlaced her riding boots and slid them off her feet. Then he reached underneath her skirts and began to roll down her stockings, making her laugh as he tickled her skin a little. Unable to stop reacting, she giggled.

"The last time I undressed ye, ye were pale and cold as death," he murmured. "I much prefer to take yer clothes off here, like this." His gaze slowly roved up her bare legs to where she held her skirts up to her knees, and then his eyes paused on her face. Her breath quickened at the primal desire that sparked inside her. She wanted his hands everywhere on her body; she wanted to feel his weight on her as he pressed her down into the grass. She was vibrating with a need that her body understood far better than her mind.

He stood up, and they shared a soft, lingering kiss before he turned her around to unlace the back of her riding habit. Now she was left standing in her petticoats and chemise, and she waited for him to loosen the stays before she let those drop to the ground along with her petticoats. She shivered at the cool breeze while Aiden removed his own clothes except for his shirt, which came down to his thighs, hiding the most male part of him from her gaze. She blushed all the same, and when he caught her peeking, he chuckled.

"There will be plenty of time to explore me later, lass," he teased. Then he waded into the water ahead of her and went hip-deep. Aiden turned and gestured for her to join him. The humming sound was stronger now, turning into a drumbeat as she dipped her toes into the water. It was cool, but not cold like she had expected. The water was as still as a mirror, despite the waterfalls nearby. Perhaps that was another kind of magic. It was nothing like the ocean she'd nearly drowned in. Anna walked deeper into the pool until she reached Aiden and he took her into his arms.

They embraced in the magical pool, and their faces turned toward each other. The water was cool on her hot skin, and the hard length of Aiden's shaft pressed intimately into her belly, making her shiver with anticipation. There was no wind, no sound except the beating of their two hearts as they exhaled together.

"Can ye swim?" he asked.

She nodded. A memory had resurfaced at the sight of the pool, one of herself swimming in a pond with her brother, Alexei. They'd laughed and splashed and dove beneath the surface and back up again over and over.

"The middle of the biggest pool isna very deep, but it does cover my head," Aiden told her. "Hold on to me."

She wrapped her arms around his neck and pressed against his chest as he moved them toward the center of the pool. He stopped when he was neck-deep in the water, and she curled her legs around his hips to keep her face the same height as his. The feel of his body and hers so tightly entwined made her feel invincible.

"Ready?" he asked.

"Y-yes."

"Hold yer breath. I willna go too deep."

Down they plunged beneath the surface of the enchanted water. The drumming she'd felt inside her head grew to a pounding in her skull as a thousand images darted through her mind.

She was being dragged through a dark forest, then shoved to her knees. The silver of a blade flashed as it was raised above her head. Her hands curled into the black soil of the earth as she heard a bellow of primal rage. Aiden was fighting someone wreathed in darkness. But he was losing...He was going to watch her die . . .

"Anna!" He roared her name, and the earth shook at his might. The sword arced above her . . . The vision changed.

Aiden stood before her bleeding, and then he stumbled backward and fell into some vast dark pit . . . never to return.

A voice spoke through the water bubbling around her: "You will take his life . . ."

Anna opened her mouth to scream, and she was suddenly fighting for air, fighting to get to the surface. She broke free of the water, sobbing and coughing.

"Anna!" Aiden pulled her to him even as she turned to push him away. "What is it, lass?"

Still sobbing, she surrendered and dug her fingers into his shoulders as she held on to him.

"*I* will cause your death. I saw it. Oh, Aiden . . . ," she moaned against his chest. But rather than release her, he only held her tighter.

"It's all right, my heart," he whispered as he took her out the water. "I ken what it means to love ye."

She lifted her head up to stare at him as he carried her toward the large stone they'd sat upon earlier. "You do?" Her chemise clung wet and cold to her skin, and she almost longed to go back into the water even though she feared what she might see.

"Aye, I do." He sat down on the stone and settled her in his lap and kissed her. "And I dinna care. Whatever may come, I dinna care so long as I have the chance to love ye as long as fate will let me."

She saw the truth in his eyes. He understood what she'd seen, had even been expecting it. How could he have known?

"But if you die because of me, if I lose you . . . What's left in the world for me without you?" she asked in a small voice.

Aiden lowered his face to hers until their foreheads touched. "There is everything, my bonnie lass, *everything*. Life will still go on, even if I'm not with ye. Ye must live, no matter what happens. Promise me ye will."

Anna wanted to shake her head and beat her fists against his bare chest, but didn't. Her mind was still caught on the vision of Aiden falling into darkness because he had tried to save her life. She was the one who should die . . . and perhaps when the time came, she'd find a way to save him, even if she perished. Resolved to that end, she managed to give him the answer he wanted.

"I . . . promise."

"Good." He nuzzled her nose with his, and the chill on her wet skin faded as desire replaced her fear.

Gripped by need, she dug her hands into his hair and kissed him. That was all it took for them both to forget where they were. Everything she felt in that moment for him, for herself, for the future she dared to dream where nothing bad could happen, all poured from her lips to his. Fire and sweetness burned between them, and she wondered if the waters of the fairy pools had somehow enchanted their kisses.

Aiden's arms wrapped around her as he stood and carried her to the soft green grass, away from the fairy pools. With every step, she felt that hard part of him pressing against her belly, and it created an ache deep within her that only he could satisfy. She arched against him, trying to rub herself against his body, and he groaned against her lips.

"Ye'll be the sweetest death of me, Anna," he growled against her lips and held her tighter to him as he finally stopped walking. She peppered kisses along his jaw and neck, feeling reckless and wild. He gripped her bottom with one hand, pressing her against his groin, and this time she was the one who moaned as the throb between her thighs increased tenfold.

"Please . . . ," she begged him.

He set her down on her feet and then retrieved the folded plaid, which he'd laid by his boots and trousers. He rolled it out on the grass and knelt so he could remove his wet shirt. Her mouth turned dry at the sight of his chest, the way the planes of muscle rolled into his rippled abdominal muscles before dipping in a sharp *V* shape just above the bones of his hips, as if directing her eyes down to the dark line of hair and then to his . . .

Her eyes widened at her first real look at an erect male cock. It was huge . . . too huge. It couldn't possibly fit inside her . . . Yet she was fascinated and afraid all at once, wanting to reach out and touch it and still hesitant.

"Will . . ." She swallowed hard. "Will it fit?" she whispered shakily.

Aiden smiled sweetly, but she saw a hint of mischief in his blue-gray eyes.

"Aye, lassie, it will. But I will go slowly at first. Ye need to stretch to take a man yer first time."

She wouldn't have believed anyone else but him. He wouldn't lie to her.

Aiden knelt on the plaid and gently urged her down beside him, and then he was kissing her again and she lay back, pulling him down with her. His large, hard body burned against her chilled skin, and whenever his hands touched her, she burned in the best way. He moved her wet chemise up with his hand on her outer thigh, and when she felt cool air kiss her mound, she whimpered in excitement.

"Part yer legs," he said in a husky tone. He moved his shoulders between her knees and kissed her inner thighs, working his way toward her throbbing mound and the pearl of desire that called out for his touch.

Anna wondered if this too was a dream, one the fairy pools showed her to make up for the sorrow the previous vision had caused. If she was still under the water, still drowning, she would be content to die in this heaven with him.

His mouth touched her core, and she cried out at the unexpected pleasure his tongue and lips brought to the most sensitive part of her body.

"Aiden . . ." She groaned his name as pleasure exploded through her. She was still dizzy as he sucked on the sensitive nub, and then she was screaming his name, the sound echoing off the nearby rocks.

As the haze of her climax began to taper off slightly, Aiden rose up, his body coming fully down over hers as he entered her, spearing her swiftly. She had but an instant to register the pain between her thighs before it was replaced by the feeling of their bodies joined together. She clung to him, their faces inches apart as he moved upon her, slowly at first, a gentle rocking against her.

His wet hair fell into stormy eyes as he gazed down at her. She was lost in him, *lost with him*. He braced his arms on either side of her head as he moved against her, driving into her with increasing force. Anna lifted her hips to meet his, the gentleness fading from their desperate mating. Each time he withdrew, she ached with emptiness, and each time he surged back, she was breathless and wild with pleasure. In that moment, they were two creatures of the wild, no different from the badgers in the hedges or the deer in the glens. They were of the land, *of each other*, and the joining was sacred.

Anna felt her body racing toward that invisible precipice, and she knew once she reached it, she would never be the same. She would never again be whoever she had once been. That Anna from before the shipwreck was gone.

"Be with me," she whispered against Aiden's lips, and he moved harder, faster, the two of them diving over the edge together, lost in the pleasure that followed.

It was some time later when Anna felt herself come back into her body. Aiden had wrapped the plaid around them like a blanket and lay on his back, her body curled up against his. Tendrils of her now dry hair drifted along his chest in the breeze, and she watched his beautiful hands play with the strands, spooling them around his fingers.

"Anna," he whispered quietly. "Will ye marry me?"

She lifted her head. "What?"

"Marry me. Be the blood of my blood, heart of my heart. Let me be that for ye too."

Part of her knew she should think about this seriously, take her time in answering. She should be rational, but all she could think was—

"Yes."

He sat up, and she sat up with him. He reached for one of his boots, pulling out a small flat blade that had been hidden in the leather. He pricked his thumb until a tiny drop of blood dewed upon his finger. Then he reached for her hand and smeared the blood on her palm. Then he gave her the blade. With a trembling hand, she pricked her thumb and smeared her blood across his palm. They then clasped their blood-streaked palms together.

"I am now of yer blood, of yer heart, *Anna mine*," he whispered, his eyes never leaving hers.

"I am of your blood, of your heart, *Aiden mine*." Anna let her voice ring off the rocks and into the distant hills. Whatever else she once was, she wasn't ashamed to be Aiden's, nor was she ashamed to claim him as hers. Whatever came next, this moment was hers, *forever*.

AIDEN MADE LOVE TO HIS NEW WIFE SEVERAL MORE times by the fairy pools throughout the day, and they took turns feeding each other fruits, cheese, and bread, along with some wine. The simple picnic he'd imagined when they'd first left the castle had become a honeymoon, where he dined not only on food but on the sweetness of Anna's body.

He couldn't get enough of her. Between moments of lovemaking, they spoke of their hopes and dreams, fears and worries, deep things and silly things, beneath the Scottish October sky. She lay in his arms now, the plaid wrapped around them like a blanket.

"I feel it's all close to the surface," Anna said. "My heart yearns to recall things. I can almost see it in my head, but it is still obscured as if behind a thin veil. When you rescued me, it was an impenetrable wall within my head."

Her gaze drifted to the fairy pools. "Perhaps it worked after all, and soon I will remember everything."

He stroked her hair from her face and tucked it behind her ear. "Ye will remember, Anna. Have no fear of it."

The sun dipped below the horizon, and at last they dressed, ready to make their way back to the castle. Both horses were resting exactly where they'd been left a few hours before.

"Time to leave, Thundir," he said to his horse who tossed his head. Bob followed suit with a nicker of greeting at Anna.

"I hope no one is worried about us. We've been gone all day," Anna mused. She'd gotten used to the rather free way in which Aiden lived. Joanna and Lydia had done their best to instill some sense of propriety between Anna and Aiden, but they had soon given up when the well-meaning pair had seen how Anna and Aiden had no desire to be parted for very long.

He kissed her before lifting her up into the saddle. "They know ye are safe with me, wife."

"My *virtue* wasn't, but I'm certainly not complaining." She laughed, and the sound filled his heart with rapturous joy.

"We will have to have a proper ceremony in the old kirk for my brothers." He mounted his horse.

"What's a kirk?"

"It means *church*." Aiden guided his horse back toward the castle, and she followed. "My mother, had she lived long enough, wanted to see her children married there, and I'm the only sibling left who wasna married until today. But I wouldna mind repeating my vows in the kirk."

"I wouldn't mind either," she replied as they rode back. It would be nice to honor his mother in such a way.

It was after nightfall when they reached the main doors of the castle. A groom ran out of the stables to greet them and yelled back toward the house that they had arrived.

"Thank God yer back, Master Aiden! Yer brothers have been searching for the last several hours for ye and only just gave up."

"What's happened?" Aiden asked as he dismounted.

"There's a message from Dr. MacDonald from North Berwick."

Aiden caught Anna in his arms and lowered her to the ground before they both rushed to the house.

Joanna spotted them as they entered and shouted for Brock to come. Soon Aiden and Anna were being dragged into the library. Brodie, Joanna, and Lydia also gathered in the room as Brock thrust a note to Aiden.

"This came for ye."

The letter had already been opened. Everyone had been hoping to hear news from the doctor. Aiden read the letter, then looked at Anna.

"What does it say?" she asked, her voice shaky.

"Some fishermen found a lifeboat of sailors from your ship. There was a woman among them who was still alive and two men. The woman said she knew ye and that ye were her lady. She told the doctor ye must get to London and that yer brother was waiting for ye. She said it was a matter of life and death."

"My brother is waiting for me in London? Alexei . . . ," Anna whispered, her eyes full of hope. Aiden knew what her brother meant to her. Memories of him had been the strongest for her, and she'd told him so many stories of Alexei that afternoon that he felt he knew the man.

"We assumed that once ye returned, ye would wish to leave for London immediately," Brock said. "We have already made all the arrangements to leave in the morning."

Aiden met Anna's gaze. "Do ye want to leave tomorrow?"

She nodded. "I do."

"Then we leave at dawn," Aiden told his brother.

"Where were ye today?" Brodie asked, now that the excitement had settled a bit. "Brock and I searched everywhere for ye. We feared we may not find ye at all, that mayhap something had befallen ye."

"I took Anna to my favorite place, a secret place," he said simply.

"We're just glad you're both home." Joanna smiled at them, but concern darkened her features. "You missed dinner. I'll have cook send up some food to your rooms."

"Thank ye, Joanna."

Anna shared a look with Aiden. She knew he was considering telling them what they had done this afternoon, but he didn't want to, not yet. It wasn't the right moment. They needed to get to London and find her brother first. Then they could share the news of their marriage when the time was right.

"You two had better change and warm up," Lydia added. "Then eat your dinner and get some sleep. We have a long day ahead of us tomorrow."

"Us?" Aiden asked his sister-in-law.

"Ye didna think we would send ye to London alone?"

Brodie snorted. "We won't stay behind while ye run off and find out who Anna is. We wish to know as much as ye do."

Aiden smiled warmly. "Very well. Ye may join us."

Brock rolled his eyes. "As if ye had a choice, pup."

"Let me take ye upstairs, Anna," Aiden said, and held out his hand. The others watched them as they left, obviously sensing something new between them, but he didn't care. He needed to speak to Anna alone.

"Wait for me in yer room. I'll dine with ye there," he said to her.

"Will you stay with me?" she asked in a low voice so as not to be overheard.

"Aye, wife. Ye cannot be rid of me, no matter what we find in London." He'd promised to stay with her through sunlight and storms, and he had a feeling they were about to face the latter.

Her hand tightened on his arm. He knew she was afraid, but he would protect her.

"Dinna be scared, lass. We're together now."

As they reached her bedchamber, she kissed him and hugged him tight. "Yes, we are, husband."

CHAPTER 11

Alexei and William stood in the center of the village of Vasler. Charred remains of homes and the slain bodies of village men filled the center of the square. There was no doubt that Yuri and the men he'd rallied to join him in his coup had done this. Alexei's men moved from building to building, seeking any survivors. The acrid scent of smoke brought back all too vivid memories of finding his parents dead in their bed as their room was engulfed in flames.

Alexei pressed his palm to his chest, suddenly unable to breathe. William put a hand on his shoulder, holding him steady when he might have wavered.

"Is there no end to my uncle's madness?" Alexei asked his friend. He knew that his uncle had always wanted to sit upon the throne, but had no claim, not as the son of the queen and her second husband. Yuri was half brother to Alexei's father, they shared the same mother, the dowager queen but the royal blood ran down Alexei's father's side, leaving only Alexei and Anna with the right to the throne. The only relief Alexei had had since this nightmare began was his certainty that his sister was safe. He could feel it in his bones that she was not in danger. It was something they'd always shared since they'd been born. That connection between them, that sense of knowing the other's feelings even when thousands of miles away. Thank God Anna wasn't here to see the results of Yuri's destruction.

Yuri had pressured Alexei's father time and again to push Ruritania into the future, to industrialize and to build armed forces. He'd even spoken of hiring Prussian mercenaries until a proper Ruritanian army could be formed. Alexei's father had always maintained good political relations with the neighboring nations and had never needed to arm the country's citizens against an outside threat. No one could have foreseen that the threat would come from within.

Alexei would never understand what made a man think he could do such terrible things to innocent people—it could only be a madness of the mind and a blackness of the heart.

"It seems not," William said, and then his voice pitched low with worry. "Alexei, I don't see any women or children among the dead."

"None?" Alexei stared at the ruins around them. "Do you think they were taken prisoner?"

William's eyes were deeply shadowed. "We would have seen footprints leading them away. We've seen only the boots of soldiers and shoes of horses."

"Then they have to be here. They . . ." Alexei didn't

finish. If they were here, they couldn't be alive, or they would have been found by now.

"Search everywhere. Find them," Alexei ordered with a desperation and fatalism that tore his heart from his chest.

No survivors were found.

"Alexei, you must see this," one of Alexei's men called to him. Alexei headed in the man's direction and slowed to a stop before the ruins of a small church, where the man stood and pointed at the ruins.

Once the church had been a place for villagers to gather in peace; now it was a mass of blackened timbers. The stench of death hovered around it, and Alexei's blood froze in his veins as he realized that not all of the charred objects in front of him were wooden beams . . . many were *bodies*.

He sank to his knees and let out a raw scream of rage. He would cut his uncle's black heart out of his chest if it was the last thing he ever did.

❧

Anna jerked awake, screaming as heartache ripped through her body.

"Anna!" Aiden's arms banded around her, holding her tight. His woodsy scent enveloped her, and she calmed a little, but she still found it hard to breathe.

"What is it?" Aiden asked.

She blinked in surprise to find herself with Aiden, Brock, and Joanna in a large coach. Lydia and Brodie were in a second coach following them. While she slept, she'd forgotten she was on the way to London, not standing in front of a burned-down church filled with the remains of women and children. For a moment the realization that what she'd seen had come to pass was too much for her, but then she knew she had to explain to Aiden since he would understand.

"The village that I saw in my dreams . . . it happened. Everyone is dead. Oh God . . ." She burrowed against Aiden's chest, shutting her eyes tight, but it only made the images she had seen all the more clear in her head.

More than ever, she was glad she had spoken her vows to Aiden by the fairy pools. He was her husband—they would be together in whatever the future brought. The comfort this gave her, knowing she wasn't alone, that her tall, dashing Scottish husband would be there, soothed her in a way she'd never imagined marriage would bring. Her mother had always spoken of love and marriage as a partnership, but until that moment, Anna hadn't fully understood what she'd meant.

Aiden said nothing for a long moment. He simply held her. When at last he spoke, she had managed to find her center of calm again. Joanna and Brock watched her with concern, but she was glad they let Aiden speak to her without interference.

"Do ye have any idea *why* ye are seeing this village? Perhaps it is where ye lived or a place ye ken?"

"I don't think I lived there. The place is unfamiliar, but the feeling of seeing the death, the destruction . . . It felt as if I was there as it happened. But I'm here with you." She could smell the burning wood and bodies, feel the wind blowing smoke into her face. She could taste the salt of the tears from her cheeks, but they weren't *hers*.

She felt like she was losing herself each time the visions overtook her. They were so strong that it robbed her of what few memories she had that she knew were her own. What if it kept happening? What if she would never be free of these horrifying visions?

The true worry that her mind kept running up against like the outer wall of a mighty fortress was, *What if everything in the visions came to pass?* Like the vision in the fairy pools. The one she'd had of herself kneeling beneath an executioner's sword. Aiden falling into darkness was the vision that haunted her the most, the one that would drive her to madness if she didn't find a way to stop it from coming true. To know her death, and the death of the man who was her mate for life, her *soulmate*, might happen . . . She had to find a way to stop the visions.

Aiden kissed her cheek and stroked a hand over her back. "Try to rest." The man's touch was positively hypnotic. It made her long for more nights in his arms where she could explore him and be lost in the passion of his possession of her body and soul. When he claimed her with his kisses, she couldn't worry about anything.

"I don't think I can sleep. What if I see something else?" She curled her fingers in his cravat, playing with the delicate folds of silk. She didn't care that Brock and Joanna could see her in Aiden's arms, and that they were openly showing such affection. It felt right to touch him, to feel comfort with him. She craved closeness to him, a craving that seemed to have been born over a decade ago when the dreams of her flight in the woods began. Someday soon they would tell Brock, Joanna, and the others that she and Aiden were married, but not now. The time wasn't right.

"Then I'll be here to wake ye and remind ye it was but a dream, lass," Aiden promised as he stroked a thumb along her jaw, the gentle touch not intending to seduce but only soothe. From anyone else, such a promise to keep nightmares away would have felt hollow, but with him, she trusted he would do what he said.

IT TOOK FOUR DAYS TO REACH LONDON. THEY STOPPED briefly to rest the horses and sleep before pushing on toward the city. It was a relief to get out and stretch her legs and walk with Aiden in a field near the coaching inn.

They talked of everything they'd done back in Scotland and all the things Aiden was keen to show her in London. He also wanted to buy her a horse from someone named Cedric Sheridan. Apparently, the man had fine taste in horses, and he and his wife were breeding some of the most beautiful horses Aiden had ever seen. It felt good to discuss normal things, things a wife and a husband would talk about even though they kept their marriage a secret. She found herself laughing at Aiden's gentle teasing, and they shared a few heated kisses behind the inn before they had to return to the coach. It helped her forget her worries.

Anna slept fitfully for the remainder of the journey, but as they reached London, she became more awake and alert. Brock and Joanna were quietly discussing things that would need to be done once they reached Rosalind's home, and how they would begin the search for Alexei. Anna's desire to be reunited with her brother was overwhelming. He was the one thing she was able to remember clearly, and she clung to those memories with a desperation that was almost frightening.

My brother could be here in the same city. That thought ran through her mind over and over, filling her with hope.

The pair of coaches rolled to a stop in front of a fashionable townhouse on Half Moon Street where Aiden's sister, Rosalind, and her husband lived when they were in town and not at their country estate.

Anna peered out the coach window at the lovely home, and her stomach tightened with fresh nerves. "Do you think Rosalind's husband can help me find my brother?"

"If anyone can, he can. The man kens everything about everyone. If he wasna on our side, I'd be bloody terrified." Aiden said this last bit with a wink, and she tried to smile back, but the expression felt forced.

Aiden opened the coach door before a footman could do it and helped Anna down from the vehicle. She smoothed out the wrinkles of her frosted-blue carriage dress and wrapped a rose-red shawl tightly around her shoulders as they waited for Brock and Brodie to assist their wives out of the two coaches.

"Dinna worry, lass." Aiden's breath stirred the loose tendrils of her hair. "Rosalind will love ye, and Ash will too."

She wasn't worried about that. Well, she was a little. She did want all of Aiden's family to like her now that they were married. But she had a terrible feeling inside her that she couldn't quite shake free. She didn't know what that bad feeling meant, and it kept her on a razor's edge.

Lydia came up to her and put an arm around her shoulders. "Anna, are you all right? You're so very pale." She gave Anna a gentle hug as they walked up the steps together.

"I had a bad dream sleeping in the coach," Anna confessed, but she didn't say much more as the Lennoxes' butler ushered them into the townhouse. The group huddled inside, quietly talking amongst themselves.

Anna took in the opulent surroundings of the home as Aiden put a hand on her waist and gave it a light squeeze. Cool white marble stairs and lovely statues filled the alcoves that she could see, and paintings in gilded frames decorated the walls leading up the staircase to the upper floors.

"His lordship and her ladyship will see you in the drawing room." The butler gestured for them to follow him as he escorted everyone to a room upstairs.

Anna drifted to the back of the group along with Aiden, and they were the last to enter the drawing room. A stunning brunette who looked like a feminine version of Aiden hugged Joanna and Lydia warmly. This had to be Rosalind. Behind her, an imperious but handsome blond man with bright blue eyes stood at her shoulder, nodding coolly but politely at the Kincade brothers as they approached to shake hands. When the man's eyes met Anna's, she saw a flash of surprise and then horror cross his face.

"You're supposed to be dead," the man gasped at her. The sudden silence in the room was deafening, and Anna's ears started to ring.

Her world started to spin and her lungs seemed to collapse inward as she fought to breathe. She remembered this man's eyes, the piercing blue, but she'd seen him somewhere else . . . somewhere . . . The images blurred, and she was seeing the tall blond man's face in a grand palatial drawing room with the faces of her parents and her brother. Even the man's voice brought back flashes of memories of someone talking about trade and politics . . . The pain in her head was pounding.

"*Dead?*" She said the single word faintly before her body crumpled and blackness swallowed her.

AIDEN CAUGHT ANNA AN INSTANT BEFORE SHE WOULD have hit the floor.

"Good God!" Ashton rushed toward him and Anna. "How the devil is she here . . . ?"

"Ashton?" Rosalind knelt beside her husband and Aiden. "What do you mean she is supposed to be dead?"

Ashton raked his hands through his pale blond hair and stared wide-eyed at Anna as if he couldn't believe she was there.

"Aiden, how did you find her? She was killed. She . . . ," Ashton muttered.

"Ash! You're scaring me." Rosalind shook his arm. "*Who* is she?"

Ashton let out a shaky breath as he reached a hand toward Anna as if to touch her cheek and see if she was real.

Aiden's grip on Anna tightened protectively. He had rarely seen Ashton Lennox ruffled, let alone at a loss for words like he was now.

"This woman is Anna Maria Zelensky, princess of Ruritania. Her entire family was murdered in a political coup by the late king's younger half brother about a month ago."

"A princess . . . ," Aiden whispered. He stared down at Anna. He had married a *princess*?

"But how do you know who she is?" Rosalind demanded.

Ash's eyes narrowed. He seemed to be thinking and strategizing even as he prepared to answer his wife.

"I met her when I traveled to Ruritania two years ago. I was there to establish a trade agreement for shipping exports of wheat and timber on my vessels. I had the honor of dancing with her once at a ball before I left. I only found out last week from one of my captains what happened. My ship's crew barely escaped the harbor after they learned the palace was on fire. The other ships in the harbor were set on fire and the crews imprisoned or killed to silence them. People were fleeing the countryside, and everyone was rushing to the harbors to escape, but even the non-Ruritanian ships were destroyed. My own crew managed to save several refugees. They all told the same story—the royal family had been slain. They were good, kind people. They didn't deserve what happened to them."

"Why haven't we heard about this in the papers? Why haven't you told anyone, Ash?" Rosalind asked her husband, clearly stunned that he'd kept this information quiet.

"Because I've been waiting to see when the news would spread. I didn't think it prudent to sound the trumpet of alarm myself and possibly upset trade routes with the Baltic nations until I could sort out the truth of the stories."

Aiden glared at his brother-in-law. "Ye and yer bloody politics . . ."

Ashton looked up at Aiden. "How . . . how did she get here? How did you find her?"

The room was silent as Aiden rose, lifting Anna in the cradle of his arms.

"We need to see to Anna first, then I can tell ye all that I know about how she came to be with me."

"Of course. Follow me this way." Rosalind stood and headed out of the drawing room. "We'll take her to one of the spare rooms."

Everyone followed as he carried Anna to the end of the corridor. Rosalind opened a door to a room decorated with bright, forest-green silk damask walls. A four-poster bed sat against the far wall. Aiden set Anna down on the bed, and then he carefully placed a pillow beneath her head. She was still unconscious, and he wouldn't leave her side until he was certain she was well. Ashton was right there beside him, looking on at the sleeping woman in the bed with concern.

"Now, tell me everything," Ashton said, his voice soft so as not to wake Anna.

"I was in North Berwick, preparing for Lydia and Brodie to arrive from France. I found Anna washed up on shore after her ship wrecked."

"And the name of the ship?" Ashton asked.

Aiden answered, which led to more questions, and soon Aiden felt as though he was being interviewed—or interrogated. But he could see that with each answer, Ashton was adding another piece to a puzzle in his head. Though to what end was anyone's guess. By the time he was done,

Aiden had told Ashton all that had transpired, except for the time he and Anna had spent at the fairy pools.

"And she truly doesn't remember who she is?" Ashton murmured. He stroked his chin, his gaze pensive. "It's not a ruse to avoid detection?"

Aiden shook his head. "It's coming back, little by little, and she tells us what she can when it does. We came here to find her brother, Alexei. She remembers him more than most other things. But she didna have any idea who she really is . . ."

"Officially, Alexei perished with the rest of the family, but if Anna is alive, then perhaps Alexei is too. It would explain some of the rumors I've heard from my ships that have carried other passengers from ports on either side of Ruritania, rumors of a resistance." Ashton sighed, the sound ancient with weariness. "We can only hope Alexei is alive, for Anna's sake, if nothing else. She'll be in danger until the matter of Ruritania's rule is settled."

Aiden didn't know anything of Ruritanian politics. All he cared about was Anna. *His* Anna. He brushed a lock of hair back from her face, unable to hide the wave of tenderness that swept through him. He'd thought the moment he first saw her that she was a fairy princess . . . and he'd been right.

Ashton noticed the tender touch and reached out and put a hand on Aiden's shoulder. "Who is she to you, Aiden?"

Aiden knew what the man was asking and couldn't hide his secret any longer.

"She is my wife."

"*SHE'S YOUR WHAT?*" A SHRILL VOICE PULLED ANNA OUT of the darkness of her unconsciousness.

"My wife. We married the day before yesterday."

"You *can't* be married to her; I would remember the wedding," Joanna said sharply.

"We married by the fairy pools." Aiden's voice was clear yet soft as Anna listened to him speaking nearby. She had the sense he was sitting close beside her, and the hand that was holding one of hers, gently caressing it, felt warm and large and likely was his.

"Fairy pools?" Lydia asked.

"Ye made a blood vow?" Brock's tone was solemn.

"Aye. And ye ken as well as I do that it is a binding marriage." Aiden's tone was hard and defensive now, as if he expected everyone to disagree.

"That may be," Ashton began, "but she has been betrothed since birth to marry one of the nephews of King Friedrich Wilhelm III of Prussia. They haven't married yet, of course, but it is expected that when she is twenty-one she will marry him. It's a very critical political marriage that will give Ruritania a strong ally should the need arise."

"Oh dear," Rosalind murmured.

Anna finally found the strength to open her eyes. Her head throbbed, and she couldn't stop a groan of pain as she tried to sit up. Aiden helped her. She looked between him and Ashton, sharp flashes of memory stirring in her mind.

"I *remember* you," she said to Ashton. "At the Summer Palace . . . You came to see my parents. We danced . . ." Memories of a grand palace with a royal court swirled around inside her head in a brilliant wash of colors. She remembered . . . *Oh God.* The memories were too much. A lifetime, *her* lifetime, was pulled sharply back into the light. And with all the beautiful memories came the bloody end of everything she held dear.

"Aiden," she gasped. "He killed them . . . My uncle killed my parents. Alexei stayed behind. He made me leave. I didn't want to. I didn't—" A flood of emotions overwhelmed her, and she wept, great sobs that tore through her so that she could barely breathe. Through the storm of her tears, Aiden held her, keeping her together when she might have fallen apart.

She was unaware of the time passing until she cried herself out. At some point, she grew too tired to do anything but lie in Aiden's arms and draw in shaky breaths. She felt empty, numb, and so very *cold.* Her parents were dead. The *Ruritanian Star* was lost at sea, and her only friend left, Pilar, was—

She suddenly tensed. "Aiden, Dr. MacDonald's note said he had rescued a woman from a lifeboat?"

"Aye, she told him she knew ye, that ye were her lady."

Anna nearly cried all over again, this time from relief. "It's Pilar, my lady's maid. Thank heavens she's alive." Her dearest friend was *alive.*

Anna gently pushed herself up so she was no longer leaning against Aiden, but he kept one arm around her shoulders.

"Do ye remember everything?" he asked.

She nodded shakily. "*Everything.*" She swallowed hard. It was strange that seeing Ashton had brought everything back, but perhaps it was because he was from her past and that was all she'd needed, a reminder of who she was. And now that meant she had to face the consequences of being Princess Anna Maria Zelensky of Ruritania, and not Anna the foundling.

"Lord Lennox is right—I was betrothed to marry someone." She reached for Aiden's other hand and clasped it in her own. "But the vow I made to you at the fairy pools is *binding* to me."

His eyes were full of sorrow. "It doesna have to be. Ye were a different person then. Now ye ken who ye are, I won't hold ye to something ye did when ye were not yourself."

She let go of his hand and cupped his cheek, turning his face her way when he tried to look away from her.

"I was *always* myself with you. That didn't change. Having my memories back only makes me more certain of my heart." She swallowed thickly at the words that held her heart. "That belongs to you, Aiden Kincade, master of fairy pools and keeper of wee beasties. My old life burned down with my home. The life I would have had is gone. I choose a new path now. I choose *you*. I know it's selfish of me to want you, now that I know the danger that awaits me back in Ruritania," she said. "But if you still want me, I'm yours. I will make that vow again with you here and now, if you wish."

Aiden's stormy eyes cleared, and he pressed his forehead to hers. "Then ye're mine, lass, and I am with ye, whatever comes next."

She pressed her lips to his, a bittersweet ache in her chest as she knew what she had to say next.

"I have to convince your king to send soldiers to help

my brother. He's fighting my uncle with only a few loyal guards. Our country is a peaceful one. We have no great armies to call upon to stop my uncle. Alexei sent me to England to find a way to save our people. I can't let him down."

"And ye won't," Aiden promised. "If there is one thing a Scot can do, it's fight, and if there's one thing an Englishman like Lennox can do, it's raise an army."

"You think so?" she asked, too afraid to hope it might be so easily achieved.

"I know so. Lennox and his League of Rogues will help us."

She adored the way he said *us* but tripped up on the phrase *League of Rogues*.

"League of Rogues?" She tilted her head as she gazed up at him. "What is that?"

Aiden chuckled, his eyes lighting up with mischief. "It's not a *what*, but a *who*."

CHAPTER 12

Anna's recovery of her memories started a flurry of activity at the Lennox townhouse on Half Moon Street the next morning. Coaches began to arrive just after breakfast, with well-dressed men and women greeted by the Lennox butler.

Anna was overwhelmed by the dashing gentlemen who doffed their hats and swirled about in greatcoats whilst their beautiful wives slid out of silk-hooded capes. It was eerily similar to the life she'd experienced at court, which should have put her instantly at ease. But the Anna she'd been before the shipwreck was not the Anna she'd become afterward when she'd spent time with Aiden. She didn't immediately join these men and women who seemed so at home with one another.

Everyone was talking, each of them so clearly familiar with the others that it was like watching a boisterous family coming together over a Christmas holiday. Anna lingered at the back of the room close to Aiden. Her hand was tucked in his, and she didn't care that the show of physical intimacy might draw judgment. As far as she was concerned, they were married.

"They dinna bite, lass," Aiden chuckled and gave her hip a squeeze before he went out to shake the hands of the men, who greeted him like a brother. Then he came back to her and grasped her hand in his.

"I'm not afraid, not exactly," she whispered. "But I still don't *feel* like myself, like the woman I used to be. The old Anna would have taken over the discussions and introductions and . . . But that doesn't feel like me anymore. I don't even know if that makes any sense," she admitted.

Aiden smiled gently and raised her hand to his lips, kissing the backs of her fingers. "I ken what ye mean."

Rosalind noticed that Anna was hiding in the alcove and came over to her and Aiden.

"Let's leave the men to their business whilst we women take tea in the sitting room. I'm sure you want to discuss your country's fate, and it's better to do it with us women —we're the ones in charge, after all. We like to let the men think they are, but really, it's us." She winked at Aiden, who simply chuckled. Rosalind tucked Anna's arm through her own in a sisterly way, and called out to the women in the entryway to follow.

Anna was ushered into a sitting room by Rosalind, who made a round of introductions for her. She was introduced to a duchess, a marchioness, a viscountess, and a young lady who were all married to the men in Lord Lennox's tight circle of friends, the ones Aiden had called the League of Rogues.

Rosalind gave Anna a reassuring smile as she poured tea

and told the other women Anna's story, from her flight from Ruritania to her rescue on the shores of Scotland by Aiden. Anna was glad for someone else to relate the tale. Her headache from the previous night had persisted. It was a dull ache now, but it still bothered her whenever she thought too hard about the past. It was a relief that the memories came now, but frustrating that it strained her head.

"You truly married Aiden next to an enchanted fairy pool?" one of the two youngest women in the room asked. This was Audrey St. Laurent, and Anna had learned she had married the younger brother of the Duke of Essex, which made her the sister-in-law of the young duchess, Emily St. Laurent, who sat beside her. The family tree was, as Aiden had warned her, very tangled indeed, but she would sort it out one day.

"I did," Anna admitted. "Have you been to the fairy pools?"

Audrey sighed. "No, I haven't. I used to think we had a fairy pool near our country estate when I was a girl, but I only recently learned it was just my brother being sweet to me after our parents died. He used to give me tea cakes for the fairies, and we'd leave them on toadstools by the fishing pond. Then he'd come back in secret and tear off a piece so I would think they had nibbled on them." She smiled, as she remembered those childhood days.

"That's wonderfully romantic," the duchess, Emily, sighed. "Men can be rather good about that when they love someone. Godric is very romantic," she added with a giggle.

Anna's face was overly warm at discussing something so

intimate in front of women who were friendly but still mostly strangers to her. It made her miss Pilar all the more, but Pilar was in North Berwick, recovering. It would be a while before she could see her friend again.

"Your husband kidnapped you," Rosalind chuckled over her teacup. "That sounds terrifying, not romantic."

At this, Emily grinned mischievously. "Well, luckily for him, he wasn't very good at it."

The room broke out into peals of feminine laughter, and Anna could feel her tension fading away. She'd never had close friends her own age before. Other than Pilar, she'd had to maintain a relative distance between herself and the other ladies of the royal court. She was expected to stay above the political intrigues, and any friendships with the courtiers would have been seen as choosing sides.

Rosalind cleared her throat. "Well, then. Ladies, we should get down to business."

The viscountess, a quiet, lovely brunette named Anne, agreed. "The men are running their war council. We ought to be focusing on ours."

"The men simply *adore* war councils," Audrey said with a laugh. "They've already had *three* this year."

Anna blinked at that.

Horatia, the marchioness, shot Audrey a reproachful look. "She's only teasing." They were the two younger sisters of Cedric, Anne's husband.

"I am not teasing. It truly was three," Audrey insisted before taking a long sip of her tea.

"As Anne said," Emily said, regaining the attention of the group, "the men are focusing on finding soldiers. We must focus on fashion."

"Fashion?" Anna echoed. "But how does that matter?" Anna didn't care about poke bonnets or the latest style of dress. She knew, of course, like all women, that dressing well or dressing in a certain fashion could affect how someone was treated, but she didn't see how a lovely gown could help her build an army.

"Fashion is quite important," Emily said, "because there is a ball tomorrow night at Lady Eugenia's home, and the king will be attending. You will attend as well, and you shall wear the finest dress anyone has ever seen." Emily gave her a clever smile. "One fit for the princess of Ruritania."

"Anna, I will have a modiste here within the hour, and the other ladies will go jewel hunting for you." Rosalind smiled reassuringly at her.

"Jewel hunting?"

"Of course—you will need something to wear to the ball," Horatia said. "You're possibly the most beautiful woman London has ever seen, but a crown of diamonds wouldn't go amiss to add to the attraction."

Audrey smothered a laugh. "The king, bless him, can be quite distracted by pretty things that sparkle."

"Audrey," Horatia warned again. "His Majesty—"

"*Loves* sparkly things," Audrey emphasized and winked at Anna.

"Lord help us," Anne muttered. "I hope the men are behaving better than we are."

Anna had been wondering that herself. Aiden was naturally quiet and often hung in the shadows when around his brothers, but this morning when the coaches began arriving and several men came into the entryway to be introduced, Aiden had stepped forward, thanking them and shaking hands as he invited them to the billiard room. Anna had seen an air of command in him that she hadn't expected, and it made her realize there was still much about him she had yet to learn.

"With the king on our side, it will be much easier to find support for your cause." Rosalind placed a hand on Anna's shoulder. Since they had met, Rosalind had been warm and sisterly, just as Joanna and Lydia had been, perhaps even more so. Anna wondered if it was because Rosalind knew firsthand what had happened to Aiden as a boy and desperately wished for her brother to find happiness and peace.

"I hope so," Anna said. If the king supported her cause, then it would be so much easier for her to help her brother and her country. Then she could focus on her life with Aiden and her future, whatever it may be.

But the worries about her mission were heavy upon her shoulders. She couldn't fail her brother or her people. Knowing she was so far away left a hollow spot inside her that whispered dark thoughts that rattled what confidence she possessed. What if Alexei was dead? She would know, wouldn't she? She would feel it—she would have to. She and Alexei had always shared a deep connection, and she had to trust that he was all right.

"Don't worry, Anna," Emily said with a confidence she wished she shared. "We will do all that we can to help you."

Most women wouldn't have the power to make or keep such a promise, but something about these women warned Anna that they were not simply society wives with powerful husbands. Each of them was intelligent and knowledgeable about social and political issues. Anna sensed there was so much more to them, though. She was only beginning to discover the strength of these women as they talked over tea.

Audrey grinned mischievously. "I think it's time for Lady Society to announce that a princess is in town and anyone who's anyone won't want to miss her appearance at Lady Eugenia's ball."

"Who is Lady Society?" Anna asked.

Audrey poured herself another cup of tea. "Anna, my dear, I will catch you up on all of our recent adventures while we wait for the dressmaker."

࿇

IF THERE WAS A GROUP OF MEN AIDEN WOULD WARN others not to get on the wrong side of, it would be the League of Rogues—powerful English lords with more resources and connections between them than perhaps anyone outside of the royal family. They had bested spymasters, foreign princes, assassins, and more. Aiden and his brothers had even tangled with them once in a tavern, which had left the furniture in ruins and all of them barred forever from returning to that tavern, but they had earned his respect. If anyone could be of aid to Anna now, it was them.

The Duke of Essex, Godric St. Laurent, did not wait long before getting everyone's attention. "Aiden, tell us about this army you need."

Aiden cleared his throat and looked at the men lounging in the billiard room. His brothers were beside him, and the League members were ringed around a map of

Europe spread across the green baize surface of Ashton's billiard table.

"Anna is from Ruritania, the small country here by the sea. Prussia is its closest neighbor,." Aiden waved at the outline of Prussia. "Anna's uncle, Yuri, is her father's younger half brother. King Alfred and Yuri shared the same mother, but Yuri's father was a Russian boyar who had no real love for Ruritania or its people and instilled in his son the same feelings. Yuri secretly turned half of the palace guards against the king and queen, and the two monarchs were slain in their bed about a month or so ago."

"Murdered in their sleep?" the Marquess of Rochester, Lucien Russell, snarled at that revelation.

Charles Humphrey, the Earl of Lonsdale, leaned on a billiard cue as he examined the map with interest. "What a bloody coward this Yuri fellow is."

"Anna's twin brother, Alexei, is still believed to be alive. He sent her here to England, hoping to secure our king's help."

"How many does the prince have on his side?"

"We don't know for certain. The royal guards were five hundred strong. If Yuri has half, that leaves him with two hundred and fifty men, but we do not know how many survived. And if the rumors from Ashton's ship captains are true, we might be facing mercenaries as well. The younger guards may have sided with Alexei, including William, who was his bodyguard. Anna believes it's possible that they may be hiding in this area here called the Dark Forest. It lies north of the Summer Palace."

"Is Yuri headquartered at the Summer Palace?" Godric asked.

Aiden shook his head. "Anna said it was burning as she fled. There is likely nothing left but ruins. She believes he may be staying at the Winter Palace in the south. It is an older, more fortified structure, more castle than palace, which means it will be more difficult to lay siege to."

"I don't suppose they'll have any access to artillery?" Ashton asked Aiden, but it was more of a statement than a question. "Yuri likely has taken control of it all by now."

"That must be our assumption," Aiden said. "I think we need men who can fight hand to hand, men who are quick of foot and quick of mind. No common soldiers. We need warriors."

Ashton stroked his chin as he studied the map. "Suppose we find Alexei. We could use him to lure Yuri's forces out into the open. I imagine he wishes to kill the rightful king more than anything. Of course . . . if we had more time and planning, we could raise our own mercenary forces, but that would take months we don't have. I think it's best if we set a trap for Yuri."

"That may be our best option, assuming Alexei will agree," Aiden added. He didn't want to risk Anna's brother's life, but given what Anna had said of him, Alexei would most likely volunteer himself before they could even ask.

"Then we will speak to the king at the ball tomorrow night," Ashton said. "Once we know if we have his support, we will go forward with recruitment for our fight."

Aiden thanked each of the me. Brock put a hand on his shoulder.

"Ye'll be going too, won't ye?" Brock said.

"Ye know I will," said Aiden.

Brodie put his hand on Aiden's other shoulder. "It's not yer fight."

"It's Anna's fight," said Aiden. "That makes it mine."

Brock grunted. "No sane man wishes to go to war."

Aiden nodded. "No, but these are insane times. It's Anna I fear for most. She's lost everything. Her home, her family . . ."

"But she has ye," Brock said. "And we ken how strong ye are, brother. Stronger than either of us."

But would it be enough? The Romani prophecy was there in the back of his mind, along with Anna's vision from the fairy pools.

"Promise me, if I dinna make it out of this and we canna take back her homeland, ye will take Anna back to Scotland and keep her safe."

"We promise," Brodie assured him. "But ye will not fail."

Aiden wished he could believe them. "I should see if Anna is all right."

He left his brothers and sought out his wife. She was standing on a chair while a dressmaker took her measurements in one of the sitting rooms. He lingered in the doorway, watching. She didn't notice him at first. She was smiling, then grinned widely at something one of the ladies in the room said. She laughed so rarely, but when she did, the sound made his heart flutter in his chest as though it wished to take flight. If he did die, at least it would be having known one of the greatest joys a person could know —to love her.

Anna's gaze drifted as she noticed him leaning on the doorjamb, watching her, and the smile she gave was brighter than any summer sun. For a brief moment, all his fears and worries vanished. She said something to the dressmaker who nodded and packed up her measuring tape and then Anna stepped off the chair and rushed over to him. He moved into the corridor out of sight of the ladies in the room as Anna embraced him. They already acted scandalous enough around each other in public, so he was trying his best to behave.

"Are you all right?" he asked as he wrapped his arms around her.

"Yes. At least, I am now that you are here." She glanced back at the doorway she had just left.

"Do you need to go back in?"

"No, we are finished." She tilted her face up to his. "Take me to our room," she whispered.

He saw a desperate intensity in her eyes and understood what she wanted. He let go of her hips but clasped her hands in his, and they went to their bedroom.

She closed the door behind them and locked it. Neither of them wanted to say the words that hung unspoken in the air between them. Each day could be their last together.

He placed his palms on either side of her head against the door. Anna peered up at him in a sultry way that made him desperate to kiss her, but he didn't dare rush this moment.

Aiden leaned in and nuzzled her nose, then feathered his lips over hers. Only when she gasped softly against his mouth did he finally kiss her. She wrapped her arms around his neck, pulling him close to her as they shared soft, excited breaths.

"Aiden . . ."

He closed his eyes, enjoying the way she whispered his name, as though it was the only thing that mattered.

"Anna," he replied, hoping she would hear it the same way.

Her tawny eyes shone bright in the late-afternoon sunlight. She reached for his cravat and began to undo the folds of silk at his throat. She took her time as she slid the cloth off his neck and tossed it to the floor. Her hands began to undo the buttons of his waistcoat, but when her fingers trembled, he caught them and raised her hands to his lips, kissing each of her fingers with all the tenderness inside him that blended with his hunger for her.

"It's all moving too fast," she whispered, her voice breaking.

"We can slow down, lass. We—"

She shook her head. "Not you and me—everything else. We've only just found each other, and now we are facing a war . . ." She faltered and then tried again. "I wish I could freeze time and simply hold on to you," she confessed.

Aiden's heartbeat quickened as he kissed her palms this time.

"There is never enough time to be with those we love." He pressed his forehead to hers. "We must take each day as we can, and for a while, we can slow time." He would find a way to give her what she needed, even if they only had a brief moment like this.

"Then don't waste it, husband," she whispered.

Anna's luminous eyes held his gaze. She freed her hand from his and, with more confidence this time, plucked the buttons of his waistcoat free. He shrugged out of the garment and unfastened his trousers. Then he removed his shirt and pinned her to the door again, kissing her ruthlessly. Her hands roamed over the surface of his chest, making him feel more alive than he'd ever felt in his life. He conquered her fears by the sheer sensual distraction of his mouth, and she moaned as he lifted her skirts up and his fingers delved beneath the petticoats to find her center.

"Hold on to me, lass," he said as he lifted her up into his arms. She wrapped her legs around his waist and her arms around his neck. He pressed her against the door, using one arm as a shelf for her body as he freed his shaft and guided himself into her wet heat.

She threw her head back and gasped as he sank into her, and they both lost themselves at the connection that went beyond mere flesh.

"Are ye all right?" he asked, holding still to let her adjust to him filling her. Then he tested himself moving inside her, gently at first, seeing if it hurt her or if he could move faster and harder.

She managed a nod. "It feels wonderful—don't stop."

He'd never taken a woman like this before, but something about Anna brought out a wildness in him, the animal that he always sensed was just beneath the surface. But rather than be frightened by his intensity, she seemed to thrive on it and kissed him harder, dug her nails into his back and shoulders and clawed at him, just as hungry for the mating of their bodies as he was.

His sweet Anna clung to him as he thrust into her, their bodies fused by desire and a love that had been born in the land of their dreams. This woman was it for him. He had but one woman who would ever hold his heart.

Anna's lips were sweet as honey as they made love against the closed door. It was part frenzied mating and part lazy enjoyment of each other as they tumbled into the explosion of pleasure that followed. He wasn't sure how he still had the strength to stand after the climax that exploded through him, but somehow he managed to carry her to the bed and, with an exhausted chuckle, collapsed beside her and pulled the blankets over both of them.

She pressed her lips to his chest in a kiss before she drifted to sleep. Aiden lay awake, his mind and heart burning this moment into his memory. If they couldn't freeze time, at least he would not forget the privilege of loving his wife.

CHAPTER 13

The Lennox coach rolled to a stop in front of Lady Eugenia's grand house on Park Lane. The faint sounds of music drifted out to the coach where Anna was sitting. She wore the new gown that Rosalind's dressmaker had made for her. A diamond-and-pearl diadem rested in the coils of her dark-russet hair. She wore elbow-length white silk gloves and a red velvet cape. Everything about her declared she was royalty.

It felt as though she was back in Ruritania, preparing to make an appearance with her family. The memories of those glittering balls at the royal court were now tinged with sorrow. Those days were gone, and the memories would fade like the smoke that had billowed up above the burning ruins of her home. Even if Alexei became king, Anna's life would never be the same.

"Are you ready?" Rosalind's voice pulled her from her thoughts.

Aiden's sister sat beside her, and Ashton sat opposite

them. Both were watching her in concern, and she understood why. Ever since her memories had come back, she kept reliving moments where her parents had still been alive, and she and Alexei had been happy. The days ahead were full of shadows, and it was hard to leave these warm thoughts of the past when she knew they would never come back.

"I'm all right." That was a lie. It was impossible to tell them how she felt. It was as though she was no longer just Anna. She was a princess, with all the responsibilities and burdens that such a title carried, and yet she was also the woman Aiden had rescued from the waves and married by the enchanted fairy pools. She felt torn, belonging in neither her old life nor her new one.

The thing she wanted most was for Aiden to be with her, but he and several of Ashton's friends had gone ahead to the ball. They wanted to make sure that it was safe. It was unlikely she was in any danger, but she appreciated their concern. What did bother her was Aiden.

They'd made love last night with a new intensity that had left her stunned and overwhelmed in the most wonderful way. She'd never felt more connected to him than she had in that moment. All that had been missing was them being in his bed in Castle Kincade and knowing his wee beasties were about. She missed Aiden's animals deeply. In just a short time, she'd grown to think of them as her beasties too, and she would have spent the rest of her life in that castle with Aiden, deliriously happy. But close to dawn, Aiden had changed subtly and withdrawn from her. She'd cuddled against him, but she sensed his thoughts were miles away.

She didn't want to worry, but given all that lay between them, it was impossible not to. She had this terrible sense that she and Aiden were tumbling down a rocky mountainside and had no way to stop themselves from plummeting into the abyss below.

"Ashton will exit first, and I will help you with your train," Rosalind explained as a footman from Lady Eugenia's home opened their coach door.

Ashton gracefully left the coach and held a hand out to Anna. She placed her gloved hand in his and lifted her skirts with her other hand as she stepped down to the ground. Rosalind followed, her hands full of the long train of Anna's gown.

The gown was red silk, with a cream bodice and cream underskirts embroidered with shooting stars and studded with pearls. Gold constellations and hundreds of pearls were embroidered along the long train. She looked every inch the princess she was.

The footman who held the coach door open gave a soft, startled sound, his lips parting as Anna thanked him. He even tripped over his boots as he tried to extend a leg out in a courtly bow. Torches and candlelight illuminated the exterior of the house as dozens of other coaches lined up to drop off their passengers. A chill in the air clung to Anna as she drew in a deep breath.

"Have courage," Ashton whispered to her as they stepped inside the house. "Remember who you are, Anna."

She nodded to herself, knowing he was right. She wasn't a lost waif found half-drowned on the shore. She was a princess, a woman born to rule a country, to lead her people, and now her people needed her more than ever.

Power flooded through her, and she knew she would find a way to convince King George to give her the military support her people needed.

"Remember who you are . . ." Ashton's voice echoed inside her head as she prepared to meet the crowds.

Dozens of faces turned at her approach, and Anna summoned the old version of herself, the proud princess, to the forefront. What would Aiden think when he saw her like this? Bedecked in jewels and in a court gown fit for a queen? Would he be like all the other men and stand in awe of her, or would he smile at her in that secret way of his that let her know he saw *her*, not the royal title she'd been born with?

Rosalind let the train fall onto the clean marble floors once they were inside, and she joined Ashton as they walked ahead of Anna, leading her to the ballroom. Music poured from the corridor as she reached a staircase where a master of ceremonies called out the names of those who entered. Ostrich plumes dipped and bowed as women leaned in to whisper to one another as she passed. Gentlemen dressed in full court attire with knee breeches and tailored coats bowed respectfully as she made her way to the staircase. She searched every face, hoping to see her husband, but none were Aiden.

The master of ceremonies, a tall man with spectacles, accepted Ashton and Rosalind's card and announced them. When it came to Anna's turn, she had no card to give, but the man's eyes narrowed in sharp recognition of who she was. He had been informed earlier by Lady Eugenia that she was coming.

"Her Royal Highness, Anna Maria Zelensky, princess of Ruritania!" His voice boomed across the ballroom.

She nodded in thanks, then lifted her skirts to descend the stairs to the crowd of dancers as they moved beneath the candlelight. The music halted as the dancers came to a stop and parted, allowing her to pass through the center of the room to where her host, Lady Eugenia, and her friends were standing watch over the ball. Ashton and Rosalind led Anna straight to their host.

"Lady Eugenia, may I present Princess Anna Maria Zelensky?"

Lady Eugenia was a petite figure, with elegant taste in clothes, and about the same age as Anna's mother. She tapped her chin with her fan before smiling at Anna, as if she had conceded victory to Anna for stealing the evening with her entrance. Lady Eugenia curtsied, and the ladies who attended her did the same. "Welcome, Your Highness."

"Thank you, Lady Eugenia," Anna said. "I am delighted to attend your ball." It was strange how easy it was to fall back into the patterns of her old life.

"I had the privilege of knowing your mother. She came out the year before I did. She was simply beautiful, inside and out," Lady Eugenia offered with genuine warmth and a hint of sorrow in her words.

"Thank you, Lady Eugenia. Every memory someone can share with me about my mother is a gift."

Lady Eugenia breached societal rules and reached out, taking Anna's hands like a dear aunt. "Someday soon you and I will have tea, and I will tell you everything about her that I remember."

Anna swallowed hard and smiled as she was overwhelmed with sadness and joy at the same time.

"I would like that, thank you."

Rosalind came up behind Anna and discreetly tucked the train up at the back of her gown, which would allow her to move freely about the room.

Lady Eugenia's smile brightened. "Only this morning I heard that Lord Erich of Prussia has arrived. He heard you were here and wished to see you. I was, of course, quite delighted to extend to him an invitation in hopes that you two might meet again."

"Erich is here?" Anna fought to control her reaction. He was the man her parents had contracted her to marry when she was born.

"Oh yes, he was in London visiting friends and had no idea you were here. He was quite concerned, given the reports of the tragedy that has befallen your family."

Anna had discovered only that morning that England had finally become aware of the her country's situation, but the story that was being published in the papers was that her parents supposedly had been killed by rebels and her uncle had done his best to restore order. Somehow, Yuri had managed to spread the story that he was a gallant hero who'd taken over the throne after the king, his older brother, had perished along with the rest of the royal family.

There were even rumors that Anna herself might be an imposter if she appeared in London because Yuri claimed she had died in the attack. Thankfully, Ashton's reach was more effective than Yuri's. Between his influence and Audrey's Lady Society column telling the truth of what had happened in Ruritania, London was ablaze with gossip and speculation that tonight Anna would reveal herself in front of London's elite society and ask the king to take her side against her uncle.

"Ah, there he is. Erich!" Lady Eugenia called out to a man in the crowd.

Anna was startled to see Erich's familiar face. She had seen him a year ago when he came to visit her as he did every year since she'd been born. Their parents had hoped it would foster a friendship that would culminate in a marriage that would take place when she was twenty-one. He was a handsome man of twenty-five. He smiled, a dimple peeping out at the corner of his mouth.

He greeted her informally, even though he made a courtly bow to her, and she noticed right away his relief at her well-being. "Anna, thank God you're all right. Rumors are all over London about recent events in Ruritania."

"Come, dear Erich," Lady Eugenia said. "Come and dance with her. Take her mind off her worries with a waltz."

Anna tried not to think about how her people were suffering while she was here in this ballroom draped in jewels and dancing. But Emily St. Laurent and the other ladies were right—her appearance tonight would win London to her side and help her people.

Erich's cheeks reddened slightly as he offered his hand to Anna. "Would you like to dance?"

Anna wished she could decline. The only person she wanted to dance with was Aiden. Her gaze darted about the room, seeking him, but finding only the curious gazes of strangers looking back at her. But she knew her role tonight. Be beautiful and charming, win over as many friends as possible, and when the king saw her, she would make her passionate plea for her country and her people.

She placed her palm in Erich's as the dancers lined up for a waltz. When the music began, Erich gripped her hand and waist as he led her through the dance.

"I heard what happened," Erich said, slipping from English into Danish to give them a level of privacy to discuss things. "I had no word of your or Alexei's survival and feared the worst," he confessed. "At least your uncle is still alive."

Anna frowned as she realized that he'd heard the false tales her uncle was spreading. "You have been *lied* to. My uncle *murdered* my parents. He has lied about everything," she said. "Alexei helped me escape the night the palace burned down, and he stayed behind to fight for our people."

Erich's eyes widened and his lips parted in shock. She understood his confusion.

"My god, it's a miracle you survived."

Anna was impressed. He did not doubt her words, did not ask if she could be mistaken or suggest that grief had clouded her judgment. "You truly believe me? Over all the reports you've heard so far?"

"Of course. I have always known you to not only speak your mind, but the truth. I've had my suspicions for some time that your uncle is not a man to be trusted. Yuri is driven by ambition, but I have no reason to doubt you. Fear not—once we are married, I will ensure you are safe."

Anna held her tongue. No one could know she was already married. Not yet.

"You've grown up," Erich said with a gentle smile. Even though they'd seen each other last year, she'd changed immensely in the last two months. The girl she'd been was gone. Now she was a princess whose country was at war with itself.

"So have you." Anna smiled, but her heart wasn't in the expression. She respected him but didn't want to play with his feelings when she knew she could never return his affections. She only wanted to speak to the king and return to Ruritania and help her brother.

"I know it's silly to be here dancing when you must be worried about your home." Erich spun her around the room. "I wish I could do something more to help."

"Perhaps you could. Alexei is fighting our uncle with only a small force of loyal guards. If you write to your uncle the king now, he may be able to send my brother military aid quickly."

"What if Alexei has been killed? You can't be certain he is still alive."

"I am sure he is. I would know if something had happened to him. Please, Erich, you must trust me. Alexei needs my help. King George—"

As if summoned, the king of England descended the stairs. She had no doubt it was him, from his exquisite clothes to the way the room fell into a hushed silence as he parted the crowds with ease. Everyone bowed and curtsied as he made his way through the ballroom. He was followed by a group of men who Anna guessed were advisors and bodyguards. The braver nobles who had connections to the Crown came forward to him at once and spoke with him at length.

Finally, after half an hour, Lady Eugenia approached the king and whispered to him and pointed in Anna's direction. Erich had stayed at her side, keeping her company while the dancing resumed around them. As the king approached her, Erich politely stepped apart.

"Your Majesty." Anna slipped into a deep curtsy and remained there until the king reached out and lifted her chin so she would look up at him. Normally she would not have shown such deference, but he was a king and she a princess. This was his kingdom not hers. Playing toward his pride might help her cause.

"Rise, my dear," he intoned softly.

She rose and folded her hands in front of her. She examined the king, a man who was obsessed with bright and sparkly things, as Audrey had put it. He was a man who enjoyed food and fashion, but despite his vanity she saw kindness in his eyes.

"You look *exquisite*, my dear," George said. "Just like your mother. I met her once, when she was a young woman, just before she married your father. She was lovely, but you . . . you are a diamond of the first water."

Anna received the compliment with politeness, but deep down she wished men would see beyond her fair looks. Erich seemed to, but Aiden had been the only man to truly see deep into her soul. His stormy eyes flashed across her mind, and she desperately wished he was at her side now.

"I was hoping to have a private audience with Your Highness," she said.

George didn't seem surprised, as he likely would have heard from his advisors the latest news from Europe. "I assumed as much, Princess Anna." He waved a hand at Lady Eugenia, who rushed over. "We require a private room. We have matters of state to discuss."

"Of course." Lady Eugenia seemed thrilled by the prospect of leading two royals somewhere private in her home to discuss affairs of state.

A small group of men followed the king.

"Your Majesty, there are some English peers I wish to accompany me as my advisors, if that is agreeable to you?" She nodded toward Godric, since he was the highest-ranking peer, and then to Ashton beside him.

"Ah yes, Essex and Lennox, they may certainly join us." He waved at them with a polite, kingly motion of his hand.

Ashton and Godric fell in step with the king's men as they came toward her. To her relief, she saw Aiden slip out of the crowd and join the escort as she and the king followed Lady Eugenia out of the ballroom. Their eyes met, and she was briefly reassured by his slight nod at her, and his burning gaze filled her with strength.

Anna's heart battered against her ribs as she rehearsed her plea over and over in her mind until they entered the drawing room. Now was the time to save her home.

ॐ

AIDEN ACHED TO TAKE HIS WIFE INTO HIS ARMS. HE AND a few of Ashton's friends, along with his brothers, had arrived early to speak with Lady Eugenia about the safety of the princess and to thoroughly familiarize himself with the house's layout.

But these preparations had kept him away from Anna,

and he'd been half-mad with worry for her until she had arrived at the ball and made her grand entrance. And what an entrance it had been. She looked *magnificent*. She looked untouchable to mere mortals such as him. That regal bearing he'd always seen in her was amplified by her appearance tonight.

Her gown was utterly bewitching, fit for a queen. It showed her figure to advantage, but it was also a reminder of *who* she was—the daughter of a king, a princess in her own right. She'd held everyone's attention, casting a spell as she descended to the ballroom floor. Aiden had been hiding in the shadows watching for any threats to his wife like a protective wolf. He'd gone unseen by her when she'd looked about the ballroom but he could tell by her searching gaze she was seeking him.

When Erich appeared and took Anna in his arms for a dance, it was easy to picture Anna's planned future. This was the man her parents had chosen for her, a man of royal lineage, the nephew of the Prussian king. He was tall with fair looks, a perfect match for a princess. As they began to dance, whispers drifted back to Aiden in the shadows.

Such an exquisite couple . . . A worthy match . . . Imagine the beautiful children . . .

Aiden closed his eyes as a pain so deep struck a place deep inside his soul. He knew Anna to be his destiny, but what would be hers after he was gone? If he died as her visions foretold, was Erich the man who would pick up the pieces of Anna's broken heart and mend them? There was a sorrowful solace in knowing that a good-hearted man would be there to take his place to love her and cherish her.

Ashton appeared at his side. His brother-in-law's face was hard as stone, but his eyes held a hint of pity as he looked upon the dancing couple.

"I assume you know who her dance partner is?" Ashton asked.

Aiden nodded.

"He is a good man," Ashton said. "He would love her and treat her well. Should you dare to let her go. He would give her the life a princess would need."

Tears welled up in Aiden's eyes, and he blinked in surprise. He had not cried since he was a mere lad, and he dared not cry now.

"Are ye telling me to let her go?" Aiden asked.

Ashton frowned as Anna twirled by in a blur of red and cream silk. The candlelight glinted off the jewels on her diadem, and the pearls gleamed like frozen dewdrops.

"I am merely reminding you that love often means a sacrifice of something. When you love someone with every part of your body and soul, that means they come first, *always*. If you love her as I suspect you do, then be prepared to do what is best for her. That might mean letting her marry the man who will be able to play the part of a prince at her side. Remember, she is royalty, and she must put her country and people first, even if that means making the right political alliances through marriage. Prussia is a strong ally and can protect Ruritania once Yuri has been removed from power. You are but one man, with no army at your back."

Ashton's words were kindly spoken, but the brutal truth of them was a knife to Aiden's heart. He was but one man . . . a Scot with no army at his back. He would never be a prince, would never do well at the balls, parades or royal events that would be expected of him as the husband of a princess. Aiden was a man who took solace in the solitude of the rocks and trees, with the cries of birds and the wind in his ears. A life away from Castle Kinkade would feel like a cage to him. He could sacrifice that part of himself, but what if it wasn't enough? What if she needed things he did not have the power to give?

"When the time comes, you will know what to do. For now, be true to your heart and stay at her side. I fear there are still dangers yet unseen." Ashton gave him a nod, and the great room fell into a hush as the king of England made his entrance.

"She will ask for an audience, and we must go with her as escorts," Ashton murmured so only Aiden could hear. The two of them collected Godric, who was a favorite of the king's and would be an additional influence, as they made their way through the crowd just as Anna requested an audience and the king granted it.

They followed Anna, and he noticed her relieved expression when she finally saw him. Once they were all gathered in a private room, Anna and the king sat in two chairs facing each other across a reading table.

"Ah, Essex, Lennox, good of you both to come. And who is this?" King George inquired as he swept a critical eye over Aiden.

"He is a bodyguard I gained while I spent time in the Highlands after my ship was wrecked off the coast. His name is Aiden Kincade.

"Ah, a Scot. Excellent choice, Princess Anna. They may be a bit wild, but Scots are fiercely loyal. Now, I assume you wish to speak to me about the unfortunate situation Ruritania is facing."

Anna settled her skirts around her, sitting prim and proper as only a princess could. "Your Majesty, I am here to ask for your military support. My uncle—"

"Yes, your uncle sent me a private envoy, who arrived almost a month ago," the king interrupted. "I heard about your parents' tragic death at the hands of the rebels. It sounds as if your uncle will take charge, and I have promised to provide support to him in crushing any future rebellions."

Anna's face drained of color. No one had known her uncle's messengers would have gotten here so quickly. It meant that he'd sent word of her parents' murder almost the day they'd been brutally slain . . . Yuri had clearly planned his coup down to every last detail, including informing trade partners like England what he wanted them to believe had happened.

Have courage and keep calm, lass, Aiden thought.

Anna lifted her gaze. "Your Majesty, it pains me to tell you that you have been deceived. I was there when the castle burned. My uncle is the one who attacked the palace. He is the one responsible for killing my parents. My brother, Alexei, still lives, fighting my uncle in secret. You must help us."

The king sat back, eyes wide with shock. He clearly hadn't expected her to say that.

"Even if his story were true, Yuri has no rightful claim to the throne, Your Majesty," Anna continued. "He is half brother to my father. His father was a Russian nobleman my grandmother married after my grandfather died when they were quite young. The throne in my country must pass to a male heir descended from the male line. By our laws, Alexei is next in line, and any male child he bears will have the next rightful claim to the throne. If he has no heirs, it falls to any sons that I might bear. Yuri is a traitor and a murderer. He has no right to rule."

For a second, Aiden realized something that hadn't occurred to him. He and Anna had made love several times —she could be with child in that moment, a child who had the potential to rule Ruritania should Alexei perish. Aiden's heart stopped beating for a painful moment. Their child . . . The thought filled him with a rush of joy, but he had to push it away and focus on the matter before them.

King George was quiet a long moment. "You are absolutely certain this is the truth of what took place? Your uncle's envoy said your brother was among the rebels responsible, that Alexei had a falling out with your father and it led to him siding with the rebels when they attacked."

Anna held the king's gaze without fear. "Alexei is my twin, Your Majesty. Our bond is unbreakable. I know him as well as I know myself. He would never have hurt our parents or made a claim to the throne until after our father died. I was there when the palace burned. I saw the tears in my brother's eyes as he told me of our slain parents and who was responsible. I saw the bodies of innocent citizens slaughtered in the corridors of my home.

"You said you knew my mother. I am her child, and the child of King Alfred and Queen Isadora. I would not lie to you, nor am I fool enough to believe the lies of others and speak them to you as truths." She drew in a breath and stood. "Will you let a peaceful nation dissolve into the darkness of an unjust war? Or will you aid Ruritania in our hour of need? I must warn you that nations who do not fight the spread of tyranny often fall prey to them. Stand with us now, and we may yet save the Continent from my uncle's greed."

The room was silent for a painfully long beat, and Aiden held his breath, afraid of what the king might do. King George slowly rose from his chair, and without looking away from Anna, he spoke.

"When I received the initial reports of the deaths of your parents, I gave my support to Yuri, obviously unaware of the truth. If I go against that decision now, it would wreck all future trade ties."

Anna's heart plummeted to her feet.

"But," King George said to her earnestly, "I do not believe in letting a king-killer steal a throne. There are ways in which I can render aid without seeming to have interfered and committing troops to a war." George turned to Ashton and Godric now, a cunning gleam in his eyes. "Lord Essex and Lord Lennox, I believe you are capable of handling this matter quietly on behalf of the Crown?"

Ashton stepped forward and bowed to the king. "Yes, Your Majesty."

The king nodded back at Ashton. "Good." Then he looked to her again. "Princess Anna, you have your secret army."

CHAPTER 14

A nna had an army.

She was so relieved that she almost hugged the king, but at the last minute she stopped herself. Spending so much time with Aiden and his brothers had broken down her royal training to stay professional and reserved.

"Now, with all that unpleasantness over with, I wish to enjoy the ball." King George crooked an arm to her in invitation. "I believe you owe me a dance, Princess Anna. Let's set the chins wagging, eh?" he teased as she accepted his arm and they returned to the ballroom. She chanced a look back at Aiden and the others, wondering if they planned to follow her.

"Go on, Your Highness. We have a few things to discuss before we rejoin you," Ashton reassured her. Aiden gave a small nod, and she tried to hide her disappointment that he wasn't coming right away.

Anna and the king rejoined the revelers in the ballroom. Lady Eugenia hovered near the entrance, waiting for them.

"Lady Eugenia, I've asked Princess Anna to dance with me. A waltz, if you please," King George said. Lady Eugenia rushed over to the orchestra to give them their instructions.

Anna spotted Erich in the front row of onlookers and gave him a gentle smile as she and the king took their places for a dance. The music started, and they began a lovely waltz.

"I am sorry about your situation, Princess Anna," King George murmured when they were far enough away from the other dancers.

"I am as well," she replied.

"You understand why I cannot take a public stand. We've only just ended a war with France, and England wishes to stay out of wars for a while. We cannot be seen openly assisting another country."

"I understand," she said, but in truth, she couldn't believe how blind the king was.

She understood that the Holy Roman Empire had dissolved during the Napoleonic Wars, leaving the entire region in chaos. Her uncle was the sort of man to take advantage of that. While Ruritania did not have any impressive military forces, she could certainly imagine Yuri would attempt to buy support from other nearby countries. He'd always talked of spreading control beyond their borders, and it would not be a stretch to see him use someone else's army to do that. But she understood King George's reluctance. If he sent troops through France, even if they were bound for Ruritania, it might ignite fresh battles, and it could also upset the fledgling German Confederation, which included most of Prussia.

Once the dance was over, the king clapped along with the other dancers and then gave a slight bow to her.

"I apologize that I cannot stay longer tonight. Good luck, Princess Anna."

"Thank you, Your Highness." She stood there in the middle of the ballroom, feeling so very alone, as King George walked away. His small retinue followed behind him, filing up the staircase.

Rosalind came to her side. "You look like you need a bit of rescuing," she said, trying to reassure her.

"I do. Is there somewhere we could go for a few minutes? I should like a chance to sit down without everyone staring at me."

Now that she had made a grand entrance and had a private audience with the king, whispers were drifting back to her. Royalty always had that effect. She'd attended many court functions in her own country and others, but the attention bothered her far more than it used to. Perhaps it was the relatively quiet and wonderfully secluded month she'd spent in Scotland with Aiden, where she'd been allowed to be herself and not a princess. Playing her royal part again felt suffocating compared to the freedom she'd tasted with Aiden in the Highlands.

"Come with me." Rosalind waved her fan in greeting at a few ladies as she led Anna back out of the ballroom. A footman stood just outside the door, and Rosalind asked him where the nearest retiring room was.

Once they were secure inside, Anna sank gratefully into a wingback chair. A few other ladies present in the room eyed them with curiosity. Their fans fluttered as they murmured amongst themselves, eyes darting between Anna and Rosalind. One woman with a turbaned head full of ostrich plumes seemed so excited by Anna's presence that the feathers quivered on top of her head.

Rosalind went over to the group of ladies. "Princess Anna is in need of a few minutes of quiet. Would you mind giving her the room? She would be very grateful."

The women nodded hastily and departed the room with beaming smiles.

"That was easier than I expected." Rosalind chuckled as she fluffed a few pillows on the settee across from Anna and then sat down. "I suppose no one wants to upset a princess."

"It's one of the few things that's nice about the role," Anna admitted, but she would have gladly given that up for the long list of freedoms she would gain by not being royalty.

"So . . . did things go as you wish?" Rosalind kept her tone light and didn't ask specifically about Anna convincing the king to give her an army.

"Yes, better than I feared, but not as well as I'd hoped."

Knowing her uncle had gotten to the king of England first had been a disheartening blow. It made her more than aware of the fact that the other countries that were Ruritania's trade partners and nearby allies had likely been approached by Yuri's envoys and told false stories as well. There would be so much political damage she and Alexei would have to undo after they'd stopped her uncle.

She let her head fall back against the chair and sighed. She was ready to go home, crawl into bed next to her husband, and feel the hard warmth of his body as he lay beside her. She had spent too much of her life at balls and official functions. Now that she had tasted freedom with Aiden, she wanted nothing more than to go back to Scotland, but she couldn't rest until she stopped her uncle.

"Well, that's good news, isn't it?" Rosalind said as she settled deeper into the settee.

"Do you suppose we could ask the others if we can go home now?" Anna asked.

"I believe so. We can make our apologies to Lady Eugenia and quietly depart. We have achieved our objective, after all." Rosalind stood and went over to the door. She opened it, but rather than exit, she halted abruptly and backed up a step. The odd movement caught Anna's attention.

"Rosalind?"

Aiden's sister backed up yet another few steps as a man entered the retiring room. He held a pistol aimed at Rosalind's chest, its barrel gleaming menacingly in the candlelight. Anna didn't dare breathe as she tried to think what to do.

"There you are, princess," the man said in Danish with a distinct accent. A chill shot up her spine. He was Ruritanian. Anna slowly rose, every muscle in her body tense. If she saw the chance, she would fight. She'd had years of defensive training growing up. One man she could handle.

"Anna, be careful," Rosalind breathed in a mix of fear and anger.

"Come with me, princess, or I will shoot this pretty bird." This time his words were in English, no doubt because he wished Rosalind to know her life was in danger.

But the man hadn't bet on one thing. Rosalind wasn't English. She was Scottish, and as such had a Scottish temper.

"Pretty bird, am I?" Rosalind growled and knocked the man's arm away. The pistol flew from the stunned man's hand and clattered onto the floor. He cursed and backhanded Rosalind so quickly that she cried out and stumbled away from him. Anna took advantage of the distraction and lunged for the pistol, but it was too close to its owner.

He bent down to grab it, and Anna changed her strategy of attack in the blink of an eye. Lifting her skirts, she kicked the man hard in the side of his knee. He slammed back into the wall with a howl of pain, but he managed to keep his fingers around the gun and point it at Rosalind.

"I warned you."

Anna stepped forward, stepping in front of Rosalind and raising her hands defensively. The man's brown eyes were cold and vengeful. A sneer twisted his face.

"My only orders were to bring you in *alive*."

She understood his threat. *Alive* was not the same thing as *unharmed*.

"Unfortunately for you, that pistol won't fire."

"What—?" He glanced down at the gun just long enough for her to take advantage of his mistake. She spun and kicked him in the lower belly. While her skirts were of bit of a hindrance, she still managed to land a fair blow. Air whooshed out of his lungs as he fell onto his back.

"Rosalind, go! Get help!" She shoved Rosalind toward the door, but her friend was thrown back as several more men filled the room, all of them armed. Two of them grabbed Rosalind by her arms. The man on the floor was helped to his feet by another man, who cursed under his breath.

"Fain warned us she'd had lessons in self-defense. I told you we needed more men," the man she'd knocked to the floor told the others.

The man who spoke next seemed to be the one in charge. "Take the princess, kill the other." He waved his gun at the men surrounding Anna.

"Wait, no!" Anna cried out. "Stop!" she told the leader of the men. "I will come with you willingly, but only if you leave my friend unharmed. Kill her, and I swear you will have to kill me as well."

"No, Anna!" Rosalind cried out.

One of the men struck Rosalind in the temple with the butt of his pistol, and she crumpled to the floor.

"Bind the princess, but make sure you cover her hands with a cloak," the leader said, and as his men followed his orders, he put his pistol away. "One of my men will stay behind with your friend. If we are stopped for any reason before we leave the building, she will die. Do you understand?"

Anna nodded, her eyes locked on his, but she said nothing.

The leader looked to one of the men. "Stay here. If you hear an alarm or are caught here, slit her throat and escape. If not, leave in ten minutes and find your way to the docks." He then turned his attention back to Anna, affecting a slight bow. "If you will follow us, Your Highness."

***

Aiden exited the private room, with Ashton and Godric on his heels. They had formed a solid plan to rally troops across London using a network of connections through the Earl of Morrey, a friend of Ashton's. It had been clear in the meeting with King George that he could not commit his own troops publicly, but there were plenty of men whom he would quietly approve of to take up the fight against Yuri's forces, either on behalf of their honor for defending a princess or because Ashton and Godric could pay them a fee. Within a week, they could set sail with Anna and be bound for Ruritania. Morrey had assured them that while many men could be gathered here in England, he could rally just as many across the Channel to aid them.

The ball was still in full swing, dancing couples still covering much of the floor.

"Bloody balls," Godric muttered in annoyance.

Aiden could empathize. He much preferred dancing in the forest with Anna in his arms and the music of song-birds in his ears.

Godric's wife, Emily, came up to him and swatted him on the arm with her folded fan. "Oh hush, Godric. You know you enjoy dancing."

"Dancing with you, yes," Godric grumbled. "Balls are bloody nonsense, full of preening fops and social pests. I much rather like hosting our own gatherings with only the people I enjoy spending time with."

Emily's eyes glinted with merriment. "By that you mean your friends and no one else."

"*And* your friends," Godric argued diplomatically.

Emily looked to Aiden with a feigned look of wifely suffering. "Still the charmer after all this time together."

Aiden chuckled. "Where is Anna?" He would have seen her in the ballroom, despite the crush of the crowd. She stood out like a star in a dark sky.

Emily tilted her head. "She and Rosalind went to rest in a retiring room for a few minutes. She looked as though she needed to sit down after she danced with the king. But I would have thought they would be back by now." Her violet eyes darkened with worry. "Perhaps we should see if they are all right."

Aiden's heart suddenly started beating fast. Something didn't feel right. He'd checked every room of this place, but in the time he'd spent with the king in that private room, it was possible the safety of Lady Eugenia's home had been breached. "Where?"

Emily pointed the way with her fan. "I'll fetch them."

"We'll come with you," said Ashton.

Godric discreetly stepped in front of her in a protective manner. "Stay behind me, darling. Aiden seems to think there is reason to be concerned."

"Oh dear, I hope not . . ." Emily's face bled of color. "I never thought anything would happen if they went to a private ladies' retiring room . . ."

Aiden, Godric, and Ashton entered the corridor, and Aiden noticed the lack of servants present. There was not one man or woman to be seen.

"Where are the footmen?" he asked Ashton. "There were at least four in this hallway when we came through an hour ago."

Ashton's eyes narrowed. "They may have been called to

some sort of emergency. But Lady Eugenia wouldn't leave this hall completely unattended." They hurried to the door at the end of the hall that Aiden knew to be the retiring room, thanks to his detailed inspection of the house before Anna had arrived this evening.

Aiden crept to the door, which stood slightly ajar. A beam of light from the lamps in the retiring room cut a thin sliver into the darkened hallway. He peered inside, trying his best to go unseen by anyone who may be in there. He thought at first it was empty, until he glimpsed a feminine hand stretched out upon the floor inside the room. Inches from her fingertips lay the diamond-and-pearl diadem that Anna had been wearing. The rest of the woman's body vanished from view behind a settee. A window that led into the gardens had been forced upward, and the curtains blew into the room, chilling it with a wintry wind.

Without a second thought, Aiden burst into the room, terrified he would find Anna hurt or even dead. The woman lying on the floor didn't move. But the body on the floor was his sister, not his wife.

"Rose!" Ashton shoved past Aiden and fell to his knees by Rosalind's limp body. He turned her over onto her back and examined her closely. "She's breathing," Ash declared, his shoulders sagging with relief. He cradled Rosalind's head in his hands and brushed her tangled hair back from her face, revealing a dark bruise forming on her temple.

"Someone attacked my wife," he growled.

Rosalind moaned as if in pain. Ashton carefully lifted her up into his arms and sat down on the settee. Aiden bent and retrieved the diadem from the floor. He could feel his heart fracturing into a thousand pieces. He saw Godric in the doorway, his face shadowed with rage.

"Godric? What's wro—?" Emily appeared in the doorway, and when she saw Rosalind in Ashton's lap and then the diadem in Aiden's trembling hand, she stopped and gasped.

"Em, darling." Godric took her into his arms, trying to comfort her. "It will be all right. We'll . . ." But he didn't have the words to lie to her.

"They took her," Emily gasped. "They took her . . ." She repeated it again, as if that would make this awful madness make sense. She met Aiden's gaze, and he saw that the young duchess understood the grief, fear, and rage swirling inside him, choking him.

Aiden clenched his fingers around the diadem until the jewels dug into his skin. He wanted to throw his head back and roar in rage and fear. But he held back those two dangerous emotions, as he always had his entire life.

"Ash, where would they take her?" Aiden asked in a quiet voice.

Ashton looked up as he held his wife tenderly in his arms, his usually clear thinking clouded by worry. "I . . . I don't know."

Godric glanced around the room, looking to the window. "There must have been at least two men. Aiden and I examined the garden tonight, and I knew the wall could only be scaled by a single man, not someone carrying a body. That means someone took the princess out another way, and this one stayed behind with Rosalind and left out the window to distract us," he said.

Godric's theorizing spurred Ashton's mind into action.

He looked to the open window, then around the room, noting its disarray. "More than two, I would say. There was a fight, given the state of the furniture overthrown, and I see dirty boot prints of at least three different sizes on the floor. The window is indeed too small for Anna to have passed through in her court dress, and we see no gown has been abandoned nearby, so they haven't stripped her of her clothing. They most likely left through a side door, a servants' entrance, I would guess. The one who stayed behind with Rosalind as a hostage could have possibly done so to ensure Anna didn't raise an alarm before they escaped. They will take her to the nearest port to sail back to Ruritania. It's what I would do in their position."

Rosalind moaned, and her dark lashes fluttered. "Ash . . ." She looked up to see her husband's pale and anxious face.

"What happened, Rose?" Ashton asked with a gentleness that he reserved only for his wife.

"Anna and I . . . we were alone when the men came. We tried to fight them, but there were so many . . ." She flinched as she tried to sit up in Ashton's arms.

Ashton stroked his fingertips over her cheek. "Did they say where they were going?"

Rosalind shook her head and realized they weren't alone. She looked to Aiden, and he saw her pity and deep regret.

"I'm sorry, Aiden. I couldn't protect her. They used me against her." Tears rolled down his sister's face as she started to weep softly. Ashton wound an arm around her, pulling her against his chest to soothe her.

Aiden could barely speak to his sister except to say, "It's

all right, Rosalind—we'll find her." The words tasted like bitter lies upon his lips. His wife had been abducted and was likely bound for her homeland, where her uncle might execute her.

"We'll send men to the harbor at once and search every ship. They can't be but fifteen minutes ahead of us. If no ships have left the harbor yet, we can lock the harbor down . . . but if they have left . . . ," Ashton began.

"We'll need yer fastest ship and yer best crew, and try to find out if they're headed to Calais or if they mean to cross the North Sea," Aiden said quietly, but his words were met with a silence so loud that it defeated him.

"Aiden. We need at least a week to gather our forces," Ashton warned him. "If the men who took Anna reach Ruritania before you, you'll be facing more than just a ship —you'll be facing an army."

"They have *my wife*. I dinna need an army to kill the bastards." If Ashton had any idea of the rage that flowed through his veins, he'd understand that Aiden would kill any man who stood in his way, a hundred if need be.

Godric exchanged a look with Ashton and sighed heavily. "Well, I'd better go with you." He pressed a kiss to Emily's forehead. "Em, you need to stay here and help arrange the transportation of the men Lord Morrey manages to pull together."

"No, Godric, you build the army with Morrey and follow us. I'll go with Aiden," Ashton interjected. "If we fail to intercept them at sea, we'll be chasing them on land. I know the country. I'll get Aiden to the Winter Palace faster. I'll take Cedric and Charles. You keep Lucien and Jonathan with you."

"Shouldn't you take them?"

Ashton shook his head. "Two more men won't make a difference where an army is involved. Any plan we come up with will have to rely on cunning and deception. Though I expect we will only be able to gather information to aid us for when you arrive."

"Very well," Godric conceded. "I'll leave tonight to meet with Morrey." Godric and Emily hastily departed.

"Aiden, I must first see Rosalind home. Then we will head for the port."

"I should go with you—" Rosalind began, but Ashton shook his head and cupped Rosalind's face in his hands.

"I need you here, my darling. I need you *safe*. I know you hate me for asking it, but please . . ."

Something soft and intimate passed between them, and watching them made Aiden's heart ache. His own wife was in the hands of her enemy, and he was powerless to help her. It reminded him too much of his dreams where he reached through the water, trying to grasp Anna's hand, never quite able to save her.

He backed out of the retiring room and stood in the corridor, trying to settle himself as a wave of panic crushed his chest like a mighty stone had tumbled down from a Highland mountain. He braced a palm against the wall, struggling to breathe. He still held Anna's diadem in his other hand. He remembered the last time he'd held this jeweled crown. It had been when he'd placed it upon her head and stolen a lingering kiss before he'd left with the others to come to Lady Eugenia's early. He'd done all that he could to prevent this, and still she'd been taken. All he had left of his princess was the crown she'd left behind . . .

Brock's voice cut through the din of his erratic and terrified thoughts. "Aiden?"

His brothers stood a few feet away, the merry lights from the ballroom illuminating their concerned faces.

"It's Anna," he rasped. "She's been taken."

Brock and Brodie rushed to him, steadying him as he stumbled forward. He'd never felt a despair like this, not even when he'd lost his mother.

"When are you leaving to go after her?" Brodie asked.

"Tonight, with Ashton and his friends."

"Then we're coming with ye," they said at the same time.

"We may not come back," he warned them. They had wives to worry about, and he couldn't ask them to make this decision lightly. He wouldn't blame them if they chose to stay.

"Aye, we ken that, but we're yer brothers, laddie," Brock said. "We'd never let ye face this alone . . . *never*," he repeated more softly. The blood Aiden shared with his brothers had always kept them close, but now, more than ever, he felt how strong his kinship with them truly was.

"Besides," Brodie added, "we're hard to kill. If Father couldna manage it, then I doubt anyone else can." Brodie's eyes gleamed at the prospect of battle.

"Dinna worry, lad. We'll save yer bonnie bride," Brock promised.

Aiden closed his eyes as the Romani woman's words echoed through his mind. *"You will die for her . . ."* Most likely he would. But he would gladly die to save Anna, because to live in a world without her was no life at all.

***

Anna woke to a bitter taste in her mouth and the sound of water lapping against wood. She blinked, her eyes adjusting to the dark. She lay on a tiny bunk with high sides, which warned her she was on a ship. The last thing she remembered was being shoved into a coach, and only then did she try to fight them, once she thought it wouldn't endanger Rosalind's life. But something had hit her hard on the head, and she'd blacked out.

Her wrists and ankles were bound with rope, and her red-and-cream evening gown was wrinkled and bunched beneath her, telling her she had been dropped unceremoniously on the bed. Her head ached from the blow in the coach. Anna struggled to sit up, but when she did manage to right herself, the dingy little room spun around her. She closed her eyes, listening to the water slosh against the hull, feeling the rocking motion. That didn't help with her nausea. They were already at sea. How long had she been unconscious?

The doors of the cabin opened, and a man lifted a lantern to stare at her. She wondered if he'd been doing that frequently to see when she woke up.

"Awake at last, princess," the man said with a dark chuckle.

Anna stared at him. She was certain she'd seen him before. He might have been one of her father's former palace guards.

"We are bound for Ruritania?" Her voice was raspy and her mouth dry.

"Yes. Your uncle is most anxious to see you safely returned."

Anna knew he was baiting her, so she ignored the comment.

"Would it be possible to have my bonds removed? I need to use the chamber pot." She nodded at the pot in the corner of the cabin opposite the bed.

The man seemed to weigh her request carefully. "If you so much as raise a hand to me, I will tie you to the bed and you can go where you lie," he warned. "There is no escape. We are hours away from England, and you would drown in the sea if you tried to jump overboard."

Anna knew he was right, and she wasn't a fool. She would let them take her back to Ruritania, and she would wait for the right moment to run or attack, whichever would prove more likely to set her free. The man set the lantern down by the door and advanced toward her, a small dagger in one hand. He knelt by the bed and sliced the ropes at her ankles and wrists.

"Thank you," she said. If he was surprised at her words, he gave no indication.

"I remember you, princess," he said softly, his tone dangerous. "Too pretty and too untouchable for the likes of me." He reached for a lock of her hair and curled it around one finger as his smile turned predatory in the darkness. "But you aren't protected now. Remember that." Then he left her alone in the room.

She shook with so much rage that her first few steps toward the chamber pot were unsteady. She knelt before the pot and then vomited hard inside it. There was nothing to stop these men from hurting her, and fighting them would do her no good, not until she was on land.

She wiped her mouth with the back of her hand and sat on the floor a long while, listening to the waves. Each caress of the water upon the hull sounded like Aiden's gentle shushing tone when he spoke to his animals. It calmed her more than she expected, and it made her miss him with a desperation that felt like a physical pain in her chest.

Think about your escape, not about your husband . . .

If the wind was with the ship, they could arrive on Ruritania's shores in less than two weeks. If the wind was against the ship, it would take a month like it had when she'd first sailed toward England and her ship had been caught in that storm. All she had to do was stay alive until then. The men aboard the ship knew better than to intentionally kill her, but if they took to abusing her, death could still result. She would have to find a way to keep them at bay.

CHAPTER 15

The wind proved to be favorable for Yuri's men. The ship carried them to Ruritania in just two weeks. But the days Anna spent on the ship were fraught with the constant fear of being tortured or raped.

Gustav, the man she'd learned was the leader of the men in charge of her abduction barely kept control of the other men on the ship. It was a shocking thing to witness. She recognized many of these men, some who had served as guards since she was a child. She'd once trusted her life to them, and now she feared for it.

The unfortunate truth was that Captain Fain was the reason the men held themselves in check. Soon after she'd arrived on the ship, she'd heard soldiers' whispered tales of his brutality as they spoke to each other over dinner or card games, and it left her cold and shaking at night. Even as far away as they were from Fain at sea, the men feared any consequences of harming her simply because of the wrath Fain would bring down upon them. She'd assumed a public execution was being arranged for her, but it seemed her uncle had other plans. It was the reason no harm had come to her on board the ship. Gustav had warned the other soldiers that Captain of Fain would not want his new bride to be sullied.

She had gleaned more information than she'd expected the few times she'd been allowed to leave her cabin to walk the decks or empty her chamber pot. She'd overheard the men talking about how her uncle had promised her as a bride to Fain, who had been her father's former captain of the guard, and was one of the reasons he had joined her uncle's cause and agreed to betray and murder her parents. Fain had been the one to kill them, but while he had wielded the sword, her uncle had wielded Fain.

The entire voyage to Ruritania, the soldiers looked at her as if she was getting exactly what she deserved, and for the life of her, she did not know why they felt wronged by her family. What words had Yuri poisoned them with? Had he convinced them that all their problems, regardless of what they were, were the fault of the monarchy? That Yuri alone could fix everything?

She remembered hearing Yuri rant to her father, his half brother, about pushing Ruritania to some glory that existed only in the fables of power-hungry men, and he had called King Alfred weak when he refused to listen to Yuri's dreams of conquest. It was not hard in hindsight to see the danger that this man had posed. But at the time she had thought him silly and delusional, even amusing in a deranged way. So had her father.

If only they had known . . .

She wondered how much her homeland might have changed, even though less than two months had passed since Yuri had murdered her family.

As the ship finally docked and sailors rushed about throwing lines out to men on the walkways, Anna stood on deck, quietly observing the scene. She wore a simple dark-blue cotton dress that had been provided for her the previous week.

One of her abductors had packed a few dresses for the rest of her journey. The lovely court gown that Rosalind's modiste had designed was beyond saving, and Anna wanted no more memories of that night. She'd folded the gown and tucked it under the bed, out of sight.

Anna curled her fingers around the deck railing. Rope bound her wrists together in front of her. It was one of Gustav's requirements when she was allowed on deck. Thankfully, none of them believed she could swim. She could, even with her hands bound in front of her. But unfortunately, she saw no advantage to diving into the sea, even now that their ship was docked in the harbor. There were too many men watching her every move to do so unnoticed.

They were at the same port she had fled from almost two months ago, but the world here had drastically changed. The once lively port was now a shell of its former self. The docks were almost empty. Only a handful of fishing vessels made berth here now. At one point she saw a child peek out a window of one of the residences in the harbor village, but the mother came and slammed the shutter almost as quickly.

This was what the war had cost her home. Tears burned in her eyes, but she held them at bay. She could not show any weakness now.

A gangplank was lowered between the ship and the dock so the sailors could unload supplies. Gustav came to her, scowling. He'd changed out of the clothing he'd worn to blend in with the English crowds and now wore a red-and-black uniform. The uniforms for her family had been white, gold and blue. Red and black must have been what her uncle had chosen for his new guards. Anna's stomach turned at the reminder that her uncle ruled her country now.

"Time to go, *princess*." He spat the word as if it was a curse.

She followed him, silent as a lamb being led to slaughter, but beneath her complacent demeanor, she was thinking through every possible scenario. One thing she had learned when the men believed her to be asleep was that she had been captured not only to keep Fain's loyalty intact but because her uncle believed it would lure Alexei out of hiding. She knew with dreadful certainty that word of her capture would draw her brother out. She had to escape, or else her twin, and her country would fall forever into the hands of her enemy.

Anna followed Gustav, and his men flanked her as they left the ship and walked toward the grouping of buildings that formed the small port city. Horses were waiting for them, and Gustav shoved Anna roughly into the arms of a hired groom who assisted her up into a saddle. She was surprised at her good luck. She stood a better chance of escaping on horseback than if they'd shoved her into a carriage again.

"I'm sorry, Your Highness," the groom whispered in apology and ducked his head as he adjusted the stirrups for her feet.

"Tie her hands to the pommel," Gustav told the groom. The poor man gave a red-faced glance at her before he complied with her captor's orders. Anna pressed her wrists together but did her best to keep them a bit apart to give her some room to move. If she worked at it, she might be able to slip her hands free of the rope later.

The groom hesitated only a second when he noticed her attempt to keep the bonds loose, but he made no mention to Gustav. A flicker of hope stirred in her chest. Her people were resisting her uncle's rule, even if it was only in small ways. Gustav signaled his men to ride. Anna had no choice but to follow when they closed in around her.

They rode into the Dark Forest, and Anna soon had an eerie feeling of being watched. They said the woods held old magic in them, but it was a magic she respected and did not wish to defy. These were the woods of her dreams, the place she was forever trying to escape, the place where Aiden came to her and tried to rescue her through the enchanted wishing well.

The soldiers grew uneasy as they rode deeper into the forest, and they fell silent. They were focused on what might come out at them that they paid her little mind, allowing her to work at her ropes in secret.

Somewhere a raven croaked, and several men jumped, their horses startling. Anna saw her chance and broke free from the group of men and kicked her booted heels into the flanks of her horse. The beast galloped madly into the woods, away from the soldiers. She bent low over the horse's neck, hanging on for her life.

The sudden crack of a pistol and a searing pain in her right arm drew a cry from her, almost blinding her. She fought to keep steady on the horse as it ran even faster from the soldiers, as if it sensed the threat they posed. A second shot echoed through the woods, and the cry of ravens taking flight mixed with the screams of her horse. The beast buckled forward, and Anna's hands were freed by the jarring movement.

A moment later, she was flung off the horse and landed on her back, the air knocked from her lungs. She tried to breathe as she stared up at the canopy of dark leaves above her. Her horse's scream was silenced by the sound of a third gunshot. Tears clouded her vision, both from the pain in her body and for losing an innocent horse to such evil. They'd killed that beautiful horse, killed it because she had tried to escape.

The ground shook as the soldiers' horses thundered toward her and surrounded her. She clutched her arm, the pain of the wound so fierce that it was hard to breathe and even harder to think.

"Better a wounded bride than no bride at all," Gustav said. "Pity you landed on your head like that, but I'm sure you'll be fine when we reach the castle." His lips twisted in a dark sneer.

He nodded to one of his men as she said, "But I didn't hit my—" just as a blow struck the back of her head and she blacked out.

***

Anna stirred in her sleep and reached for Aiden. Pain shot up her arm and through her head, causing her to groan. Her eyes fluttered open, and she stared in confusion at her surroundings.

This wasn't Castle Kincade. She lay in a bed she recognized, but it wasn't the bed she should be in. It was her bed in . . . the Winter Palace. Yuri's stronghold.

Anna moved to sit up, and pain lanced through her upper arm. She pulled away the bedsheets and saw that her arm was heavily bandaged.

Flashes of her race through the Dark Forest came back to her. Gustav or one of his men had shot her, and when that had failed to stop her, he'd shot her horse out from under her. A the wave of nausea swelled up in her stomach as she struggled to get up. The instinct to escape was so overpowering that for a moment she couldn't think rationally. The bedchamber was empty, but sunlight peeped in through the blue-and-gold brocade curtains half covering the window.

Her bare feet touched cold flagstone as she stood. She wore only a nightgown. Her stomach turned at the thought of who might have changed her out of her dress. A robe was draped over the edge of the bed. She hastily slipped her arms through the sleeves and belted it around her body, glad for the extra warmth and concealment. She used the wall for support as she crept to the bedchamber door.

She wasn't sure what she would find on the other side. A guard, most likely. The handle turned beneath her palm, and she breathed a sigh of relief at not being locked in. But when she opened the door, *two* guards were there to block her path, one on either side of the doorway.

The men turned to face her, but Anna didn't dare show fear. If there was one thing she'd learned from Aiden about animals that could be applied in this situation, it was to never show a predator fear.

"Tell Yuri the princess is awake," one guard told the other. The subordinate stood to attention, turned, and left, leaving Anna alone with the remaining guard.

"How long have I been here?" she said in her most commanding tone.

The soldier reacted to the natural authority in her voice. "A day. They brought a doctor in to see to your arm and your head."

She had lost an entire day . . .

"Have a servant bring me food and water."

At this, the guard snorted. "You do not give orders anymore, princess."

"You are mistaken. As I understand matters, I am to be the wife of Captain Fain, your commander. Starving his future bride will likely earn you a nasty punishment," Anna bluffed.

The man's eyes narrowed as he considered her threat. "You can eat after your uncle speaks to you."

"Then take me to him," she snapped.

"You are hardly dressed for an audience," he sneered back at her, his gaze far too familiar for her liking.

Anna stared him down, acting as if she didn't care that she wore a nightgown and robe as her only armor.

"Take me to him, *now*. Or you will regret disobeying me."

"There's no need for that." A voice carried from down the hall. The second guard returned with her uncle Yuri and Captain Fain.

Her uncle waved a hand at the guard, and he stepped back. Having nowhere else to go, Anna retreated into her bedchamber. Her uncle gripped her uninjured arm and dragged her deeper into the room. Rage flared inside her, and she jerked free, stumbling a little and catching one of the bedposts to support herself. She faced the two men responsible for the loss of her parents, her home, and her country, clutching at a bedpost, her body weak with pain, exhaustion, and fear.

"Yuri," she said with cold fury.

"My dear niece, you have been *most* troublesome." His tone was full of boredom.

Captain Fain watched with a gaze that made her skin crawl. She recognized him as one of the captain of her father's royal guards, but she'd had very little contact with him before now. It made her shiver to think he'd been watching her all this time, coveting her the way a dragon coveted gold.

Anna focused on her uncle. "What are your intentions toward me?"

Yuri was a tall man, like her father, but he shared little else with his half brother. He was fair-haired with a touch of silver at the temples, and he had cold gray eyes. He was fit, and she knew he was good with a blade, bow, and pistol. Once she had thought him a posturing fool, but he was dangerous, had *always* been dangerous. Only now did she realize how much.

My family was so blind, she thought with quiet despair.

Alexei's last words came back to her. *"The devils were inside the walls."* Her father had been too moved by compassion for shared blood to see the viper in the grass.

"You will be sent for execution tomorrow morning at dawn. That, of course, will draw Alexei out. Once I have him, you will be granted a reprieve and marry my captain of the guard." Yuri gestured at Fain, who stared at her with a cold, almost reptilian look.

Such a simple plan he had, yet it would destroy what was left of her country with one death and one marriage. Anna's mind played out a thousand scenarios, but feigning compliance was the only way she could possibly win. But they would not believe it unless it seemed she had been convinced of their position.

"You expect me to cooperate when you tell me to my face you intend to kill my brother?"

"You don't exactly have a choice, Anna," said her uncle. "Your brother is dead, whether it happens tomorrow at an execution or a month from now, hunted down and shot in the forests. But the longer he stays free, the more he will hurt Ruritania and its people. The more people will die fighting for a hopeless cause. Already so many have suffered in this pointless struggle. If you truly care for the people of this country, it would be best to allow me to do what must be done and end this conflict so that this nation can heal."

She wanted to slap him, saying such words as if he was not the cause of all the suffering he claimed to want to end.

She looked down at her feet, as if in meek acceptance. She could not endorse his words, for he would not believe it, but she could not oppose him either. He had to see the fight had been taken out of her. The more she convinced them she was not a threat, the more lax they would be in her treatment. But that laxity would take time to build, and she had only a day to find a way to avoid her brother's capture.

"You see? She understands now. There is no point in resisting what must be. See to her needs," Yuri told the captain before he left the two of them alone.

Being alone with Fain afforded Anna a new opportunity —to test where she stood with him and what she could get away with. "If I am to marry you tomorrow, then you had better have a proper gown made. I will not become a bride in rags, nor will I do it on an empty stomach."

The captain of the guard walked over to her and reached out, brushing a lock of hair back from her face. It took every ounce of Anna's willpower not to flinch at his touch.

"When we are married, you will not order me about like that. You will do as I say, and only then will you be treated well. Remember, *Anna*," he said, caressing her name, "I could have claimed any woman in the world when your uncle asked for my allegiance, and I chose you."

Fain left and closed her bedroom door. Anna stared at the door a long while, then crept to the window of her chamber, which overlooked the courtyard below. She pushed back the curtains and saw the scaffolding where a chopping block awaited her. Whatever came next, she had only one thought that gave her a sliver of peace. Aiden was not here to die. Her visions from the fairy pools would not come to pass.

***

Alexei and William snuck out of their hidden camp a few hours before dawn and rode south toward the Winter Palace. Word had reached him the previous evening that his sister was Yuri's prisoner and was to be executed at dawn, along with the terms that would spare her life.

He and William had almost come to blows that night, but in the end, Alexei knew what he must do. He must surrender to Yuri. William pointed out the futility of it, that there was every chance that Anna would still be executed alongside him, but he had to take the chance of saving her.

When he and William rode to the palace, hundreds of villagers and townsfolk from miles around flooded the road leading to the palace and the courtyard. They had come to see Anna's execution, but not one face held any joy over the fact. They looked beaten down, their gaunt faces lined with misery. Perhaps they'd come hoping for a miracle, just like he did.

Alexei kept the hood of his cloak shadowing his face as he dismounted, and William followed suit. They pushed through the crowds and entered the gates of the fortress.

When they reached the inner courtyard, they saw Anna being led out from the castle, hands bound behind her. An execution block sat on the wooden platform that had been erected in the middle of the courtyard. A hush fell upon the subdued villagers at the sight of the princess, wearing a simple gown, her hands bound behind her back, her long hair tumbling free down her shoulders.

Seeing his beloved twin facing death sent a punch to Alexei's gut. It was a trap for him, but what could he do? Either she'd die or he'd surrender and pray his uncle would spare her. She was no use to Yuri, after all—Yuri saw no value in her, and as long as she bore no child, she would have no way of taking the throne from a usurper.

Alexei shot William a look. His friend gave a subtle shake of his head, trying to discourage him, but Alexei's mind was made up. Anna would not pay with her life for his.

A hand grabbed his arm, halting him when Alexei tried to move forward. William's eyes were dark with sorrow. "Without you, Ruritania is lost."

Alexei smiled sadly. "Without my sister, *I* am lost." He could never fully explain to anyone how deeply bonded to Anna he was. It was a connection forged in their mother's womb. It could never be broken. "Goodbye, Will."

William's eyes were overbright. He blinked, and his hand fell away from Alexei's arm.

A man in a black executioner's hood walked toward Anna where she knelt on the platform and forced her neck down against the chopping block. The brute wearing the black hood adjusted the grip on his ax and then raised it up.

"Halt!" Alexei bellowed. His voice carried across the courtyard. Everyone turned to stare at him. The executioner, his blade aloft, looked between Alexei and Yuri, who watched from a nearby balcony. "I surrender!"

"My dear nephew." Yuri's voice carried over the gasps that filled the courtyard. "Come inside and we will discuss the terms of your surrender." Yuri then gave a signal to the executioner, who lowered his weapon and yanked Anna to her feet.

Alexei felt the eyes of his people on him as they parted

to let him pass. Hands touched his shoulders and arms, quiet whispers of *"Long live the king . . ."* gave him the strength to keep moving forward. His people still believed in him, and yet he was giving himself over to the man who had hurt them and would continue to hurt them. He had failed his people. He could only pray that William and the other guards would fight on after he died.

He reached the platform just as Anna was led down the stairs, and they fell in step beside each other. She looked at him and he looked at her. That silent way of communicating by gaze alone passed between them. She'd known he would come for her, and he knew she'd hoped he wouldn't. But none of that mattered now. What was done was done. At least they were together for a little while longer before . . . it ended.

Yuri waited for them inside the castle, his smile as cold as winter.

"At last, I have the pair of you. Take the prince down to the dungeons," Yuri told the guards who came up behind him. Alexei did not struggle when he was restrained by them.

"You will spare my sister?" he asked his uncle.

Yuri glanced at Anna. "She is spared from execution. Now she has other obligations to satisfy."

"What obligations?" Alexei growled.

Yuri laughed, clearly delighted by this turn of events. "She will wed the captain of my guards, the very man who slit the throats of your beloved parents. And he will do the same to her if she doesn't prove to be a pleasing bride to him." His uncle fisted a hand in Anna's hair, wrenching her head back to expose her throat. "Such a pretty neck . . . I imagine she'll do whatever she must to keep it." Yuri released Anna and walked off, laughing. There was a note of madness in the sound.

"Anna!" Alexei shouted, but the guard holding Anna dragged her away to the staircase that led to the rooms above, while he was taken to the dungeons.

Once there, he was shoved into a cell. The three guards who'd taken him down to the dungeons were smiling darkly as they advanced on him. Knowing what was coming, he raised his fists. The first man who lunged toward Alexei caught Alexei's fist on his chin and he stumbled back, but the other two rushed at Alexei. He jammed his knee into one man's stomach, but the other grabbed him from behind in a choke hold. Alexei kicked out, but the lack of air made his vision narrow as the other two men advanced on him. When they were done long minutes later, Alexei was still able to stand by sheer will alone, but he braced himself against the wall of his cell and spit blood into the hay at his feet. His ribs ached and he guessed a few were bruised, but hopefully not broken. It hurt to breathe, but it wasn't impossible.

The guards slammed the door shut and locked it. Alexei waited until they were gone before he sank to the straw-covered floor. Every part of him hurt like the devil, and yet he tried to ignore it and focus on his sister and finding a way to help her before . . . before his uncle got what he wanted.

Part of him had imagined some grand opportunity to escape would present itself for him and his sister, but it had been a fool's dream. The last of his hopes died in the darkness of that cell. William was right. Ruritania was lost.

CHAPTER 16

Aiden placed a hand on the hilt of the knife tucked in his belt as he settled onto the back of his horse. The Dark Forest was eerily quiet. Behind him was a train of his companions, Ashton, Brock, Brodie, Charles, and Cedric, along with a handful of men recruited the night of Lady Eugenia's ball who were able to leave England immediately.

It had been two weeks since his wife had been abducted, but it felt as though he had aged a thousand years. The *Lady Fair*, Ashton's fastest ship, had chased the horizon, searching for a glimpse of the vessel that had taken Anna, Aiden and his companions hoping that they could board the ship before she reached port.

Once, before a storm, they thought they had spotted the other ship, but then the wind rose and the skies darkened and they had to take in the sails to ride out the storm. Once the skies cleared, any sign of the other vessel had vanished.

They reached Ruritania's coast and sailed along the shore at night when only a sliver of moon graced the skies. It had been too dangerous to dock in any port under Yuri's control. Once they landed, they met a village of farmers, and thanks to Ashton's fluent Danish, they managed to procure horses with the provisions they'd brought with them off the ship. Once prepared, they had saddled up and ridden directly into the woods.

Aiden studied the surrounding trees. Many were gnarled, with nearly black bark and treacherous roots that seemed to crawl across the paths, tripping anyone who moved without care. These were the woods he and Anna had dreamed of since they were children. They were vast and full of danger and death. Aiden took the lead, but a horse soon moved up to walk alongside him. Aiden saw Ashton's face in the dim light.

"We have a two hour ride before we reach the Winter Palace," Ashton said. He spoke quietly, as though the trees themselves were listening.

"And then?" Aiden asked.

"The only way in is through the front gates. If they are open, we must enter in a way so as to escape the notice of the guards."

Aiden considered this as he adjusted his grip on his horse's reins. "We should find some guards on patrol and take their uniforms if we think they willna be missed. It willna be easy to fool anyone, but it might get us inside." He paused and then cleared his throat. "It will likely be a fool's errand. I should go on alone."

Ashton sighed heavily. "Aiden, we are all fools when it

comes to love, and doubly so when we make such brash declarations. Not one of us here will let you go on alone. You've *never* been alone in this," Ashton said.

Once Aiden would've denied those words and insisted that he had been alone all too often. His eyes had been opened during their voyage as he realized the men who had followed him into the mouth of hell did so out of loyalty and love for him and his kin.

"Thank ye, Ashton," he said. "Ye've been a brother to me."

"Don't get sentimental on me now, Scot. I need you at your most bloodthirsty."

Aiden grinned, but it was more of a sneer. "Oh aye, I'm plenty thirsty." In the last two weeks, he had thought of little else besides what he would do to Anna's uncle if he had the chance.

They rode through the forest and into the farmlands in the south. As they reached the village that abutted the fortress, they slowly let their horses drift apart so that it didn't appear that they had been riding together. Aiden searched the villagers for guards. There was a pair of men in red uniforms who were walking toward a tavern. *Perfect.* Aiden caught Charles's eye, and the two of them dismounted, tied their horses up, and followed the men inside. Ashton and the others moved past them on horseback and dismounted farther down the road.

When Aiden and Charles entered the tavern, they found it empty, except for a barkeeper and the pair of guards they had tailed. The guards seemed to be harassing the man for free drinks.

As much of the discussion was conducted in Danish, Aiden followed some of it thanks to the Danish lessons Anna had been giving him before they'd left for London. He approached the two men, and Charles walked up on the other side.

"Are they bothering you?" Aiden asked the barkeeper in Danish.

"N-no . . ." The man's eyes widened, and he backed up. The barkeeper knew trouble was coming, and he wanted no part of it.

"Who are you?" One guard whirled to face Aiden, but he never got a chance to draw his blade. Aiden's fist landed, and the guard dropped like a stone. His companion was about to call for help, but Charles slammed the man's head into the bar rail, and he crumpled to the floor.

The barkeeper stared at Aiden and Charles in horror, putting as much distance between himself and them as he could. Charles put a finger to his lips as he met the frightened man's eyes and winked.

"Aiden, ask this fellow if he has any good, stout rope for us to use." Charles glanced about the little tavern.

Aiden asked the man, and he nodded, gulping as he hastily made his way to a storage cupboard near the back of the taproom. He handed Aiden a coil of rope.

Aiden thanked him, and then he and Charles dragged the bodies of the guards through the door at the back of the tavern into the alley, where they stripped the uniforms off the men and bound them with rope and gagged them. By the looks of the narrow alley, Aiden guessed few people came back this way, so it would be a while before these men were discovered. He lifted the red military coats from the guards and handed the second one to Charles.

"This bastard is too small," Charles complained when he tried on the first coat. "Switch with me." Aiden tossed him the one he'd been about to put on. Charles wasn't as tall, but his shoulders were broader than Aiden's.

Once they were dressed, they went back to the tavern, much to the dismay of the poor barkeeper. Then they exited the tavern back onto the street. Ashton and Cedric had acquired similar military guard uniforms. Aiden didn't see any sign of the hired men who'd come with them. He guessed that Ashton had given them orders, and his plan, such as it was, was fully in motion.

Aiden headed straight for the castle, and he and Charles were able to pass through with only a brief nod to the guards by the entrance. It seemed Yuri had recruited men who were more lax in security than the guards who had likely gone with Anna's brother during the initial fight at the Summer Palace. It was possible that Yuri's forces were stretched, then, and he'd sent his more trained soldiers into the countryside to keep down any rebellions while recruiting local men to stand guard in places he it was less likely rebel forces would attack.

The courtyard was empty, save for some guards milling about and a few servants. Aiden kept his breathing calm as he approached a large door that seemed to open into the main part of the castle itself. It was clear Yuri felt there was no threat from rebels here, and Aiden dreaded to think why Anna's uncle could feel so confident.

Aiden and Charles moved quickly through the corridors in the castle but tried not to show their haste. He eavesdropped on some of the conversations of the men around him. A pair of guards at the end of one hall were laughing. From what Aiden could understand, they were mocking Prince Alexei. Taking a risk, he walked up to them and spoke in Danish.

"I have been recruited from the country. Do you know where I should report?"

One of the guards studied him curiously, clearly noticing his odd accent and stiff grasp of the language. "What part of the country?"

"Near Nalia." That was the village where they had purchased the horses when they'd first landed, and it had a blended population from many other countries due to it being close to the border. Coming from such a place would hide Aiden's odd accent.

"You should report to Lieutenant Lewig, but I'd say wait a day—Captain Fain is about to get married to the princess."

The other guard started laughing again.

"What's so funny?" Aiden asked, faking a smile.

The first guard spoke. "The prince gave himself up two days ago, and the rebellion's in disarray. We're to have a wedding and an execution tomorrow. Captain Fain promised as much wine and ale from the palace stores as we want tomorrow."

Aiden, still feigning a smile, clapped the nearest guard on the shoulder. "That's good news indeed." He didn't know who this Captain Fain was, but he planned to kill the man.

As he and Charles walked away to find the dungeons,

Charles asked him what had put the guards in such a good mood.

"The prince surrendered a few days ago, and the rebellion's collapsing. He's in the dungeons. My guess is the dungeons will be this way if I know anything about castles. They plan to kill Alexei tomorrow . . . and Anna is to marry someone named Captain Fain."

"Oh . . ." Charles's eyes narrowed. "Those louts weren't very intelligent, were they? I wonder why Anna's uncle hired such idiots?"

Aiden shrugged. "Often brute strength doesna need intelligence. As long as a man has an army of mean-spirited men, they don't have to be smart as long as they can fight. I double these men are real soldiers either, but instead locals recruited to handle security. I imagine some of these men were desperate enough to join to feed their families, and the rest simply like to stir up trouble."

"Ah." Charles nodded. "Of course Yuri would send his seasoned soldiers out into the forest to hunt down Prince Alexei."

After casually searching the castle, they found the staircase that led into the dungeons behind a tall, faded tapestry. They slipped behind the fabric and then crept down the stairs. Aiden's breath quickened as he prepared to meet dozens of guards who would be watching over the prince. They'd no doubt have to fight their way out.

But there weren't any guards. The row of cells was empty except for one at the far end. A young man sat on the floor with his back to the wall. Torchlight illuminated his face as he glanced at them. When he saw their military uniforms, he pushed himself up to stand and face them, raising his chin proudly. Aiden's heart stuttered as he reached the cell and saw that Prince Alexei was so similar to Anna in his features that Aiden's chest clenched with fresh heartache.

"Prince Alexei?" Aiden whispered the name carefully.

The young man's gaze was wary. "What do you want?" he growled, clearly thinking they were Yuri's men.

"My name is Aiden Kincade. Anna sent me."

Alexei still looked suspicious. "Anna? How do you know my sister?"

Aiden slipped into English, letting his Scottish accent roll. "Her ship wrecked, and she washed up on the shores of Scotland. I was the one who found her. My friends and I have come to rescue ye both."

"You must save Anna, not me. Go before they find you down here," Alexei warned.

"Not without ye." Aiden approached the cell, studying it for a way to open the door. "Who has the keys?"

A cold voice echoed from the end of the hallway. "I'm afraid I have them."

"Fain, you bastard!" Alexei cursed at a man who stood at the base of the stairs leading out of the dungeons. The man held a pistol, and behind him a dozen guards moved to block Charles and Aiden's way out.

"Who are your friends, Alexei?" the man called Fain asked in English. He'd clearly overheard Aiden's words.

"They aren't friends. Just drunk fools who wanted to see a prince behind bars. Take them away and throw them out of the castle," Alexei growled.

Fain's laugh was even colder than his voice as he and his

guards now filled the aisle between the cells, pinning Charles and Aiden against the dead end of the dungeon.

"Well, in that case, they can share your appointment with an ax tomorrow." Fain gestured to one of his guards, who took the keys Fain held out and unlocked the cell door opposite the prince.

"Get inside," Fain commanded. "Or I'll shoot you where you stand and the prince can watch you bleed out for the rest of the day."

Charles shot Aiden a look asking a silent question: *Do we fight?*

Aiden shook his head in a silent response: *Not yet.* There were too many of them and so little room to maneuver, no hope to fight them all.

Aiden stepped into the open cell, followed by Charles. The door clanged shut, and a guard locked them in. Only when they were safely behind bars did Fain approach them, curious.

"You are not Ruritanian . . ."

"Oh, this one's clever," Charles snorted.

Fain's eyes snapped to him with deadly rage. "English . . . interesting. I wonder how you got here?"

"We took a wrong turn at Copenhagen," said Charles.

Fain was not amused. "Perhaps torture will loosen that tongue of yours."

Charles grinned like a jackal. "I went to school at *Eton.* If you think you know what torture is, you have no idea."

Fain ignored him and turned his focus to Aiden. "You, however . . . You aren't English."

Aiden curled his fingers around the bars. "I'm far worse. I'm a Scot." As he spoke, he let part of the rage he kept buried inside leak out. The iron bars creaked ominously beneath his powerful grip.

"You know what the English say about Scots?" Charles added, his words soaked in deep humor. "You can't kill them, you can only slow them down a bit."

Aiden kept his gaze on Fain, and he noticed the slightest twitch in the man's face.

"I think killing both of you tomorrow along with the prince will be easy enough." Fain's expression was smug.

"It will be *so* much fun to disappoint you, old boy," Charles said.

"I'll enjoy the pleasure of killing you myself," Fain promised.

"Not if I have the pleasure first," Aiden said. "Sleep well, Captain. It will be yer last. When ye reach hell tomorrow, ye can tell the devil himself I sent ye."

Fain stared at Aiden a long moment before he turned and walked away, his guards following behind him.

Charles looked at Aiden with new respect. "You're supposed to be the nice Kincade brother . . ."

"There is no nice Kincade brother—I'm merely the *quiet* one."

"Ah," Charles muttered. "They do say it's the quiet ones you have to worry about. But still, you seem to be taking things rather personal . . . I mean, beyond the whole 'captured and going to be executed tomorrow' thing."

"It *is* personal. That man is the bastard who plans to marry my wife."

"Excuse me?" Alexei interrupted them. "Wife? You mean *my* sister?"

"Aye." Aiden was still squeezing the bars, listening with satisfaction as the iron groaned.

"*You* married my sister?"

Aiden looked at Alexei and nodded after a long minute.

"How did that happen? She was betrothed to Lord Erich of Prussia . . ."

"'Tis a long tale," Aiden warned.

Alexei glanced about his cell. "We don't seem to have any other pressing engagements."

"Aye." Aiden sat down and got comfortable. "Fair enough."

"I love a good tale," Charles said with a look of childish delight, even though he knew the story already.

***

Ashton let the body of the guard fall limp at his feet. Cedric took the guard's legs and dragged him out of sight. Ashton took a person's life seriously, but he didn't hold back when the men he fought were involved in evil deeds. As he and the others had moved through the village outside the fortress, he'd heard whispers about the murder of entire villages, burning women and children alive.

While much of the castle was being garrisoned by locals from the village, either desperate for work or afraid of repercussions if they refused, a number of the dangerous former royal guards still remained. They were the ones Ashton knew they had to worry about. The ones who needed to be dealt with first. The conscripts were more likely to scatter or surrender to any significant show of force once the fighting started.

Ashton knew he could be a cold bastard, but the idea of anyone killing women and children set a rage burning inside him. That left no mercy for the guards who'd aided Yuri in such bloodshed.

"How many more do you think we can remove without being detected?" Cedric asked. "They don't seem to be that aware of how many guards they even have inside the fortress. I've never seen such an unorganized lot of men in my life. I'm rather surprised Yuri has stayed in power."

Ashton had noticed that too, the seeming haphazard behavior of the guards. It was as though Yuri had managed to recruit the worst men, both in intelligence and temperament. It would make Ashton's job easier, but it left him worried about the unpredictability of the patrols, among other things.

"I want as many of the seasoned guards to be subdued," Ashton said. "The rest will likely run or switch sides if our men gain the upper hand once the fighting starts. Some of these new guards are villagers, most of them just men trying to survive, and I won't have innocent blood on our hands. We need to be in control of the castle tomorrow. We need to stop that wedding, as well as the execution."

"What about Aiden and Charles?" Cedric asked.

They'd heard the guards talking about two Englishmen who were locked up in the dungeons with the prince, but Ashton knew that they couldn't save their friends right now. They'd have to wait out the night.

"We'll handle that tomorrow as well. I don't want Yuri to notice anything is amiss. Right now, we have to keep an eye on the captain of the guard. We'll blend in with the servants and start gaining their trust. I want eyes and ears on Yuri and the captain, and the servants will help us with that."

"Right . . ." Cedric kicked the guard's booted foot deeper into the closet they had shoved him into. By the looks of the cobwebs inside, the closet must rarely be opened, which meant the body would go unseen for at least a little while.

Yuri was clearly a man who did not care about the commoners, and no doubt the palace servants feared for their lives. Ashton had every intention of enlisting their aid in what was to come.

They could lock crucial doors when a signal was given, forcing the royal guards to go down the paths Ashton wanted them to go, or they could create distractions. He didn't want to risk servants' lives, he knew they weren't fighters, but they could contribute in other ways.

"We have work to do," Ashton said before the two of them slipped away down a darkened corridor, merging with the shadows.

***

Anna tensed as someone knocked at her bedchamber door.

"Who is it?"

"Your future husband. I've come to escort you to dinner," Fain said.

Anna wanted to hurl a vase at the closed door, but no matter how good it might feel at the moment, it wouldn't help her situation. Fain wasn't her husband. Her husband was back in England. Anna would have given anything in that moment to be in London, in bed with Aiden, his strong arms wrapped around her as he told her stories and made love to her. She would have given her soul for one more kiss . . . but even that was a bargain beyond her reach.

She went to the bedchamber door, reluctantly opening it. Since she had arrived at the Winter Palace, she hadn't been locked in, but was always followed by at least two guards.

Fain stood in the corridor wearing a black evening coat and trousers. She was so used to seeing him in uniform that it startled her to see him dressed as a nobleman. He'd even taken care to comb his wavy black hair, and the scent of cologne drifted toward her, burning her nose.

His eyes roamed over her, approving of the dark-green velvet gown she wore. It was one of her older dresses, most likely found in a trunk in an attic, but she was grateful for the long sleeves and full skirts to keep her warm in her room, since the servants weren't allowed to light a fire in her chamber, nor was she allowed to have any candles. Everyone must assume she might set the palace alight in revenge. Honestly, the thought had crossed her mind.

"You look well," Fain said, attempting a chivalrous tone.

Anna stared at him. Did he honestly expect her to swoon at his compliments when he was the man who had murdered her parents?

"When I compliment you, Anna, it is in your best interest to thank me." His tone held a warning, but she was in no mood to placate him.

"Captain, you seem to forget I'm not a trained spaniel who sits upon command. I am the daughter of a king, the king *you* murdered. Within my body beats the heart of a queen. I'm not a creature to be broken. If you want a wife who bows to your every command and whimpers in fear when you scowl, then you have chosen poorly."

She pushed past him and began to walk toward the stairs that led to the dining room. For a moment she didn't think he would follow her, but his boots rang out on the stone a moment before he grasped her arm. He spun her into the nearest wall, pinning her there and wrenching her arm painfully behind her.

"If I but twist another inch, *princess*, your arm will snap. And a broken arm will not stop me from claiming your body after we are wed."

Anna twisted in the direction that alleviated the pain in her arm, and broke free of the lock he had on her, but in doing so, it brought her face-to-face with him. His eyes widened slightly in surprise that she had managed to reposition herself out of what he likely believed was a hold that should have kept her still.

"I may not live that long," she said and shoved him. She aimed for his shoulder, knocking him off balance more easily than hitting him square in the chest. "Now, leave me be so I can enjoy dinner." She once again left the captain standing there staring at her in utter bafflement.

The few extra seconds it took him to recover gave her just enough time to hide the dagger she'd just stolen from him in her skirts. He had several blades tucked on his body, and she prayed he wouldn't miss this one. Now all she had to do was survive dinner without him noticing she had stolen a weapon.

Thankfully, the heavy velvet gown had a hidden pocket sewn deep into the folds. Nearly all of her gowns did. They had been created for the express purpose of concealing a pistol or a dagger. Her father had taken her safety seriously.

Anna smiled as she reached the dining room. When she saw her uncle, she wiped her face of any hint of triumph, and instead looked defeated. If she was to dine with devils, she had to beat them at their own game.

CHAPTER 17

Anna's hands trembled as she held still in front of a tall cheval mirror while a maid finished lacing up the back of the pale-blue satin wedding gown she wore. The gown had been taken from one of the minor noble families who had a daughter close to her age. Most of Anna's court gowns had burned in the Summer Palace, and when she'd insisted on a fancy gown, in hopes of slowing down the wedding, her uncle had apparently taken what he wanted from someone else.

Her uncle had delighted in telling her over dinner how he had made the noble families fall in line by executing "a few" of the eldest sons of the most powerful men in the country. Facing threats against the lives of their remaining children and wives, the noblemen had conceded to Yuri's control of the throne. Alone in her room after dinner, she'd wept for those young men, men who'd been friends with her brother. Men who were good and kind, men who would have followed her brother to the ends of the earth. They'd paid for their loyalty to Alexei with their lives. Then as her tears had dried, Anna had felt a rage unlike anything else in her life burn bright as a newborn star in the sky. She would have vengeance on her uncle, Fain, and all of the other men who'd helped kill her family and hurt her people.

Now in the light of a new day, Anna still felt that burning desire to get revenge, but she was thinking more clearly than she had been the previous night. Drawing in a deep breath, Anna stared at her reflection in the mirror and saw a stranger looking back. In an hour, she would be Captain Fain's property, and by tonight her brother would be dead. If ever hell existed on the mortal plane, this was surely it. But she would not give in to this fate without a fight worthy of a queen of Ruritania.

"I'm finished, Your Highness," the maid said, her brown eyes welling up with tears. "You look beautiful, but . . ." The young woman didn't continue. Anna understood what she dared not say. She should not be marrying Captain Fain. "Don't give up hope, Your Highness," the woman whispered so softly Anna almost thought she'd imagined it. "There are those who would help you . . . if the time came to fight."

Anna grasped the woman's hands and held them, their eyes meeting as she let the woman know she understood.

"Well, at least you look presentable." Her uncle's voice from the doorway made both her and the maid flinch. She looked beautiful, but she knew he would never pay her a compliment. Yuri's joy in life was cruelty. He'd always been mean-spirited, but now that he ruled Ruritania, it seemed to have magnified.

"Your betrothed is waiting for you in the great hall,"

Yuri said with far too much pleasure. "It's time for your wedding."

Anna quietly thanked the maid and followed her uncle out of the bedchamber. She took the stairs carefully, not because of her appearance or her gown, but because she had Fain's small dagger tucked in the garter above her stockings on her right thigh and didn't want it to shake loose. She resigned herself to the fact that today she would kill Fain or she would perish trying. She was surprised he hadn't noticed it was missing. Perhaps he had, but hadn't made the connection that she was the one who'd stolen it. Hopefully, he would continue to underestimate her.

When she reached the bottom step and walked toward the great hall, two guards opened the doors for Yuri, and she came behind him as she saw the crowds of noble families lining the interior of the hall. They had no doubt been required to attend her wedding. The white-blue-and-gold banners that had hung from the vaulted ceilings of the hall had been torn down and replaced with the red-and-black banners that represented her uncle's rule.

Fain waited ahead of her, and just beyond him stood a single throne. Her mother's throne was gone. The sight of that missing chair somehow cut Anna deeper than any of the desecrations Yuri had made in the great hall. Yuri believed in himself and no one else. He would likely not take a queen, at least not a willing one. Perhaps his rule would end without heirs, and the world would right itself again. That thought gave her a small measure of hope.

She held her head high as she walked alone down the center of the great hall toward her fate. There was no sword above her, no dark woods, no death of the man she loved. Only the death of her soul loomed in the future.

When she reached the front of the hall, she faced her uncle, who was already seated on the red and gold chair, lounging comfortably on his stolen throne. Fain gave an icy smile as she stopped a few feet from him. A nervous priest stood in attendance, and the poor man swallowed audibly as he clutched a Bible in his hands and tugged at his collar.

"You may proceed in a moment, Father. The bride must first see our esteemed guests." Yuri waved a hand to the guards near the back of the hall. She turned, her heart pounding as three men were escorted down the center aisle and shoved to their knees beside her on the stone floor. She'd expected to see her brother, but the other two men couldn't possibly be there . . .

Charles, the Earl of Lonsdale, and . . . Aiden . . . were staring straight ahead, not making eye contact with her. Their stubborn avoidance of her, rather than upset her, kept her calm and her thoughts clear. No doubt they didn't wish her uncle to know she knew them. She had to play along too, if there was any chance she could free them.

"I find it very curious that two Englishmen would be in my dungeon attempting to free your brother, princess," Yuri said in that infuriatingly bored tone. He spoke English to them since most of the nobles in the crowd were fluent in the language.

"I'm not English," Aiden growled. "I'm Scottish."

"It doesn't matter," Yuri said. "You will soon be dead and thrown in an unmarked grave. So, is that all your meeting with the king got you?" Yuri asked Anna. "Two fools to play the hero?" Yuri then looked to Fain. "I told you George wouldn't have the stomach to interfere."

Anna wanted to plead for their lives, but doing so would only make her uncle more likely to kill them.

"Let's begin." Yuri clapped his hands and pointed a finger at the trembling priest. The priest began his service, but a minute into his long preamble, Fain interrupted him.

"Move to the *relevant* parts, Father."

The priest fumbled briefly and then asked if Fain agreed to take Anna as his wife. Fain said yes. Then Anna was asked simply to honor and obey Fain and not whether she actually *agreed* to be his wife. Anna spoke a simple yes, but of course it was a lie. She was already another man's wife. The vows made by the fairy pools were binding to her. Fain might claim her body, but the rest of her was free of him and there was nothing he could do to change that.

"Does anyone ob-object to these two marrying?" the priest stuttered.

"Of course I do!" Charles spoke up. "This is rot and nonsense."

Anna, stunned, turned to look at the English earl. He shot her a wink, but one of the guards struck him hard on the back of the head. He grunted but took the blow easily, where most men would have doubled over in pain.

"Please note my objection as well, Father," Aiden added. "The princess already *has* a husband."

"She—she does?" the poor man dared to ask. "Who?"

"Me," Aiden said as he turned to look not at Anna, but Fain. Anna saw challenge in his eyes. The kind, compassionate man she loved was, right now, buried beneath violence.

Fain drew his sword out of its scabbard, and his gaze fell on Anna. "Is this true?"

Anna's lips parted, and her hesitation sealed Aiden's fate.

"Then I shall marry a widow. Take that one out to the courtyard. I will deal with him in a moment." Two of the nearby guards dragged Aiden away.

"If this is how you treat visitors, I believe I'll cancel my next visit to Ruritania," Charles muttered loudly. A few people nearby in the crowd dared to laugh before they were silenced. Yuri stood and walked down the steps to stand before Charles and Alexei.

"I think it's time we had our execution. Fain, you may take your bride now. I'm sure you wish to consummate your marriage."

Fain grasped Anna's arm, and pain from where Gustav's bullet had grazed her a few days before made her cry out.

"Anna!" Aiden bellowed. He fought the men who were already dragging him away.

"No . . ." She spoke the word to him and him alone. "*No*, Aiden," she repeated. She wanted to make him save his strength, to just give her time to find a way to save him.

"Captain, spare that man and the Englishman. He is not truly my husband. He is but a lovesick fool who thinks a declaration of affection is binding. It isn't. You and I both know, I need a marriage to a strong man with power. It's what a princess deserves." She softened her voice and lowered her gaze, not in submission but to hide the anger she knew he wouldn't miss in her gaze.

Fain held up a hand to stay the men attempting to drag Aiden away.

"*Now* you see the advantage of marrying me?" Fain asked, his voice just as soft.

"Yes," she said as she curbed her anger and lifted her face to peer up at the captain from beneath her lashes.

"What would you have me do with these men? Especially the one who claims to be your husband?"

"Put them on a ship bound for England. Send them away. They would not dare come back. And since he is not my husband, he has no legal claim to me." Anna felt Aiden's eyes on her, and she knew he understood that her words were empty. Those vows at the fairy pool were etched on her heart so deeply they would never be undone. But Fain would never know that.

Fain seemed to briefly consider it, and then he chuckled darkly and looked at Yuri. "She is a convincing liar. I almost believed her."

"I warned you, women are duplicitous creatures," Yuri said. "Take your bride away, Fain, and do as you will. I will see these three men dead within the hour. You have two days to enjoy the girl, then you must report back here for duty." Yuri dismissed Fain and Anna with a wave of his hand.

Anna was pulled away from the dais despite the priest's insistence that the ceremony was not finished. Fain dragged her from the hall and out to the courtyard, where a coach waited for them. Fain wrenched the door open and shoved her inside before climbing in after her.

"I will enjoy you however I like, princess, and it's in your best interest to please me."

Fain shouted at the coach driver to move. The horses bolted, and Anna fell back against the seat. The dagger was still strapped to her thigh, out of sight. All she had to do was wait for the right moment to strike.

***

Aiden and Charles were shoved to their knees on the execution platform.

"Well, this is not how I imagined dying," Charles muttered. "I always thought I'd go out in a duel, or perhaps a noble battle fighting the French. Bloody shame, this is."

Anna's brother was already in front of the chopping block, his face blank of emotion. Aiden knew what the young man must be thinking about.

Anna was in the hands of the man who had murdered her parents. None of them wanted to think about the horrors she would face as soon as Fain had her completely alone. Aiden tried to calm down and think rationally, but his blood was roaring in his ears. All he wanted to do was go after his wife and save her.

The gathered crowd was quiet, the nobles forced outside to watch. Alexei's hands were bound behind his back. The executioner towered over him as he tested the edge of his sword with a fingertip.

"This is bloody medieval. Even the French use a guillotine," Charles said scornfully, but no one but Aiden seemed to hear him. Not that Aiden was fully listening. He was focused on Yuri, who stood on the platform facing the crowd.

"Today, you shall witness the end of the old ways that held us back. Tomorrow, Ruritania will become a nation that others will fear and respect. We will show our might by growing our army. Growing our borders. This is Ruritania's future," Yuri declared proudly, then faced the executioner.

"You may begin."

The executioner pushed Alexei's neck down onto the block and leaned in close, as if to say something to him. Alexei's jaw flexed and the rope that bound his hands creaked as he fought his bonds.

Aiden's heart pounded against his ribs as he pulled at the rope around his own wrists. The rope began to tighten as he pulled on it. The executioner took a few steps back and practiced his swing. His face was hidden beneath a mask that made him a target for Aiden's blind rage. Aiden had but one instant to notice that the executioner's boots were shiny and . . . expensive looking? Not like the sort of boots an executioner in a rural country would have.

The executioner lifted his blade high in the air. Aiden's anger roared out of him like a tidal wave, smashing into the rocks and sending a wall of water towering into the air. The ancient blood in him, the blood that came from the Vikings who had settled Scotland centuries ago, left a berserker's power in him. Always before he had held back, but not today. His hands would have the blood of his enemies upon them before the day was through.

The ropes on his wrists tore free against the sudden pressure he forced on them, and he surged to his feet with a mighty roar. But he didn't aim for the executioner— instead, he flung himself at Anna's uncle.

Aiden hit the would-be king hard, sending both of them flying off the platform. He didn't give Yuri a chance to fight back. He swung his fist down, striking the man.

Blood exploded from the Yuri's shattered nose. Aiden raised his fist to strike again.

"Aiden! Go after Anna!" someone shouted.

Aiden looked up at the platform. Alexei was on his feet, and the executioner stood beside him. The man had ripped his mask off to reveal that it was Godric who had yelled at him.

"Go, man! We have control of the castle. Save the princess!" Godric shouted again. As he shouted this, men in the crowd were throwing back their farmer's cloaks and revealing the white-and-blue uniforms of Alexei's loyal guards.

Aiden spotted his brothers among the men who'd been hiding in the crowd. They shot him quick nods that he should go, and then they dove into the fray with war cries born of their Highland blood. The battle broke out between the contingent of guards Yuri had with him and Alexei's men. With a breath of relief, Aiden knew that he could leave and go after Anna.

Aiden left Yuri on the ground. The man was screaming for his guards, but none came to his aid.

A farmer in the crowd grasped Aiden's arm. "You, Englishman!" Aiden didn't bother to correct him. "I have a good horse, a fast horse. Go! Rescue our princess." The man pulled Aiden with him out of the courtyard. Aiden glanced back once to see Alexei had leapt off the platform, now wielding a sword. As he advanced on his uncle, the people of Ruritania closed in around them.

"Here, this way." The farmer led Aiden to a small stable outside the castle courtyard and quickly brought out a horse. The beast only wore a bridle with reins, no saddle.

"I saddle him for you," the man said in broken English.

"No time." Aiden clicked his tongue, and the horse stood still as he swung himself up onto the horse's back by gripping the base of the horse's mane. Aiden nodded at the stunned farmer, then dug his boots into the horse's sides when it stood. He prayed the horse was as swift as the man claimed. He thundered down the road, praying he would not lose the trail of the coach on the path.

***

"Where are we going?" Anna asked. The coach had just passed by the fields beyond the castle. She knew they were going north toward the Summer Palace, but they couldn't be going there.

Fain unbuttoned his military coat and tossed it to the side. "I have a small home waiting for us. We will spend two nights there before I must return to the castle."

She stared at the coat that he had removed. Next, he took his sword off his belt and set it on the seat across from them as well. "What are you doing?" she asked, though she already suspected she knew the answer.

"I am taking no chances. You will learn who your master is, and I will break you like any good horse until you can be ridden without a fight."

He reached to grab her, and she doubled over, gagging and retching. Nothing came from her but dry heaves, but still he drew back in clear revulsion. He opened the coach window and shouted for the driver to stop.

The moment the vehicle stopped moving, Anna opened the door and stumbled outside, still gagging, but it was all a ruse. The coach had stopped. Now all she had to do was wait for the right moment. She continued to pretend to be sick while she fussed with her skirts as if overheated from the nausea, and in so doing she freed the dagger that was strapped to her thigh.

"That's enough." Fain was on her, grabbing her left arm. She spun around and plunged the dagger into him. But the pain from her bullet wound weakened her strike, and he was able to knock her hand aside before she could plunge the blade into his heart. Her dagger sank only a few inches into his shoulder instead, staining his white shirt crimson with blood.

"So that's where it went," Fain snarled as he gripped her wrist and squeezed until at last she released the dagger.

She was shocked by how unaffected he was by the wound she'd inflicted.

"You disappoint me, Anna. It's clear you don't know when you have been beaten." Fain leered at her with cold violence in his eyes. In his gaze, she saw the bodies of her parents, the blood of her people, and the burning of her home.

"You haven't beaten me," she said. "Even my death will be a victory over you." She flung her head forward, striking him in just the right spot. He grunted at the unexpected impact and let go of her wrist. She ran. It was the only choice she had left. He was too large and too strong compared to her, and with an injured arm she could not use any of the protective moves she had learned from her brother and William.

Straight ahead of her was a forest . . . the dark forest of her nightmares. Too late, she realized that the visions she had seen at the fairy pools might yet come to pass. She bunched up her skirts to run faster.

Fain charged through the undergrowth, shouting her name. The sound echoed around her, booming off the trees and confusing her as to where he was. She stopped twice, listening to his howls of rage, before continuing on in the direction she hoped was the safest path away from him. The trees seemed to all look alike, and she quickly became lost in the dense foliage. She stopped again to catch her breath as she leaned against a gnarled old tree. In the distance, she saw a shape that filled her with dread. A wishing well. *The* wishing well . . .

"It can't be . . ." She spun to run in the opposite direction, but Fain broke through the trees ahead of her, and in his hand was his sword. Fain must've gone back to the coach for his sword. Fate had caught up with her, it seemed, but she would not make it easy for Fain to kill her.

"Give up, princess!" Fain shouted as he spotted her. She broke away from the tree she'd been hiding behind and sprinted toward the well. She had no choice but to run past it, but she would not dare stop there.

A hand grabbed her hair, and she screamed as Fain yanked and threw her to the ground. She landed on her stomach, the dark rich soil like black dust beneath her fingers as she braced herself against the fall. Flashes of her visions from her dreams and what she'd seen within the fairy pools blurred with the reality of what she knew would be her final moments.

"Kneel, princess." Fain forced her to her knees by gripping her hair again. "If you will not yield, you can join the rest of your family." Just as he lifted the blade up in the air, a voice cried out, filling the forest around them.

"Anna!" It was Aiden!

Fain spun as Aiden broke through the clearing on horseback. He slid off and charged at Fain with a short sword in his hand.

"Aiden . . . no!" She struggled to her feet and threw herself at Fain as he raised his sword to strike at Aiden.

Fain struck Anna's face with the back of his hand, and she fell like a stone. She didn't pass out, but the pain was so fierce that her head felt as if it had been split open. She panted and blinked hard as she tried to banish the black dots clouding her vision.

Aiden and Fain were grappling, their swords abandoned on the ground. Anna crawled toward it, her fingers digging into the earth to propel her to move faster. Every second was agony. She couldn't lift the sword, but she could drag it away, hide it, so that Aiden had a fair chance. The second her fingers curled around the hard leather-bound grip, she heard a shout of triumph.

She turned and saw Fain had Aiden pinned against the wall of the well. The hilt of a blade jutted out of Aiden's stomach. Fain sneered as he stepped back and pulled the dagger out. It was the dagger she had stolen, the one she had tried to kill Fain with. Horror began to suffocate her. She couldn't breathe. Aiden had been hurt by the blade *she* had stolen. She had tried to deny fate, and fate was proving its point that it would not be denied.

"Aiden!" she rasped, her voice hoarse.

Fain sneered at her, then Aiden. "So this is the man you chose . . ." Fain smiled coldly at Aiden. "She will never be yours." He struck Aiden in the jaw, and Aiden stumbled back. Everything seemed to slow down as Anna screamed a warning, but it was too late.

Aiden fell back over the edge of the well and vanished into the darkness of that terrible void.

Anna's world closed in around her, shrinking from a vast life of endless joys and possibilities to one small, dark space that barely left her room to breathe. She had survived losing her parents, her home, being separated from her brother, leaving everything behind, even her own memories.

But Aiden . . . Aiden was the one thing she could not lose, the one thing she had jealously guarded as her gift from the heavens. But she'd thought she could deny destiny, and now it had cost her everything.

"You will kill him," a woman's voice said in her head. *"But death is perhaps not the end . . ."*

Anna lifted her face up as Fain stepped toward her. Her hands were still on the blade. She tried to stand, tried and failed to wield the sword, but the pain in her head and arm were too much for her, and she was off balance. He wrestled it from her hands. She collapsed, her knees too weak to fight anymore. Fain lifted the blade, the dying light of the setting sun flashing a stark red-gold over the steel of the sword.

Her gaze fell on the well. If fate had any mercy left, she prayed that her soul would join Aiden's in that quiet, dark mystery of things that continued beyond death.

CHAPTER 18

A iden was sinking into darkness. The cold black well water swirled over his head as he was lost in that place between the living and the dead. Every moment of his life, both large and small, good and bad, played across his mind in brilliant colors, as if in one final quest to find meaning in it all.

He felt each lash of his father's whipping cane, the cool water of the fairy pools knitting his soul back together, the smiles on his brothers' faces as the three of them ran free in the hills in those rare moments when they knew peace. The feel of the fresh heather in his hands as he presented a bouquet to his mother. The way she smiled as if that simple act had taken every sorrow away from her, even if only for a few hours.

He relived the night Rosalind had fled into the darkness, and the letter he'd received a month later saying she had married an Englishman and would not be coming home. He remembered his father's deathbed, watched as the man drew his last breath and a flame guttered on a candle that burned too low nearby.

It seemed as if his life had only ever held darkness, but then he saw the light, the love that had always been there for him. His friends and siblings had never truly left him. It was he who had left the world . . . until Anna. She had chased him back into the light. She had given him back his life, and now he had failed her . . .

"Death is perhaps not the end . . ." The Romani woman's voice echoed around his head. She had never said those words to him that night she'd cast her warning, when he'd been but a boy, yet he heard her voice now clear as a bell, as though she were speaking in his ear. *"Pass through the water and save her . . ."*

He pushed away the encroaching darkness and the weariness of death stealing through his limbs. His hands spread out, catching on the rough stones of the walls of the well, and he pulled himself up, breaking the surface of the water as if breaking the barrier between worlds. He gasped, drawing air into his lungs. That sweet, glorious air sent strength back into his arms and legs. He climbed, gripping the cracks and crevices with his fingers, and fought against the pain in his abdomen where the dagger had pierced him. His body shook violently with pain and weakness as he tried to force his way up the steep stones. The opening of the well seemed so far away, and he was so very tired, but the Romani woman's voice urged him ever onward.

"Save her."

He reached the top of the well. The last princess of Ruritania was on her knees, hands digging into the soil as Fain wielded a broadsword high over her head. The small dagger still gleamed red with Aiden's blood, abandoned on the ground by the base of the well. Aiden climbed over the top of the well and fell to his knees, grasping the dagger in his hand. Then he pulled back his arm and summoned the strength of every Kincade ancestor into that single throw.

The blade sailed true and sank deep into Fain's back. For a second, Aiden feared the blade hadn't gone deep enough. But then the broadsword slipped free of Fain's hands, and he stumbled a few steps before collapsing to the ground.

Aiden leaned back against the well, breathing hard as the pain in his lower belly grew too great for him to ignore. He covered the wound with his hand, trying to keep pressure on it. He didn't think the blade had gone that deep, since the dagger was small, but he wouldn't be sure until he saw a doctor.

"Anna . . . it's all right, lass," he gasped.

She opened her eyes and stared at him in shock. "Am I dead? Are we . . . ?" She blinked as tears rolled down her cheeks.

"No, lass. Ye're not dead." He held out his free hand to her. "Do ye trust me?"

Her tawny brown eyes moved from his face long enough to see his outstretched hand. Then she was on her feet, running to him, and she flung herself at him, wrapping her arms around his neck.

"*Oof.*" He winced as his wife settled against him and buried her face in his neck. He brushed the loose strands of her russet hair away from her face so he could kiss her cheek.

"You came back," she whispered over and over. He curled one arm tight around her.

"I promised I would never leave ye." He took in the scent of her hair, the soil, and the trees. The once frightening forest seemed to have softened around them, now feeling more like a peaceful ancient wood. A soft breeze blew in from the north that smelled of the ocean and dreams of distant hills and fairy pools. For the first time in his life, there was no room for sorrow. No room for the demons of the past to haunt him. There was only room for love and hope for the future.

He wasn't sure how long he and Anna sat by the old stone well, but after a time, she wiped her eyes and then kissed him sweetly upon his brow, then his closed eyelids, then his cheeks and finally his lips.

"You died for me."

"Only a little," he teased, but she didn't laugh.

"I tried to stop you from coming here . . . ," she sniffled.

"I'd die for ye a thousand times, lass," he vowed. "It's all right, Anna. We survived. We willna have any more dreams to fear now."

"You don't think so?" She still seemed unsure. It was understandable. They'd both had this nightmare countless times over the years.

"I think those dreams were a way of preparing us," he said. "I think it was meant to test our mettle, prepare us for when this day came and we'd have to fight to be with each other. It's over now."

Anna's eyes suddenly widened. "But it's not over, is it? Aiden, we have to go back. Alexei—"

"He's fine, my heart. When I left him, he was free. My brothers, Godric, and his friends were battling the guards."

She let out a long breath as her eyes misted. "I am so weary of death, of fighting. I hope it's truly over." She got to her feet and shook her skirts free of dirt and leaves.

"It is," Aiden promised.

Using the last of his strength, he pushed up against the well and braced one hand on it. He slowly turned and then peered down into the water. It had been black and fathomless when he was beneath its surface, but now it reflected the purpling skies above. Anna joined him by the edge and looked down into the well with him.

"It all seems so very strange," she said, her tone soft and a little wistful. "All these years we've wanted to avoid this moment, but in truth we've been running toward it."

"Toward each other," Aiden said. "And I'd do it all over again if it meant we'd be together." That was what life was. Every pain, every anguish, every lonely night and dawn of heartbreak were to fight toward the singular moments where the suffering ended and there was only joy and love. He realized now that joy had never truly been that far out of reach.

He remembered something his mother once said. "We fight on toward the dawn of new days and the hope of blessings those days bring."

He was a blessed man, and always had been. He had family, friends, and now the love of a woman he didn't deserve, but he would try to earn her love every day until he died.

Anna linked her arm with his and pressed her cheek

against his shoulder as she spoke to the enchanted well. "Thank you for granting my wish."

Aiden almost asked her what she'd wished for, but he was weary and his stomach hurt. He needed a doctor, and the walk to the Winter Palace would be too long.

"Can ye help me bind this wound?" he asked.

Anna examined the wound with anxious eyes, but her hands were steady as she ripped a long strip of cloth from her petticoats and circled his waist with it. Then she cinched it tight to stanch the bleeding.

"I think that will hold until we can reach the palace. We could try to find the coach Fain left on the road . . . Oh, look!" Anna pointed, her face full of surprise and delight. He saw across the clearing that the horse he had ridden here was grazing contentedly, eyeing them cautiously.

Aiden clicked his teeth, and the horse snorted and lifted its head before trotting over to them.

"Good lad," he praised and gave the horse a pat on the neck, then he clicked his teeth again and the horse nickered softly. Aiden helped Anna up before climbing up behind her. Then they headed back toward the road that would take them to the Winter Palace.

***

Anna held her breath as they reached the village. Scores of townsfolk filled the road, and many were crying, but she noticed there were smiles and hugs and laughter among the tears.

My people are free.

She knew that many of her uncle's men were out there, spread over the countryside, but they could be caught and dealt with soon enough. If her brother and William had the upper hand, they could round up those men or drive them out of Ruritania.

"Princess! Thank God you're alive!" William's joyous shout caught her attention as her brother's dear friend came beside their horse when they entered the courtyard.

"Hello, Will." He caught her waist and helped her down. "Where's my brother?"

Grinning, William pointed out Alexei standing with members of the League from London. "There."

Ashton and his friends had formed a circle, standing with crossed arms as they listened to whatever Alexei was saying. She saw with a pang of bittersweetness that her twin had changed over the last two months. He seemed more like a king and now carried the weight of their country's needs upon his shoulders.

But ruling Ruritania was not a right one should be born with, no matter what others might think. It was an honor to be given only to a man who would put the needs of all others above himself. Yuri had never understood that, but Alexei did.

Her brother's gaze drifted, and he halted whatever he'd been saying as he spotted her.

"Anna!" He bolted toward her and caught her in his arms. She buried her face against his chest, crying in relief. When she looked up at her brother, she saw he was crying too.

"You're all right?" he asked.

She managed a nod. Alexei looked past her to Aiden, who'd kept his distance.

"Thank you for saving my sister, Mr. Kincade."

"It was my honor, Your Majesty," Aiden replied.

Anna's throat constricted as powerful emotions warred within her.

"Anna, we must talk," Alexei said.

She turned to Aiden, but he waved a hand. "Go on, lass, I need to see to this." He held a hand against his abdomen, which was still bleeding. She didn't want to leave him, but the stubborn look on her husband's face told her he didn't want her to see whatever a surgeon would likely have to do to him. Not that a stubborn Scot could stop her from doing anything, but she did need to speak to Alexei soon.

"I don't want to leave you. You're hurt—" she began.

"*Go*, lass. I'll be fine." He gave her a gentle smile of reassurance before he walked toward Ashton and his brothers. Anna reluctantly followed her brother inside the castle. She'd speak to Alexei quickly, and then she'd go find her husband and see that he was all right.

"Where is Yuri?"

"Dead."

"Did you . . ."

Alexei gave a curt nod. "After you and Fain left, the executioner turned out to be a friend of yours—Godric. Apparently, the fellow and his friends won over the castle servants, and they assisted in the battle, along with William and my guards who'd snuck into the courtyard without being recognized. We had quite the fight. Yuri fled into the castle, and I chased him down. We fought and I won. The man is dead." Alexei didn't seem to want to say more than that, and Anna could feel her twin's grief at having to take a life. He was and always would be a kind and compassionate man, and while courageous, he did not like to kill.

She leaned in and curled her arms around her brother's neck and held him for a long moment. Alexei breathed a soft sigh as they broke apart.

"I'm so glad you came back, Anna. So damned glad," he confessed. "I couldn't have survived this without you." They walked in silence until they reached the great hall.

The hall was empty now yet felt strangely full of ghosts. Alexei sat at one of the long tables that had been pushed against the wall for Anna's ill-fated wedding to Fain, and Anna sat beside him. Alexei took her hands in his, holding them as he studied her.

"I plan to create a change in the royal charter and establish a constitutional monarchy. I would love for you to stay, to see our people through the coming days with me."

Anna held her breath, knowing she would soon face an uneasy choice.

"I will stay," she assured him, but in her heart she worried about Aiden. She knew he would stay with her, but this life, the life of a prince consort, would break his heart. To be away from his brothers, away from his wild Scottish mountains and glens, it was like taking his very soul away.

"Kincade told me all that befell you since we last parted." Her brother changed the subject, startling her. Aiden had told her brother everything that had happened, the good and the bad?

Anna's eyes burned. "He did?"

"We shared a *long* night in the dungeons together."

"Did he mention that we are married?"

"He did. But, Anna, he said he would not hold you to

the vows if you choose to marry someone else, like Lord Erich. He said he saw you dance with Erich in London and that, well . . . the pair of you would make a strong alliance by marriage between Ruritania and Prussia. I don't think he wishes to stand in the way of your duty. The choice is yours. He won't demand you return to Scotland."

My duty . . . Those two words had been on her shoulders since the moment she and Alexei had been born. Unlike her brother, she wasn't destined to be queen, but if Alexei died without an heir, any sons she had would be next in line for the throne. Even if she returned to Scotland, there would still be that knowledge that her children might one day rule Ruritania. But that didn't answer the question that Alexei had presented to her. Should she do the right thing for her country and marry Erich, or should she do the right thing for herself and uphold her vows to Aiden? And if she did . . . should they leave or should they stay?

Anna's shoulders dropped slightly. "What would you do?" she asked her twin.

Alexei's smile was rueful. "What *I* would do and what *you* would do are perhaps for the first time in our lives as twins very different answers. I accepted my role as king the moment I first fought against Yuri, the day the Summer Palace burned. That means I must always put this country first. But you . . . you don't have to.

"Just think on it. No decisions must be made until we settle the matter of Ruritania's future." Alexei squeezed her hands, smiling sadly before he looked down the hall at the unoccupied throne and the empty space where a second should be. "It will never be the same without them, will it?" He sounded almost like a lost child, but the vulnerability he showed only to her was quickly buried beneath a kingly composure.

"No, it won't. Sometimes I think perhaps it's all a bad dream and that I'll wake up tomorrow and everything will be just as it once was." A tear rolled down her cheek and dripped off her chin onto her sullied wedding gown. "But we cannot live in such fantasies." She'd never really understood what it would mean to face such a choice between duty and desire and that the weight of that choice would affect so many lives.

"I suppose we should get back. There's much to do," Alexei said.

Anna stood with her brother and had the strangest feeling that they weren't alone. As if the ghosts of the past were there with them, watching . . . waiting. Alexei rose, and they started to walk once more away from the single throne at the end of the room, and she felt the loss of her parents so deeply in that moment she couldn't breathe. She glanced over her shoulder at the empty golden chair and fought off fresh tears as her soul wept for the past. Then she turned to face the future.

***

"Well, you'll live," Ashton pronounced as he examined Aiden's wound. "You Scots have the devil's own luck."

Aiden lay on a table in a cottage that belonged to one of the merchants in the village. Beside Ashton, a doctor was opening a black medical bag and nodding in agreement. "Lord Lennox is right," the man said in heavily accented English. "The blade missed your organs, by some sheer bit of luck. It happens from time to time when the puncture is in the right spot. Your muscles are thick down there, and the silk shirt you were wearing did help slow the blade a bit. The Mongols used to wear silk to battle for that very purpose—"

"Doctor . . ." Ashton gently interrupted the beginning of the doctor's historical lecture.

"Right, my apologies. As I was saying, it was harder for the blade to reach anything vital."

"That's a relief." Aiden laid his head back down on the table.

"You'll still need stitching," the doctor warned. "And you must watch out for fever."

"Stitch away, Doctor. Just give me some whiskey first."

Ashton laughed. "Find the man a drink," he called out to the crowd of Ashton's friends standing around.

"Right here." Charles pulled a silver flask out of his coat and handed it to Aiden, who took a long draw before he sighed and lay back down on the table. Brock and Brodie were on either side of his shoulders, looking on with concern as the doctor started to stitch up the wound. Despite the pain, Aiden only made a few small sounds of discomfort. This was nothing compared to the things his father had done once a upon a time . . .

"Ashton . . ." Aiden grunted, trying to ignore the sting of the needle. "How did Godric end up in the executioner's uniform? I didn't think he and the others would reach us in time."

"After we left London, Lord Morrey said he'd follow us with backup forces. He told Godric and the others from our group to leave that same night we did. Godric and his half of his men arrived only half a day after we did, and they met up with Alexei's second in command, a fellow named William. William had been marshaling the prince's rebel army and was planning to storm the castle to stop the execution. Cedric and I managed to work our way through the palace posing as servants and gained their trust to help when the battle broke out. We learned you and Charles were in the dungeon, so we met with the others and hatched a plan to stop the execution and fight Yuri's men. After you rode off to save Anna, William's forces revealed themselves in the courtyard and fought the guards still left here in the palace. With the help of the servants, we were able to funnel the guards into a part of the castle and trap them. Then they faced a surrender-or-die situation. Naturally, they surrendered," Ashton said with no small amount of pride.

"And Yuri?" Aiden asked. The last thing he'd seen was the villagers and Alexei closing in on the man.

"Alexei chased his uncle into the great hall, and they dueled with swords. Yuri perished in the fight."

Some of the tension left Aiden's body. The threat to Anna was gone at last.

"Morrey's forces will be here any day, and once they are, we'll make sure they can round up the remainder of Yuri's men in the countryside and establish order. Villages need rebuilding, and the men and women of Ruritania need food and work. Morrey's men will help them rebuild what Yuri destroyed," Ashton added.

"We'll all go home soon, brother." Brock gave Aiden's shoulder a squeeze.

Not all of us, Aiden thought. That was what Aiden was afraid of. It meant either staying here with Anna, being parted from the land he loved and his family, or Anna having to choose her country over love. No matter what, not all of them would be going home.

But in truth, it was no choice. If Anna chose to stay married to him, he would live here with her. No matter how much he would miss his home, his animals, his friends, and his siblings, he would always put her needs before his own. Love was a sacrifice . . . but it was also a precious gift, and he would do whatever he had to in order to be worthy of it.

"It's a pity we never got to have a decent battle," Charles grumbled. "We handled Yuri's men so quickly it was rather dull, wasn't it?"

Ashton rolled his eyes.

"I think storming a castle with rebels makes for a decent story," Godric said. "Besides, it's not really an adventure if Charles's head doesn't almost get chopped off."

Charles scowled at Godric and shuddered dramatically. "That isn't the least bit amusing. I like my head where it is, thank you very much."

Aiden closed his eyes, a slight smile tugging at the corners of his lips as he listened to his brothers jump into the conversation with good-natured insults about where Charles's head should be. He would miss them all fiercely, but Anna was his future, and if she would have him, that meant letting go of the past. But that was all assuming she chose him and not Erich. He would honor whatever choice she made, even if it broke his heart.

CHAPTER 19

Four weeks later

Anna stood a few steps behind Alexei in the great hall as he knelt before a priest and received the royal crown of Ruritania. A cheer erupted from the crowd gathered to witness the coronation. Anna watched the late-autumn sunlight streaming through the stained-glass windows, painting the stone walls with a rainbow of colors and she snuck a glance at Aiden in the crowd who watched her with soft eyes that made her skin warm with a blush. She forced herself to focus back on her brother's coronation.

"Rise, King Alexei III of Ruritania," the priest announced. Alexei stood and turned to face the crowd, and his red cloak lined with white fur swirled behind him. He surveyed the room. Beneath it, he wore the royal Ruritanian military dress of white and blue, with their family's gold lion emblem on his chest. He looked magnificent, and so much like their father that Anna's heart ached.

Four weeks had passed since the death of the Pretender, as the locals now called Yuri. They seemed determined to deny the man any place in their history. In that time, Alexei had met daily with nobles and commoners representing every major village to discuss the country's future.

The royal charter had been revised to convert Ruritania's government to a constitutional monarchy. The noble families had been happy to stand in support of the move, along with the commoners. It seemed the people of Ruritania had never lost faith in the rebel prince. Anna clapped along with the crowd as her brother walked down the aisle and headed out into the castle's courtyard.

Anna remained behind in the hall and listened as the cheers continued outside. She walked over to the throne and touched the carved crown at the top of the chair. She felt those same ghosts again pressing in upon her. In the pocket of her dress, she held a letter that she'd received before the ceremony. Now that she was alone, she removed it from her pocket and finally broke the seal to read it.

My dearest Anna,

I am coming to join you in Ruritania to renew my suit. Although our parents already signed our betrothal contract, I believe it should be a binding promise only if you wish it to be. But I wonder if perhaps when I arrive you shall not be there. For I saw something in London that has given me pause. I saw you look at another man the way I have looked at you. My heart feels that perhaps another holds you in his arms even as I write this, and that in his arms is perhaps where you truly belong.

If that is so, please know that I believe it is a good thing that you have followed your heart. There was a summer once when I came to visit you, your mother spoke to me privately. Her words have always been at the back of my mind. She said that Alexei was born to live in Ruritania, but you had a destiny that would take you far away to a place that held no crowns, where you would be free to pursue other dreams.

She looked so sad when she said this to me, as if she'd always known that one day you would leave Ruritania. But if there is one thing I've learned, it's that we should not deny who we are, nor deny our calling, regardless of what form it takes. If I arrive to find you gone, I will know your answer. I will be sad, but at the same time there will be peace within me to know that you chose your path freely.

Yours always,
Erich

She pressed the letter to her chest. The last bit of guilt she felt at the thought of leaving was gone.

"You always knew I'd leave, didn't you?" she whispered to the air, and for a moment she thought she felt a caress upon her cheek. "But I won't be gone forever," she promised. "I'll be back," she said.

"Anna?" Her brother's voice at the far end of the hall made her spin.

Alexei walked toward her. The heavy crown was gone from his head, and the cloak no longer covered his shoulders. He was simply her brother again, yet also a king. Someday it would be hard to remember the days when they had been young. There would be so much of her brother's life she would miss when she left Ruritania, and she would no longer be here to act as Alexei's private counsel. Before, they'd shared almost everything of their lives, but that was coming to an end, as all things must someday.

"Anna," he said again as they met in the middle of the great hall.

"I—I have made my choice," she said. The words caused actual pain inside her. She'd never handled saying goodbye very well.

"You've decided to leave, haven't you?" He placed his hands on her shoulders, his eyes a reflection of her own sorrow.

She nodded. "I will be leaving as soon as a ship can be made ready."

"To Scotland?" he asked, but it was more of a statement than a question.

She nodded again, and the joy of the thought of her new home drew a smile from her.

"What's it like there?" he asked curiously. "Perhaps one day, when things are peaceful here again, I shall visit you."

"You had better," she said. "I think you would like it. The land is wild, untamed, yet it welcomes you with its endless skies and fields of purple heather. Magic still exists there in the ancient forests and fairy pools. It's home." She hoped someday her brother could understand what it meant to feel the call of home like she did.

"And Kincade? You'll stay married to him?"

"Yes, but I want to renew our vows before his family and our friends. There is an old kirk, a church upon a hill, that means a lot to his family. I should like to have a second wedding there. It's not as if we won't visit you at least once a year, but we can't stay here." Anna wiped away a tear. She wished she could have had a ceremony here with her parents, but that was forever out of reach.

"You'll be happy with him? You won't mind giving up life at court?" Alexei asked.

Anna reached up to cup his cheek, the thread of invisible connection with him as strong as ever.

"I never really thought about happiness, not true happiness, until Aiden found me that day on the shore. It was as though everything missing within me was suddenly found. I didn't feel alone or out of place. I felt I belonged, not just to him or the land, but to myself. Does that make any sense?"

Her brother smiled. "Love *always* makes sense."

Anna knew from the look in her brother's eyes that he wanted to ask her to stay here permanently, to make Aiden stay here with her, but it wouldn't be right for Aiden or for her. Their lives were in Scotland.

"He and I . . . we're so alike, you see. I could not imagine staying at court any longer and letting the rules of others dictate my life. It wouldn't make me happy."

Alexei leaned in and kissed her forehead. "I shall miss you beyond words," he said, his lips twitching as he tried to smile, but he seemed unable to manage it.

"I think that's the best and worst part of loving someone. Someday you have to part, and the thought is painful, but not all parting is forever. We will come back, Alexei, every year, I promise."

"I know you will." He hugged her tight, and Anna held her breath, foolishly thinking it would ease the breaking of her heart.

"You had better go tell your Scot the good news. He's

been far too quiet these last four weeks. I think he fears losing you."

Even though she and Aiden had been sharing a bedchamber, they'd seen surprisingly little of each other in the last month, between her helping Alexei, and Aiden assisting Lord Morrey's men in rebuilding the villages. Often they'd missed entire days with each other, and one or the other of them would come back to find the other dead asleep in bed. It proved her theory that if she stayed, she'd hardly get to spend enough time with Aiden to enjoy a real life with him. Returning to Scotland was what they both needed.

"You're right." She sighed, and the two of them let go of each other. She was smiling despite her tears as she looked at her twin. "Long live the king."

His eyes lit with adoration. "Long live the *princess*."

***

Aiden rode his borrowed horse down toward the Winter Palace and reined the beast in as he saw the distant crowd of people still filling the streets. The coronation had ended two hours ago, but the people who had come from far and wide to be there seemed content to continue celebrating. He couldn't blame them. They had had their country torn apart by war and greedy ambition. Now was a time of peace, a time to return to normal, and yet things had certainly changed as well. Anna's brother had formed a parliament, and while it was in its infancy, she believed it would in time become a good voice for her people.

During the ceremony while everyone else had looked at Alexei, Aiden only had eyes for Anna. She had worn a red-and-cream gown, much like the one she'd worn in London at Lady Eugenia's ball. Pearls gleamed all over her skirts, and more pearls were threaded through the intricate strands of her coiffure. She looked like the radiant princess she truly was. He realized that he had a lot to think about, both for his future and for Anna's. In the last few weeks, Anna had been busy with the new governmental changes and the preparations for the coronation. Aiden had helped Lord Morrey's forces settle into their role of rebuilding villages and chasing down Yuri's guards still roaming about the country. It had kept him busy and focused.

Ashton and his friends had stayed a week or so after Yuri's death to ensure the stable transition of the men Morrey sent, and then they'd boarded a ship for home. Aiden's brothers had gone with them, and the memory of that parting was still an aching wound in Aiden's chest. They'd said their goodbyes, not for forever though, because he planned to visit them in a year, but Brock and Brodie had understood that he wasn't going to live at home with them again. He'd made his choice.

He would find a way to be more like Erich, to become dashing and sociable and play the part of a prince consort so that his wife could fulfill her duties as a princess of Ruritania. Even if it meant leaving his home and family, he would do it for Anna.

Aiden entered the courtyard of the palace and slid off his horse. One of Alexei's guards spotted him and came over.

"Mr. Kincade, the princess has been looking for you."

Aiden nodded. "Where is she?"

"I believe she has retired to her chambers for the evening, sir."

Aiden thanked the guard and headed into the castle. The corridors were full of bustling servants, and the extra staff members were working hard to restore the palace to its former glory. He climbed the stairs that led to Anna's bedchamber and found her door open. Anna was by the window, silhouetted against the setting sun.

"Lass?" He spoke the word uncertainly.

She had one hand on the glass windowpane, fingers splayed as she gazed at the countryside. When she turned, her slender gold crown caught the light and sparkled like the flash of a shooting star across the night sky.

Aiden's heart stopped, and every doubt he'd ever had about leaving his home and family vanished. He *loved* this woman, loved her more than his own life, and he would do whatever he must to make her happy.

"You went riding without me," she said.

Aiden wondered if she was teasing him or hurt by his actions. He couldn't tell. "I had a few things to think about," he said.

"As did I." She crossed her arms in front of her as if she was cold. "Could we sit down and talk?" She nodded at the chaise at the end of her bed. He sat down at one end and joined her. He noticed that she had somehow found his tartan plaid among his travel cases and had unfolded it on the settee like a blanket. For a moment, neither of them spoke.

"Aiden, I—"

"We should—"

They laughed nervously. "You first," she insisted, her hands clamped together in her lap.

Aiden noticed she twisted her fingers together, and he

gently stilled her hands, covering them with one of his own. "Ye belong here. Ye belong with yer brother and yer people. I would never ask or expect ye to leave that for me. So I've decided to be the man ye need me to be, if that's what ye wish."

Anna's eyes grew dark and luminous. She withdrew a letter from the pocket of her gown and held it out to him.

"Please, read this." She pressed the letter into his hands, and he unfolded it and read the words that shattered his heart. He swallowed thickly and gave it back to her.

"What are ye trying to tell me, lass, that you choose Erich?"

Anna reached up and with delicate fingers brushed the hair back from his eyes, then smiled at him.

"Foolish man. I'm not choosing Erich. I'm choosing *you*." She read her mother's words, the part she'd been too shattered to focus on after seeing that Erich had wanted to come to renew his suit. She emphasized the part about how she'd always been destined to leave.

"I'm not staying here in Ruritania, Aiden. I want to go home, to *our* home. I miss Lydia, Joanna, and Rosalind. I miss the hedgehogs, pine martens, and owls. I miss Bob and Thundir. I miss little Cameron, and I miss *our life* there most of all."

For a moment he found it hard to speak. "You dinna want to stay here and help yer brother rebuild yer country?"

She shook her head. "Alexei and I will always be connected, but my destiny and his have diverged. I belong in a place where I'm free to be myself. Free to share the rest of my life with you. Besides, I think it would be good for England to have me as an official envoy for Ruritania, when needed. King George does like me, after all." She winked at him mischievously.

"Aye, that he does, lassie, that he does." Aiden was quick to agree. Anna would never be short of admirers in England and Scotland if she decided to use her political influence there.

"Does that reassure you, husband?" she asked him in a soft, husky voice that made his breath catch in his throat.

"It does . . . but a kiss wouldna hurt to add to that reassurance." His own voice was low and gruff.

She leaned in and kissed him, and Aiden forgot to breathe. He hadn't known kisses could show a man his future, but Anna's kiss did. He could see them returning home to Castle Kincade, welcoming their first child, and then several more. He saw them in their twilight years as they sat by the fairy pools and watched the clouds drift over their heads. He saw the exquisitely beautiful life Anna's kiss promised. A life he never thought he would have.

He cupped Anna's face, kissing her harder, hungrier, and soon she crawled onto his lap, wrapping the plaid around them to keep them warm as the sun fell past the horizon. After a long while, he dropped the plaid and scooped his wife up in his arms and carried her to bed. He set her down on the edge of the feather tick bed and cupped her face again, kissing her harder this time. Then he let go and stepped back, simply admiring the princess sitting before him. *His princess.*

"Are you going to ravish me, oh devilish Highlander?"

she teased with a silky laugh. "Or stand there staring at me?"

"Ye want to be ravished, lassie?" he growled playfully.

"By you? Always . . ." She reached up and removed the golden circlet upon her brow and gently set it on the table beside the bed. Then she began removing the pins from her hair until it tumbled down her shoulders in wild russet waves. It reminded him of the first time he'd met her, when she'd washed up on the shores of Scotland like a selkie princess.

He took over then, by kneeling at her feet and removing the fine jeweled slippers she wore. She lifted her skirts up to her knees so he could roll her stockings down. He kissed every inch of her, taking his time in a way he hadn't had a chance to before. Until now, every minute with her had felt as if it would be their last. For the first time since he'd met Anna, he could savor her, with the knowledge that this was only the beginning.

When it came time to remove her gown, she rolled onto her stomach on the bed, and he crawled up over her and carefully straddled his knees on either side of her hips as he worked his fingers through the buttons and hooks at her back. Then as he peeled her gown off her shoulders, and leaned over to kiss the back of her neck. He traced her spine with his lips until she shivered and whispered for him to hurry. That only made him smile as he shushed her.

"If I'm to ravish ye, I'll take my time, wife." His scolding made her giggle as she buried her face in the crook of her arm. The sweet, girlish sound made his chest ache. She was letting go of her fear of the future, of her worries, and that made his entire body hum with a joy he'd never thought possible.

Anna lifted her hips so he could slide the voluminous gown off her body, leaving only her stays, chemise and petticoats. He was quick to remove the stays and petticoats, but when he got to the filmy chemise, he simply tore it down the back and lifted her into his arms as the cloth fell away.

"You can't do that to every chemise, you know," she warned with an impish grin as she turned in his arms and kissed him.

Her breasts brushed against his chest, and he growled in delight. He didn't bother to tell her he rather liked ripping her clothes off sometimes. Perhaps it was the old Celtic warrior within him, to want to claim his woman so roughly sometimes. But now, now was a time for sweetness, for long, torturous delights, and he would enjoy every minute of it.

He cupped the back of her head and kissed her deeply, his tongue miming what his body would soon do to hers.

"Please, Aiden, you're wearing far too many clothes to kiss me like that," she moaned, and her hands frantically tugged at his shirt, trying to pull it free of his trousers.

He gently laid her back on the bed, and removed his shirt, and kicked off his boots. He nearly fell off the bed trying to get rid of his pants and stockings, and then he was on her again, laughing with her as he came down on top of her. Her legs parted, and he was sinking in, basking in the welcoming heat of her body as if the heavens themselves had opened for him.

"I love ye," he whispered as he began to move inside her. "I love ye so much it hurts."

Her inner walls clamped down on him in response, and she threw her head back with a cry of pleasure. When she seemed to have come down from her climax, she buried her hands in his hair and stared up at him, love shining in her eyes.

"I love you too, Aiden. So much it hurts. But it's the most wonderful sort of ache, isn't it?"

He knew exactly what she meant. When his heart was as full as it was in that moment, it actually did hurt, and the hurting was a thing of beauty to him, just as she was. He made love to her, taking his time, making her come apart twice more before she begged him to let her rest. He allowed it with a sensual, rumbling laugh. She was asleep moments later, and he simply stayed awake watching her. Then in the hours before dawn, he gently roused her once more.

When she parted her thighs and he sank into her, they both shared a soft gasp as they became one in those wee hours before dawn. Anna gave in to her passions with fresh fervor, and Aiden drew out her pleasure until she wept with desperation for him to satisfy her. As sweat dewed upon their bodies, he nuzzled her neck and kissed her ear.

"I hope that we made a life between us just now," he whispered.

"So do I." She stroked her hand through his dark hair, and he was thankful that his tears of joy were hidden by the fading night.

"I told my brother we would sail to Scotland when a ship could be made ready," she said.

"Are ye ready to leave so soon?" He was happy to think they would be going home, but he didn't want her to rush her goodbyes.

"Yes. Your brothers and the others left weeks ago, and I long to be home with them, to be home with you. I told Alexei we would come back next year and visit."

He kissed her. "We certainly will visit as often as ye wish, lass."

"Good." She smiled sleepily at him. "Then we leave tomorrow. For home."

"*For home,*" he agreed.

She cuddled closer and splayed a hand on his chest. "You promise to chase my bad dreams away if I have any?"

"Lass, from now on ye'll only have good dreams, and we'll chase them together."

EPILOGUE

December *1821*
Scotland

A coach pulled up in front of Castle Kincade one wintry morning. Brock spotted it from his bedchamber window upstairs while he was dressing for the day. He wondered who would come visit them at such a cold time of year.

Travel on the rural roads to reach the castle couldn't have been pleasant. Whoever had just arrived was determined, to say the least. Brock let his valet finish fixing his cravat, then left his bedchamber and called for his wife.

"Joanna! Who's at the door?" He had grown accustomed to shouting for his wife because she was somewhere deep in the castle. It was a vast place with dozens of rooms, and he could never quite find her without a shout or two. He did so enjoy it when his proper English wife hollered back at him like any good Scotswoman, her cheeks flushed and her eyes lit with mischief. When he found her, and if she was alone, he'd often take his time reminding her why she'd agreed to marry him. Stolen kisses in libraries were still one of his favorite pastimes.

He'd only been home from his adventure in Ruritania for about a month, and Joanna was anxious for him not to leave again anytime soon. He suspected she was with child but wasn't telling him until she was sure.

Both Joanna and Lydia had been frantic with concern when the Kincade brothers left to rescue Anna. He had understood their fears, but neither he nor his brother could let Aiden face the dangers overseas alone. Joanna had feared every day that he might not come back, and no word of their safety had reached London until he and Brodie sailed back into an English port and were able to greet their wives at Ashton's townhouse.

Brock had made a pledge not to leave Scotland or England again for a long time. But with that promise came heartbreak. It meant he had lost his brother, just as the old Romani woman had said he would. Of course, he had thought *lost* meant dead. Aiden wasn't dead, but he was far away, and it might be a long time before Brock would see him again. He'd promised to visit Scotland, but being married to a princess would mean Aiden would be busy with royal duties, and it would not be so easy to come home frequently.

It didn't feel right to not have his youngest brother here. The animals that belonged to Aiden seemed restless, as though they knew their gentle-hearted master would never again return. But that was the price of love. It meant giving things up to form a partnership with the one you loved. Aiden had chosen a princess, and he had done the right thing by staying with her when she had her royal duties to fulfill.

"Brock! Come quick!" Joanna's voice held surprise and excitement, which sent him running for the stairs. He skidded to a stop when he saw snow already blowing in through the open front door. A woman hidden beneath a heavy blue cloak was hugging Joanna and Lydia. Brodie stood beside them, grinning as though Christmas had come early. The young woman pushed back the hood of her cloak, and Brock saw Anna smiling up at him.

"Anna?" If the princess was here, that meant his brother . . .

Another figure swept into the castle, and the Kincade butler hastily closed the door to prevent more snow from getting in. He removed his hat and shook his great cloak free of snow before slipping it off and handing it over to the butler. Brock's heart clenched so tight he couldn't breathe.

Aiden had come home.

"You're just in time for the holidays," Lydia announced.

"We are," Anna laughed. "I hope that's all right?"

"Of course it is, sister." Brodie took his turn to hug Anna as Brock hurried down the stairs to join the merry gathering. He could barely contain his joy.

"How . . . ?" He cleared the lump in his throat as he looked between Aiden and the princess, trying not to get his hopes up. "How long are ye staying?"

Anna's responding smile could have outshone the sun itself. "Forever, if you'll have us."

"Forever?" Brock echoed.

Aiden stepped toward him and held out a hand. "Forever, and perhaps a little longer after that," Aiden said with a warm smile.

Brock saw no shadows or sorrow in Aiden's eyes. The pain and loneliness he'd carried for so long had been banished completely.

Brock pulled his youngest brother into a hug and then pulled Anna in as well, embracing them both as tears filled his eyes. Anna could never know what she had done for him by saving Aiden, but he would be forever in her debt.

"Ach! We canna breathe, brother," Aiden groaned good-naturedly.

Brock let go of them, and Aiden ducked his head, blushing as if embarrassed at the show of affection.

"Ye didna used to be the hugging sort," Aiden said.

"I am now. I have much to be grateful for." Brock saw Joanna press a palm against her still-flat belly, but the broad smile she gave him hinted that more to be grateful for was on the way.

Brodie cleared his throat, trying to sound gruff. "Well, it's about time ye were back. Yer wee beasties have been in a right state without ye. I've been playing mother hen to wee Prissy for the last week." He opened up his waistcoat pocket and passed Aiden a very excited, squirming hedgehog. Chuckling, Aiden tucked Prissy into the crook of his arm.

A boy's shout echoed in the hall. "Aiden! Yer back!" Suddenly, a boy had rushed over and was now clinging to Aiden's waist.

"Cameron, lad," he greeted and then tousled the boy's hair with one hand. "How have ye been?"

"Great! I have so much to show ye! I learned all about the horses, and now I'm learning to read and write . . ."

Aiden smirked. "*All* about the horses? I doubt that. I think I can still teach ye a thing or two."

Cameron's eyes grew round as he looked to Anna. "Is it true, Miss Anna, that yer a princess? That's what Joanna said . . ." The boy dipped his head and then shyly touched the toes of his shoes together.

Anna leaned down and winked at Cameron before putting a finger to her lips as if it was a secret.

"I am, but don't tell anyone. Now I'm a Scot, just like you."

"Ye are?" He beamed at her. "Oh boy, wait until I tell Bob. She's been missing ye something fierce."

"Has she?" Anna laughed. "Oh, come and tell me all about it while we warm up with some tea."

"That's a lovely idea. Cameron shall regale us with his tales." Joanna and Lydia and Anna left the three brothers in the hall.

Once they were alone, Brock placed his hands on Aiden's shoulders.

"Ye really plan to stay? What about the royal court and all of that?"

"I told her I would do whatever I must to make her happy, and she said what she wanted most was to come home. She's to be Ruritania's ambassador to King George. We'll visit Alexei at least once a year, but she wants to live her life *here*. She said this is the place where she feels free to be herself. I still canna believe it, but here we are."

Brock swallowed hard. "We thought we lost ye . . ."

Aiden smiled. "I was lost for a long time, but Anna

found me." For the first time, Brock realized that the Romani woman's words had a second meaning. That *lost* perhaps didn't mean Aiden's death or that he'd never return to Scotland, but rather that part of him, the part that had been so wounded, so hurt . . . was gone. Perhaps that dark part of him being lost had always been a good thing, and he simply hadn't seen it until now.

"Thank God for shipwrecked princesses," Brodie said, and all three brothers laughed.

"Thank God, indeed," Aiden replied.

"We must write to Ash and Rosalind!" Brock announced. "They'll want to know ye're back."

"We've already seen them. We landed in London first and spent a few days with Ashton and Rosalind. We wanted to thank them again for all that they did. Then we made a short stop at North Berwick to see Dr. MacDonald and his new wife."

"New wife?" Brock was not following this at all. "Dr. MacDonald married?"

Aiden chuckled. "Aye. Ye remember how he found a woman from Anna's ship and was helping the lass recover?"

"Aye, the woman he mentioned in his letter." Brock nodded for him to continue.

"Well, that woman was Anna's lady's maid, Pilar. While we were off saving Ruritania, Pilar and Dr. MacDonald were here falling in love. They were married two weeks ago. So it seems Anna has a bit of Ruritania left here in Scotland with her."

"We should invite them here for Christmas," Brodie suggested.

"Aye," Brock said. "We should invite Rosalind and Ash too, if they arna busy."

"They might be," Aiden said. "I think Emily St. Laurent is husband hunting for Charles, and it might keep everyone in London a bit occupied."

"Charles married!" Brodie snorted. "The lady who takes him for a husband would have to be a saint."

"Perhaps it's best we stay away from London, if that's the case," Brock added. "Why don't we join the women and have some tea?"

Brodie shot Aiden a brotherly look of mischief. "Only if we tip a bit of whisky into our cups."

"I second that," Aiden said with a laugh.

***

Christmas morning

Anna placed her chin on Aiden's bare chest and drew patterns on his skin as he slept. The morning sun reflected off the snow outside and sunlight flooded their bedchamber. Aiden's tame pine marten was curled up on the armchair. It stretched and yawned before curling right back up to sleep, tucking its tail around its body. Anna smiled, feeling exactly the same. She didn't want to leave this warm bed for at least another few hours.

"What are ye thinking about?" Aiden said.

She giggled. "I didn't know you were awake."

He stroked a hand through her unbound hair.

"I woke when ye did, lass."

"Happy Christmas," she said, barely able to contain her joy. She had been holding on to a secret for a long time, a full month to be certain, but now she couldn't wait.

"Do you want your present?" she asked seductively.

"My present?" He seemed intrigued by the idea.

"Yes . . ." She scooted up his body a little so that she lay even with him, their faces close together on his pillow. Then she took his hand and tucked it under the warm blankets and placed it on her belly. She expected him to be surprised at what she was hinting at, but instead he smiled mischievously.

"I was wondering when ye planned to tell me."

"You knew?"

"Ye've been very passionate in bed, more than usual, and yer breasts have grown larger and more sensitive. I can feel the changes in ye."

"Oh . . ." She was a bit disappointed that it wasn't a surprise to him.

"Since the moment I realized ye were with child, I've been bursting for ye to tell me."

Anna nuzzled her nose with his before kissing him. "Truly?"

"Truly." He cupped her face and deepened the kiss, slipping his tongue between her lips.

"Well, I had to be sure before I told you."

"I thought that might be why. I didna want to upset ye by pushing ye." He was quiet a moment, and then his gaze sharpened on her face. "Anna, do ye mind if I ask ye something?"

She nodded, curious as to what could be on his mind.

"That day at the wishing well, ye said the well granted yer wish. What did ye wish for?"

Her gaze turned solemn as she recalled those terrifying moments. "Every time I dreamed about you in the well, I wished that you'd find a way to save me, to break through the water and come to me. You did. You saved me that day, the way I'd always hoped you would. And I don't simply mean that you saved me from danger. You saved me from a life that would never have been my own. You've given me love and happiness, and a life that will always be mine."

"Perhaps the well granted yer wish because I wished for that too. I was desperate to save ye, to break free through the water, take yer hand in those dreams, and not only to save ye but to love ye . . . and how it felt to finally surface in the well after that fall and somehow not die. A wish was certainly granted that day. A very powerful one."

"I agree," she echoed before kissing him.

When they finally broke apart, Anna traced his lips. "I'm glad I got lost in Scotland." She drew her fingertips down the line of his nose, and Aiden's eyes were clear of the storms that once haunted them. She chuckled. "Lost with a Scot . . . Sounds like a wonderful adventure, doesn't it?"

Aiden stroked her hair, his eyes searching hers. "It was a wonderful adventure, finding ye, and ye'll never be lost again, not so long as I'm with ye," he promised.

She kissed him again. This time, she was lost in the best way with her Scot.

***

Masilda, an old woman and the matriarch of her clan of Travellers, sat by the warm fire, draped in a colorful cloak sewn with care by her beautiful daughters as a gift. They camped out at the edge of the forest to keep the winter wind from the coast of Cornwall from creating too much of a chill in their bones. Their wagons were well built, but Masilda had lived many years and knew that winter was hard upon the wood. She wanted to preserve their wagons as long as she could before they'd need to consider making repairs.

She watched the flames dance as her people sang merry songs, drank warm drinks and celebrated the winter solstice. The world faded away, and all Masilda could see were the flames, and she heard the messages that whispered to her through the cracks and pops of the fire.

"So death was not the end for you after all." She smiled as she saw the little Scottish boy she'd warned all those years ago embracing his princess, both now safe. He had loved his woman despite knowing what it might cost, and fate had given him his life back for that loyalty to love.

The sound of a horse approaching stilled the revelry of her people, and she looked up at the dark-haired and dark-eyed *gadjo* who stopped near their camp. His great cloak swirled as he slid off his horse and approached the fire. He was blessed with looks that would make the devil himself green with envy.

Masilda spoke as she stood to face him. "Are you seeking something, sir?"

The stranger glanced around at the camp and the people.

"I seek a place to warm myself before returning to my home. I live *there*." He pointed to the distant manor house that belonged to the lord who owned the lands they were currently passing through.

Masilda beckoned to him to sit next to the fire. "Then come and warm yourself." The man settled on the bench close to her and stared at the flames. Masilda poured him a cup of hot tea, and he drank it with a murmured thanks.

"We will not stay long on your land," she promised.

The man's eyes glinted with amusement. "Stay as long as you wish. My mother was one of your people. I welcome you on my lands anytime."

Masilda chuckled. "I thought you had the spirit inside you. You also have trouble and mischief in your eyes. You, I think, are never satisfied."

"You know much, old mother."

The way he said *old mother* showed he had some of the knowledge of their people.

"I do." Masilda looked away from him and turned her attention to the fire again. The prophecies were still whispering to her between the pop and crack of logs.

"What do you see for me?" the man asked, as if he knew she was listening to the future.

"I see you running from the thing you long for most," she said.

He tilted his head before sipping his tea and eyed her curiously. "And what is that?"

"A woman."

The handsome stranger barked a laugh. "I've never run from a woman in my life."

"You will when you realize you love her," Masilda said.

She could see the man in the fire, waltzing with a beautiful woman in his arms. A woman he had fashioned into a dream for all other men to desire, as though he'd molded her from clay. But what he secretly wanted was the woman before she had transformed into the creature he had created.

"I've never been in love and never will be. Women are too boring and predictable."

Masilda cast her gaze heavenward as she heard the challenge the man had just issued to destiny. "Only because you never give women the chance to be what they wish, and not what you expect of them."

The man finished his tea and set the cup down. "Thank you for the tea and the warm fire." He stood and glanced around the camp before turning to walk away.

"What is your name, my lord?" Masilda called out.

He paused at the edge of the camp's firelight and gave her a darkly charming smile.

"Trystan Cartwright, the Earl of Zennor." Then he mounted his horse and rode away, the night swallowing him.

TURN THE PAGE TO READ A FASCINATING HISTORICAL note about the literary inspiration for *Lost with a Scot*.

HISTORICAL NOTE

THE INSPIRATION FOR LOST WITH
A SCOT

The Prisoner of Zenda . . .

Have you heard of this novel? If you haven't, that's not surprising. It was published more than a hundred and thirty years ago in 1884 by a man named Anthony Hope and was so popular it was turned into a board game by the Parker Brothers company in 1896! I bet you're wondering what a book that old that you probably haven't heard of has to do with Aiden and Anna's sexy Scottish romance.

Well, that's where the fun begins. If you're like me and you love books, especially old books, or you like the history of literature, you'll be fascinated by what I'm about to share with you. As you'll recall, the country where my heroine, Anna Zelensky, is from is called Ruritania. I chose this name for a reason. Ruritania has already existed in the world of literature. It was the feudal Germanic country that formed the setting for Anthony Hope's *The Prisoner of Zenda*. Now, it is important to note that my Ruritania and Hope's are different in many ways. However, my Ruritania was chosen to be a tribute to Hope's fictional country, and here's why . . .

For the last one hundred years, readers have been entertained with stories about characters, usually royal in nature, who come from fictional foreign lands. Now it's almost seen as a cliché. Books like *The Princess Diaries* by Meg Cabot (which has been made into two movies) and even the Christmas Hallmark movies about fictional foreign princes and princesses are all considered "Ruritanian romances," even though they do not use the name Ruritania.

So what are Ruritanian romances, exactly? They are any fictional story, whether it be a novel, play, or screenplay, where a foreign country with a fictional name is used as the setting, and the stories often involve a royal character either as a romantic interest or in the lead role, and the stories must involve adventure, danger, and love. In other words, Ruritanian romances are, in some ways, the original romance novels, only the stories like mine that exist today that are clearly defined by the romance genre have happy endings. Ruritanian romances did not always have happy endings.

When Hope penned *The Prisoner of Zenda*, he brought into existence an entirely new type of novel. Before his book, the world of fiction had only seen "novels" as either gothic in nature or sentimental. I could write an entirely new historical note devoted to those types of stories, but suffice it to say that nothing like an adventure novel written in fast-paced and modern language had yet been written until *Zenda* was born.

Even though novels like *The Three Musketeers* by Alexandre Dumas, adventure stories with passion and romance, did exist, they were not written in the verbiage of the modern speaker, nor with the fast-paced style that would come to define the late Victorian dime novels. Writers like Edgar Rice Burroughs, who created *Tarzan of the Apes*, would find that a more down-to-earth style, no less lyrical or poetic, but more accessible and modern in word choice, would appeal to the masses of people who would not always sit down to read. Think of it like this: When *Fifty Shades of Grey* was released, many people who didn't read books that often actually sat down and read *Fifty Shades of Grey* to see what all the fuss was about. The book (no matter what your personal opinion of it is) appealed to a large amount of people, whether by actual interest or mere curiosity.

Hope's novel *The Prisoner of Zenda* was the late Victorian age's popularity equivalent of *Fifty Shades of Grey*. But what about *Zenda* made it so fascinating, other than that the style of writing was more accessible to a greater number of readers across a variety of class levels?

Let's break it down into its basic elements. The hero is an Englishman with a love of travel and adventure. He tours Europe and stumbles upon a quaint little "pocket kingdom" called Ruritania, and he remembers hearing that his family has distant relations living there. He ends up falling in love with a princess who is destined to marry the current king of Ruritania, and he also resembles this king so strongly that he is recruited to play the king's double for safety reasons. What follows is a madcap series of adventures that puts the handsome young Englishman in the role of the king, and he falls for a princess and defeats a dastardly villain.

This plot sounds familiar, doesn't it? You're thinking you've read a million of these stories by various authors or seen plenty of movies with these plots. Well, you're quite right. But *The Prisoner of Zenda* was the very first story to have a plot and themes like this. What I think is the most interesting thing isn't just that Zenda was the birth of modern adventure romances—it was also a way for authors to examine current political situations in the world through the lens of a "pocket kingdom."

Pocket kingdoms are tiny fictional kingdoms that are often feudal in nature, where a king rules over a relatively medieval kingdom. This country may be facing a civil war, a tyrant ruler, a usurper, a dynasty in peril for lack of heirs, a court full of treacherous nobles, or war with a neighboring country. When authors use these pocket kingdoms as a literary device, they are safely able to pose rhetorical, philosophical, or political questions in a way that allows the reader to form less biased opinions.

For example, if a reader who doesn't approve of the style of government they currently have in their own country reads about a fictional pocket kingdom with a similar government, they aren't immediately or at least consciously noticing the similarities. But they are taking in the story and the questions raised as if it's an entirely different country, and it broadens their perspective rather than limiting it. It is one of the many reasons fiction is such a powerful form of expression. You may be reading a fun steamy romance, but deep down, you're also processing bigger concepts and broadening your mind and thoughts.

That's why literature is an amazing gift. Knowing all of this, I wanted to make my story a tribute to Hope and *The Prisoner of Zenda*, his incredible novel. Aiden in many ways plays the Englishman hero character of Rupert, while Anna plays the role of Princess Flavia, Rupert's forbidden love. While the stories play out very differently upon the page, *Lost with a Scot* is my tribute and contribution to the continued literary tradition of Ruritanian romances. I hope you enjoyed the novel and this historical note.

If you're interested in diving deeper into a study of what I've briefly discussed in this historical note, please read Nicholas Daly's *Ruritania: A Cultural History, from the Prisoner of Zenda to the Princess Diaries.*

Thank you for reading this book, and please don't forget to leave a review! Even one sentence of what you loved about the book or how it made you feel makes a world of difference for authors.

Lauren Smith
November 2022

*Next up in the series will be Trystan Cartwright, The Earl of Zennor's story. Turn the page to read the first chapter!

THE EARL OF ZENNOR

Penzance, England, April 1822

"You know what's wrong with you, Trystan?"

Trystan Cartwright, the Earl of Zennor, arched a dark brow at one of the two men seated across from him at the table in the grimy little tavern.

Graham Humphrey, a blond-haired gentleman with gray eyes lit with dangerous mischief, grinned at Trystan. His companion was Phillip, the Earl of Kent, a solemn man with a nature so honest he made up for Trystan and Graham's roguish ways. Graham and Phillip were two of his most trusted friends, the only ones who could rein him in when his recklessness began to spiral.

"What?" Trystan asked, his tone laconic as he lifted his glass and downed the scotch within it.

"You're bored. You get testy when you have nothing to do," Graham observed.

"He's not wrong," Phillip added. "And often, what entertains you is not anything I would recommend." He hesitated before continuing in a more careful tone. "What you need is a wife."

Trystan snorted. "No, not yet. Perhaps not ever. Wives can be useful, but they are hardly entertaining. They are shackles that bind men to early graves."

"Wives can open doors that men cannot," Phillip said sagely. "Take a woman with breeding who has been raised to be familiar with the ins and outs of society, women like Audrey St. Laurent or Lady Lennox, who have a knowledge of business and politics. They have a vast amount of power and influence in not just feminine circles."

"But what do I need with power and influence? I have plenty already," Trystan replied. "Besides, you can turn any woman into a society creature. Feed her the right lines, put her in the right clothes and she'd fit like any goose with a gaggle of geese."

"Are you joking? You can't take just anyone and turn them into a lady. Ladies are raised from birth to think and behave a certain way," Graham argued.

"Maybe that's the problem. Perhaps I'd rather converse with a street urchin than another boring lady of society. They all bore me."

Graham chuckled. "You need a *mistress*, not a wife, obviously," he said, and took a swig of his ale. "Mistresses are amusing, but they require funds to keep them happy. My last mistress cost me a townhouse and half the jewels in London to keep her happy." Graham frowned, as though he hadn't really considered the cost until that moment. That was to be expected. Graham rarely gave anything much thought. He simply did what he wished and damn the consequences. It was why he and Trystan got along famously.

Trystan sighed. "I'm afraid even mistresses bore me." His gaze wandered over the shabby little tavern. Its grubby wallpaper was peeling in places, the tables needed more than a good scrubbing, and the man they'd paid for drinks looked as though he had gone a few rounds in a pugilist match.

Trystan preferred their usual club, Boodle's, but they were far from London and bound for his home in Zennor, which meant reputable places shrank in number the further they strayed from civilization. Zennor, despite its rural location, wasn't all that bad; Trystan could admit that much. His ancestral home was built near the coast of Cornwall, and he liked the way the wind swept in off the sea and how the deep blue water burst into white foam as it careened into the rocky cliffs that banked the sea.

As much as he enjoyed the pleasures of a city like London, he felt an undeniable draw to his home, the many rooms of the rambling manor house full of memories of an adventurous, though sometimes lonely, boyhood. After his mother passed away when he'd been but a boy of ten, he and his father had grown close. He'd learned to appreciate the land and the home that had only a few years ago become his when his father had suffered a stroke and joined his mother.

After his father's death, Trystan had taken to the life of an earl with relative ease. He did not squander his family's fortune on drink, gambling, or other vices. His recklessness came in the form of what entertained him... usually something that would cause Phillip to frown and lecture him on responsibility. His two old school friends were the proverbial angel and devil on his shoulders, offering temptation and temperance in turn, which in its own way was an entertainment.

Trystan swept his gaze over the tavern again, this time taking in the occupants. Everyone here came from a hardscrabble life. Most looked to be dockworkers or sailors. It was possible even a few pirates still sailed into the seaside village.

As aristocrats, Trystan, Graham, and Phillip stood out from the crowd, and because of this they were earning more than a few curious looks from the more brutish men who huddled by the hearth on the opposite side of the room. The speculative looks these men were sending his way could result in trouble, which only made Trystan smile.

Perhaps these men would attack them in hopes of getting some coin. Wouldn't that be a nice change of pace? He could do with a good brawl. He had studied for years at Jackson's Salon with the best boxers in London, and had even managed to give the legendary Earl of Lonsdale a few good swipes.

Graham waved the barkeeper over to bring them more ale. "What you need, my friend, is a challenge."

"I do, but I cannot think of a single thing that could hold my interest." He played with the rim of his cup, gently stroking a fingertip along its smooth edge.

"How about a wager?" Graham said.

Phillip rolled his eyes. "You two and your bloody wagers. Didn't you learn anything the last time when you freed that bear in that dogfighting ring?"

Trystan laughed. "I've never seen so many men run and scream like children when that poor beast got free." he said. "You have to admit we did a good thing, though, Phillip. That bear should never have been held in chains and forced to fight like that."

Phillip closed his eyes and rubbed them with his thumb and index finger. "As much as it pains me to admit it, yes, but the only reason no one was mauled to death was because of that Scottish fellow who was there to calm it down. If he hadn't had such a gift with animals, you both might have been killed, and the beast as well."

Trystan remembered that night all too well—and the surge of power he'd felt at freeing the beast and watching it chase the men who'd tormented it. But Phillip was right, the bear would have eventually killed someone if Aiden Kincade hadn't been there to soothe the creature and trap it in a coach outside the warehouse where the beast had been held captive.

"All's well that ends well. The bear is now in Scotland and we're still here to wager yet again on something ridiculous." He was, however, far from convinced that there was anything new he could bet on that would entertain him for long.

A serving boy brought them more ale, slamming the tankards down hard enough that the ale sloshed out of the cups.

"Ho, there! Watch it, boy!" Trystan snapped at the lad.

"Watch yerself, milord!" the boy countered sharply and stalked back to the bar.

"Impertinent lad," Graham observed. "As I was saying—"

There was a loud crash near the bar. The boy had tripped and a tray of mugs now lay shattered on the ground.

"Daft fool!" The barman swung a hand and cuffed the boy across the face. The boy crumpled to the floor with a sharp cry of pain.

Trystan, Graham, and Phillip all tensed.

"He was impertinent, but he didn't deserve that," Graham said.

"Do that again and I'll sell you to the whorehouse!" the barman roared. He kicked the boy's ribs as the lad got on his hands and knees to collect the pieces. He fell onto his back and his cap dislodged, sending a tumble of long dark hair down in a messy, oily tangle.

"Bloody hell... It's a girl," Trystan murmured to his friends as they all stared in amazement at the creature on the floor. She was small, dirty cheeked, not the least bit attractive, and had a waspish tongue, but she was still a girl and shouldn't have been hit like that.

"You try to sell me, and I'll cut your bloody heart out and sell it to the bleedin' butcher, you bastard!" the girl shot back at the barman. Despite his best intentions, Trystan found himself smiling at the girl's courage.

"There's a girl with fire in her belly," Graham said. "That's a female who would never be tamed into a quiet, biddable lady of society." he laughed, but Trystan wasn't laughing.

He stared at the girl as she picked up a piece of broken mug and hurled it back at the barman. The clay shard smashed against the wall next to the man's balding head. Then she ran outside before the bellowing pig could catch her.

For a second the taproom was silent. Then everything went back to normal, laughing and jeering and drinking. The little hellion was gone and no one seemed to care.

"Fancy that. A drink *and* a show," said Graham.

Trystan's lips twitched as he stared at the door the girl had vanished through a moment before.

"Christ, he has that look again," Phillip muttered.

Graham was less concerned and looked hopefully at Trystan. "What is it? What's your idea?" He knew his friend too well.

Trystan leaned back in his chair, a smug smile now spreading across his face as he gripped his mug of ale.

"I wager I can turn that whelp of a girl into a proper lady in one month."

"*That one?* The hellcat who threatened to cut a man's heart out? I just said you couldn't possibly make a girl like that a lady," Graham sniggered. "You might want to be careful she doesn't cut yours out."

"Yes, *that one.*" Trystan smiled wickedly at the thought of such a challenge.

"If you turn her into a proper lady, one to rival a duchess like Emily St. Laurent, I'll pay you two hundred pounds." Graham volunteered the vast sum of money as if it barely mattered.

"Throw in that black-and-red racing curricle and your

fastest pair of geldings, and I'll take that bet," Trystan offered.

Graham eyed him thoughtfully. "What if we make it more interesting? Lady Tremaine's ball is in a month. If you bring that girl to the ball and she fools everyone, you win. But if *anyone* sees through her disguise and you fail, you owe me..." Graham drew out his next words in wicked delight. "The deed to your hunting lodge in Scotland. I rather fancy it."

"High-stakes indeed, just the way I like it." Trystan chuckled. To have so much to lose only heightened the excitement of the wager, and his friends knew it.

"Now, hold on a minute," Phillip interjected. "This is a *woman*, albeit a rough and ill-mannered one. We must set some rules for propriety's sake."

"Rules?" Graham scoffed at the same moment Trystan replied, "Propriety?"

"Yes," Phillip insisted. "If you both do as you're planning, that woman will be under your control, Trystan. You will be responsible for her. That means you cannot turn her into a mistress or take advantage of her. You must think about her future. What reason does she have to accept your terms, and what will you do once the wager is over? Toss her back into this bar and tell her to carry on as before?"

Trystan laughed. "You honestly think I'd take advantage of *that* creature? Lord, Phillip, I have standards. I thought she was a bloody boy, for Christ's sake. The little hellion has nothing to fear from me. I shall not touch her. Not even if she begs me and not unless I lose my own sanity." He was still chuckling at the thought. He had his pick of women to share his bed, and certainly wouldn't choose a bloodthirsty guttersnipe like the creature he'd just seen.

"Good." Phillip relaxed. "You *both* must deal with this girl with some sense of decorum and chivalry."

Trystan snorted, and Graham only laughed into his mug of ale.

"Enough talking," Graham said. "Get to it, Trystan. Claim the girl, and let's be on our way."

Trystan stood, took his time dusting his waistcoat off, and then he walked over to the barman. He braced his arms on the bar and leaned forward to speak to him.

"Was that hellion whelp yours?" he asked the man.

"Whelp?" The barman seemed confused by the word.

"Yes, the girl you kicked like a starving dog."

The heavyset gray-haired man scratched his chin, eyes narrowing in suspicion at Trystan. "What if she is mine?"

"Then I wish to buy her from you." Trystan expected the man to show at least a minor concern for the girl's treatment or at least pretend to care what Trystan might do with her, but he didn't so much as ask about Trystan's intentions.

"How much are you willing to pay?"

Trystan stared at the man before he reached for his coin purse and tossed fifty guineas on the table.

"There's fifty," Trystan said.

The man smacked his lips and decided to press his luck. "I could make double off her if I sell her to the whore-house, plus profits on top of that."

"No madame at a brothel would split any profits with you. She would buy the girl and that would be the end of it.

You and I both know it. And she certainly wouldn't pay you fifty guineas for that girl."

"Throw in another five then. She is my stepdaughter, after all, and I love her dearly."

Trystan let out an exasperated sigh. "I'm sure you do, old chap." He slapped another five guineas down beside the rest. Then he returned to his friends at the table and finished his mug of ale.

"How much did she cost you?" Graham asked, trying to hide his devil-may-care grin.

"Fifty-five guineas." He wouldn't miss a single coin, not with the excitement of his wager to look forward to.

Graham whistled. "Expensive girl."

Phillip looked heavenward and cringed. "You two are absolute barbarians."

"Perhaps we are, but what a challenge this will be." Trystan smiled with relish. "I assume you'll come with us to watch over the girl and play her nursemaid?"

His friend gave a weary sigh, but there was a hint of humor in his eyes. "I suppose I had better. Although, I would argue, you two are the ones in need of a nursemaid."

Ignoring Phillip's remark, Trystan looked about the taproom. "Now, to find the little hellcat..." He started for the door and his two friends followed. He was a little more drunk than perhaps he ought to be, but he was quite looking forward to the adventure of turning this hellcat into a fine lady.

***

Bridget Ringgold huddled against the side of the tavern, cloaked in shadows while she nursed her wounds. Her stepfather's blow had split her lip, and her ribs ached.

She'd be damned lucky if they weren't broken. Her chest would be purple in a few hours after the kick she'd taken. Blood filled her mouth with a foul taste, and it stung each time she ran her tongue over her lip.

She shivered against the brisk fall wind that blew in off the sea. She wished desperately she could sneak back in the kitchens and warm herself, but the odds of her stepfather finding and striking her again were too high. That meant she would be sleeping in the stables tonight.

Bridget needed to find a way out of this town and into a new life, one that did not involve spending time on her back in a brothel. She was old enough to be on her own—nineteen, in fact—but had few decent options open to her. She could cook a little, could clean a bit, but not well enough to earn a decent living at either. She'd had plenty of men offer her marriage, but none of them were good or decent men. One had almost certainly been a pirate. If only her mother had been here to offer advice, to help her find a way in life either by counsel or helping her find someone to share her life with.

Her mother had died ten years ago, leaving Bridget with a beast of a stepfather. She'd been too young to learn any skills that a woman ought to learn from her mother and had been too busy just trying to survive the dangers of living with a man like her stepfather.

Pushing away from the side of the tavern, she crossed the cobblestone courtyard and ran into the stables. The loft above was quiet and no one ever came up there, aside from the occasional stable boy who forked down hay for the horses. Bridget climbed up the ladder and crawled through the haystacks until she found her nest made of blankets that formed her bed. She had nicked the blankets here and there over the last year from drunken travelers not minding the belongings in their coach while they went into the tavern for a drink.

She checked for the cloth bag that contained her few treasures, something she did out of habit every night before she settled into sleep. The comb and the mirror had been her mother's, along with several shillings she'd made by whittling wood into the shape of animals.

People passing through Penzance seem to like her figurines. She'd managed to sell or barter three or four of them each week for the last few years, which gave her a little money to afford extra food and clothes as she had grown older. She never wore dresses. Aside from the expense of having gowns made, it was easier and safer to wear clothing meant for men. The locals knew she was a woman, but with a grimy face and hair pinned up beneath a cap, she managed to avoid the interest of most men who passed through the tavern while she served drinks.

Even those fancy gents tonight hadn't known when she'd served their drinks. She'd been watching them too, out of the corner of her eye, and had been rather nervous when her stepfather had ordered her to take more ale to them. But she'd done what she'd always done when she got nervous—she overcompensated with confidence. She couldn't afford to be a fragile flower; she couldn't fake her strength or confidence.

But that had been a mistake. The three men had paid more attention to her because of her impertinence than she'd meant them to. They were a handsome lot, with their finely embroidered waistcoats and polished boots that gleamed in the lamplight. Even the one who'd come in leaning heavily on a cane had been a handsome fellow. Men shouldn't be *that* attractive, Bridget thought with a frown. Especially the one with dark hair and honey-brown eyes. He had an intensity that she didn't like one bit, as if he could read anyone's thoughts simply by meeting their gaze. That one was dangerous.

"But I'm out here, and they're in there," she murmured to herself. No one ever disturbed her up in the loft, because no one thought to look in the haystacks.

She busied herself by inventorying the rest of her possessions, which included a small carving knife that was tucked away in the back of the bag. Once she was assured her treasures were safe, she settled down to sleep and tugged her blankets up over her. She heard the horses below, nickering softly as they ate oats and hay. The scuttling of mice somewhere on the rafters, rather than frightening her, assured her she was safe. Mice always moved about when no one else was around.

She had closed her eyes and started to drift when the scurrying mice stopped and the stables turned quiet. A moment later, low voices whispered to each other from below.

"She must be in here. I saw her cross the courtyard as we came out," a man said. His cultured voice was one she recognized, belonging to one of the fancy gents. His voice was smooth as warm brandy, and she remembered his eyes were the same color. Bridget slid free of her blankets and moved silently along the floor of the loft so she could peer over the edge. Three men stood in the center of the stables, looking around.

Bridget ducked down as far as she could to avoid being seen by them.

"Trystan, no one's here," one of the other men said.

"She's here," the first man said with a soft chuckle. "Aren't you, little hellcat? Come out, child! I bought you from that wretch who claims to be your stepfather, and I'm here to discuss your future."

"Trys, you'll scare her. Tell the girl what you plan to do for her first, or she'll think you mean her harm," one of the men argued.

The loft vibrated as the man began to climb up the stairs of the ladder. Bridget would have shoved the ladder away and sent the man crashing to the floor, but that would leave her no easy way to escape. If she tried to make that drop, she would most likely break an ankle or her neck, and she was injured enough as it was.

Thinking quickly, she dug through her bag until she found her whittling knife. It was a small blade, but it could still cut them if they tried anything. But her best chance was to not be seen at all.

The man reached the top of the loft, searching the dim, hay-strewn platform. It was just dark enough inside the stables that he might miss her.

Please don't let him see me, please.

She held her breath, and the blood roared so loud in her ears she couldn't hear much else.

"Gotcha!" With his feet still planted on the top rung of the ladder, the man lunged for her. Bridget scrambled back, but one of his hands gripped her ankle and dragged her toward him. She kicked at him with her foot and caught his chin. He grunted in pain but didn't let go. Instead, her fight seemed to light a new fire in him. He climbed fully into the loft and dove at her. Bridget raised the knife just as he landed on top of her, and she felt the blade scrape across his arm.

"Christ, she has a knife!" The man bellowed as he pinned her flat on the floor.

He grasped her wrist, stopping the hand holding the knife, and pressed it hard against the floor beside her head.

"Let go of it, hellion!"

"No!" she spat.

"Let go!" His grip tightened to the point of pain, forcing her to drop the knife. His grip instantly eased and the pain vanished.

"Er... I say, Trystan. Let's be quick about this," one of the man's friends said. "It looks as though we're kidnapping this girl, when that's not really the case. I don't wish to be here long, lest we find ourselves in trouble. Our coach is ready."

Trystan stared down at her, the hard angles of his face too perfect for any man, especially one as wicked as the devil himself.

"Listen, little cat," he growled. "I bought you tonight from that swine who claims to be your stepfather. I have no plans at all to hurt you, except to spank that ass of yours if you dare to stab me again."

"I ain't no whore!" Bridget spat angrily. "Don't you dare touch me!"

"Of that, I'm very aware," he replied. "And that's not why I bought you. Come down with me, and my friends and I will explain just what I plan to do with you."

Bridget didn't want to go anywhere with a man she didn't know, let alone *three*.

"Go to hell," she snapped, but she was all too aware that he was fully on top of her and could do anything he wished to her if he wanted. His weight didn't crush her, but she was fully pressed into the floor by his body, trapped and helpless. Something wild fluttered in her lower belly that made her feel strange.

"Graham, find some rope, please. The little cat refuses to withdraw her claws," Trystan shouted over his shoulder to one of the two men waiting below.

"Miss..." the third man's voice gently called out. "We really mean you no harm."

Bridget spat, "You're trying to bloody nab me. Ain't nothing innocent about that." Her protest was silenced as Trystan rolled his eyes and shoved a wadded handkerchief into her mouth.

"There, that's better." He grasped both of her wrists in one hand and dragged her toward the ladder. She fought valiantly, and he soon seemed to realize he could not force her down the ladder. He peered over the side of the loft and then before she could stop him, he scooped her up and tossed her.

She screeched and a second later landed in a wagon of hay just below. Trystan climbed down the ladder and pulled her from the hay.

"Rope, Graham." Trystan held out his hand.

The one not leaning on a cane passed Trystan a coil of rope, which her captor used to bind her wrists tightly together. Then he held her still, with one strong hand gripping her arm. She was trussed up like a sheep for slaughter.

"We need to get her into the coach. I don't want that barman changing his mind. She's got too much spirit to end up in a brothel," Trystan announced.

Confused by his words, she stumbled along as Trystan pushed her to follow his two companions into the waiting coach. She panicked, trying to spit out the gag. Her bag, her things... all that she had in the world was still in the stables. Tears streamed down her face, and one of the men noticed.

"We aren't going to hurt you," said the one who used his cane to walk about. His eyes were gentle as he looked upon her. "Please don't cry, Miss. Everything will be all right. Now please, don't scream. I give you my word no one will hurt you." He removed the handkerchief from her mouth just as the other two men sat down. The dark-haired devil named Trystan chose the seat directly beside her, and she was suddenly warmed by the heat of his body.

"Please—please, milord. My bag... I ain't got nothing else."

Trystan lifted up her cloth bag. "You mean this?"

She sighed in relief. "Yes, that's the one."

"I'm tempted to search it for weapons," he mused as he started to open the mouth of it.

"Trystan, really. Give the girl some peace, will you?" the kind one said. Then he turned her. "My name is Phillip Wilkes. I'm the Earl of Kent."

"An earl...?" Bridget said, relaxing a little. On the one hand, it seemed inconceivable that a man of high birth would mean her any harm. Then again, it also meant if they did, there was nothing anyone could do to stop them.

LAUREN SMITH

"That's right. The man beside you is Trystan Cartwright, the Earl of Zennor."

"Two earls? They just handing out titles to anyone these days?"

Kent smirked and nodded at the third man. "And that is Graham Humphrey."

"Not as fancy as your friends. No title to wave about?" she taunted. Graham's gray eyes narrowed on her.

"Some of us don't *need* a title to wave about. Some of us are wicked enough without it," Graham warned her. But something about him didn't scare her like it should have. He seemed like a man who would tease a woman and make her laugh, rather than threaten her.

Trystan burst out laughing. "Lord, what fun this will be!"

"Fun? What do you plan to do with me?" Bridget demanded. "I'll not share your bed if that's—"

"Heavens, no! On that we agree," Trystan tutted before he dramatically shuddered. "No, no, my little hellcat. Graham and I have made a wager, about *you*."

Bridget didn't like the sound of that. Wagers were made by either bored men or desperate ones, and she didn't want to be involved with either.

"I have one month to turn you into a proper lady, Miss... Lord, I don't even know your name."

"It's Bridget. Bridget Ringgold. And wot do you mean a proper *lady*?" Bridget echoed, drawing out the word. "Why would you want to do that?"

"Because I am bored," Trystan supplied.

A bored gentleman. It was as she had feared.

"I ain't no doll to dress up and play with," she argued.

"It's 'am not,' and yes, you are my doll, girl. I *bought* you. For the next month, I will dress you and teach you to do things that I want you to do. In one month's time, you will walk, talk and look the part of a duchess, by God. By the end of all this, you will likely be able to catch some man in a parson's mousetrap, and you will have a far better life than the one you currently have. You will be singing my praises instead of trying to turn me into a pincushion."

She plum forgot she had pricked him with her blade, but he didn't seem to be hurting.

"You ain't hurt none, milord. If you was, you'd be bleeding all over the blooming place," she pointed out sourly, secretly wishing she'd had better aim and had stabbed his heart.

"I *am* hurt, but I'll deal with it later." He nodded toward his sleeve, and she realized that she'd cut through his coat and down to his flesh. Even in the dim light of the coach, she could see he was bleeding now. If he was hurting, what sort of man could hide a pain like that? Bridget fell into a worried silence.

"Trystan is right," Kent said. "In a month's time, you will have a whole new set of skills. I expect you will be able to find a man to propose to you who can offer you a fine life with fancy gowns, a coach at your disposable, and a life without worries. Wouldn't that be lovely?"

She shot Kent a sour look. "An' who says I need a man?" she fired back.

Graham was the one who laughed this time. "Christ, you're right, Trystan. This is going to be fun."

Fun for them, perhaps, but Bridget wanted no part of this silly wager. She'd take advantage of a roof over her head and food while she planned her next move. Perhaps she'd nick a bit of that fine silverware the toff no doubt possessed and start a new life with the money that silver would fetch her. Then *she* would be the one laughing.

*The Earl of Zennor will be available for a limited time in the Wicked Earls Forever collection online (you can preorder it now). After that it will become available in April or May of 2023 as a single title: The Earl of Zennor.

ABOUT THE AUTHOR

Lauren Smith is an Oklahoma attorney by day, author by night who pens adventurous and edgy romance stories by the light of her smart phone flashlight app. She knew she was destined to be a romance writer when she attempted to re-write the entire *Titanic* movie just to save Jack from drowning. Connecting with readers by writing emotionally moving, realistic and sexy romances no matter what time period is her passion. She's won multiple awards in several romance subgenres including: New England Reader's Choice Awards, Greater Detroit BookSeller's Best Awards, and a Semi-Finalist award for the Mary Wollstonecraft Shelley Award.

To connect with Lauren, visit her at:
www.laurensmithbooks.com
lauren@Laurensmithbooks.com